Beastly
BEAUTY

GIRL AMONG WOLVES 2

USA TODAY BESTSELLING AUTHOR
LENA MAE HILL

I am riding a mountain lion. I cling to his back, my arms circling his neck as he climbs steep slopes and slips between towering boulders. My head swirls with questions and my ankle throbs with pain where I twisted it during my escape from the valley of the wolves. Adjusting my hold, I shift the glass lantern against my chest, but it still bites into my skin. Inside the lantern, instead of a flame, a little grey mouse huddles. The mouse is Mrs. Nguyen, my childhood babysitter, next door neighbor, and tonight's hero. The mountain lion is my father.

As we crest one of the giant, rolling hills that make up the Ozark Mountains, a chorus of howls sounds behind us, echoing through the valley. My chest tightens, and I hope that isn't the mourning cry as the pack finds their new Alpha in a mangled heap in the woods. I hope it isn't my sister being caught and punished for trying to run away with us. But more than anything, I hope they don't catch us.

The mountaintop flattens into a plateau under us as my father makes his way along the ridgeline. The land folds, pushing up into more hills and down into valleys. From here, I can see all the way across the wolves' valley to the next mountaintop, where a white lookout tower stands guard over the valleys on either side.

"Where are we going?" I ask, but of course my father can't answer now. I'm so sick of being in the dark, of never having answers, that all I want to do is slide off his back and demand he shift into his human form and tell me everything. Instead, I cling tighter when I hear a roar echoing up from the wolves' valley, where they are fighting with the shifters.

Dad increases his pace again, moving down the far side of the mountain. The howls dissipate, their lonesome sound sending chills along my arms as it fades into the distance. Inside my head, I whisper a goodbye to my sister, hoping she can somehow hear it through our twin bond. But she's in wolf form now, and I don't know if she can sense my presence drawing further away, the way I can sense hers.

At last, when my arms ache from the strain of holding on so long, and my sternum is raw and bruised from pinning the lantern between my chest and Dad's back, he slows. He lopes across a dirt road and into a driveway.

"What is this place?" I ask, slipping from his back. I clutch the lantern in front of me, as if Mrs. Nguyen can somehow protect me.

Dad shifts into human form in seconds. After seeing the wolves transition in such a slow and gruesome way, with bones and cartilage snapping, it's still a bit of a shock to see a shifter do it so easily.

"It's where Efrain held me captive," he says. "He wanted me to ask around about a girlfriend who took off on him. When I didn't do it on his time schedule, he locked me in his shed."

I shudder, but I can't stop the suspicions circling in my

mind. Mrs. Nguyen says he left his body, so is this really him? What if someone else has projected into his body, and this isn't my father at all? Suddenly I'm sure it's Mother, waiting to grab my hands and say I'm caught, and that I'm going right back into her attic where I belong.

My hand goes to my throat, and I swallow hard. "What did you get me after we went to the zoo?" I ask.

"Your necklace," he says. "Why are you asking about that?"

I don't know what to say to him. How to admit I don't know if I remember his voice well enough after only three years to trust that it's him, or that I don't believe in hope enough to trust that it is. I've learned again and again that trusting anyone here is not an option.

"I want to make sure it's you," I say at last. Dad's not the type to get his feelings hurt over reasonable answers. But as he laughs, a chill goes through me. Mother knows I wear that necklace. I might have even told her it was from my dad. "Why did you get it for me?" I press.

"Because you loved the tigers, so I got you a tiger eye," he says. "So you could think of me and my promise to take you back to see them."

"It is you," I say, my throat suddenly thick with unshed tears.

"I'll give it to you as soon as we get out of here."

"What do you mean?"

"Yvonne gave it to me—before she projected," he says, faltering so strangely that my suspicions rise again. But before I can ask more, he goes on. "Right now, we need to focus on getting that mouse back to her human body." With that, he turns and circles the shabby stone house.

Yvonne, known to me as Mrs. Nguyen, peers out of the lantern with beady black eyes.

I hurry to catch up with Dad.

Behind the house, two rusted-out cars crouch on blocks, and a small tin shed sits next to a large walnut tree. For a second, I want to tell Dad that I have learned to recognize one tree from another, that I've read books on native plants and animals of the Ozarks. There's no limit to the things I would do to stay sane in the months of sheer boredom when I was a prisoner. But Dad seems more interested in the shed than making conversation, so I follow along, averting my eyes so I won't see his nakedness.

"Why are we here?" I whisper, glancing back at the house.

"I told you. To get Yvonne's body," he says, surveying the ground around the shed.

"This is where you were kept?" I ask, not bothering to hide my shock. "In a shed?" Here I thought my mother was cruel for locking me in an attic. Suddenly, I'm filled with pity for my father. I can't imagine what he went through at the hands of the shifters. Compared to this, the attic was a five-star resort.

"She got me out," he says. "I need to get her out. They'll use her magic for their own purposes. She's more valuable to them than I was, that's for sure."

"But why would they want you?" I ask. "If you're one of them?"

"Found it," he cries, pulling a crowbar from under the edge of the shed. He braces it against the padlock and yanks. With a screech of metal, the tin bends away from the wooden frame of the door.

"How did you get out?" I ask.

"They let me out because I agreed to fight alongside them. But when they threw her in here instead of me, I told her I'd come back for her."

"They must have known she could leave her body and project into the mouse," I say, peering into the lantern. "Since they caught her in this form, too."

"Now she just needs a human body so she can communicate with us. Here, help me pry this open."

With my help, Dad yanks the tin free of the doorframe, leaving bent nails and splintered wood behind. We peer into the dark opening of the shed, and a chill passes over me.

"Why didn't you break out as a mountain lion?" I ask.

"They had a spell on me so I couldn't shift." He steps inside and crouches, feeling around on the ground. At last, he scoops up a body and steps out. The plump old woman who lived next door to us for the past ten years sags in his arms, as limp as a dead person. It reminds me too much of the day I found Dad's body and thought he was dead.

"Let's get out of here," he says. "I'll explain everything later."

But I'm tired of those words, tired of waiting for explanations. "Dad," I say. "I found your body. How could you let me think you were dead?" My throat tightens painfully at the memory of it, but a swell of confusion and betrayal is seeping over the memories of sadness. He was alive. Somehow, some way, he could have gotten a message to me.

"We need to get to someplace safe, and then we can talk," he says, laying Mrs. Nguyen's body gently on the fresh green grass sprouting in the backyard. I'm touched by his care and tenderness, the way he always was with her, even when he joked around. Back then, I didn't understand why he liked spending time with an old lady so much.

Dad takes the lantern from me and looks it over. "I think she's trapped in here," he says. "It's got some kind of magic keeping her inside. Let's break it open and see."

With that, he takes the crowbar and strikes the glass lantern. I bite back a yelp, but Dad laughs when the glass cracks. A few more blows and he's broken out a pane of the lantern. He takes the mouse in his hand and slips it into Mrs. Nguyen's pocket.

We sit back, waiting.

"What if she can't project back?" I whisper.

"She can."

After a minute, when she doesn't move, he steps back into the shed. Seconds later, he returns, a string dangling from his fingers. At the end of it hangs the tiger-eye charm. I start to reach for it, but he slips it into Mrs. Nguyen's breast pocket with the mouse.

"It has a protection charm of sorts on it," he says. "I had her put it on the stone to keep you safe."

Touched, I start to answer, but before I can, Mrs. Nguyen draws a noisy breath and sits up so suddenly that I stumble back.

"They'll be coming back from the fight by now," Dad says. "Hurry and get on my back." Without waiting for our agreement, Dad shifts back into his mountain lion form.

"I always did fancy a lion ride," Mrs. Nguyen says with

6

a sly smile. She hops up as if nothing happened and attempts to climb on Dad's back. I give her a boost, then look at him doubtfully.

"Are you sure you can carry us both?" I ask.

His huge head swings around and he growls low in his throat.

"Okay, okay." I climb onto his back, holding onto Mrs. Nguyen, who lays forward and grips his neck. Dad is much slower this time, and he keeps to the road. By now, it's sometime between midnight and dawn, and we have the dirt road to ourselves. After only five or ten minutes, he steps off the road into another driveway. My heart nearly stops when I see his faded red pickup in the drive.

"Home sweet home," Mrs. Nguyen says, straightening.

"What?" I ask, sliding off Dad's back and holding out a hand for her. As soon as she sets foot on the ground, Dad shifts into human form.

"It's where I grew up," he says, gesturing to the house. "Come inside. I'll call Dr. Golden to come have a look at your ankle."

"Dad," I say, my voice stronger than I expected. "Can we sit down and talk about the last, oh, I don't know... fifteen years or so?"

He sighs. "Okay, let me get some clothes on, and then we'll talk."

"Fine," I say, because I really don't want to talk to my dad when he's naked, no matter how dark it is.

He jumps up onto the porch and disappears inside.

"I'll get us something to drink," Mrs. Nguyen says, shuffling up the sagging steps. I don't want to be ungrateful, but I'd really like some time with just my dad. He has

7

so much explaining to do. But for now, it will have to be enough. Maybe Mrs. Nguyen can answer more of my questions, and after all, she did get me out of the wolf valley. Quelling my disappointment at her presence, I head for the porch swing.

The house is small and plain, with siding that should have been replaced a decade ago, a sagging roof, and a porch that looks like it might detach from the house at any second and collapse into a heap of boards and cinderblocks. When I step closer, I can see that the porch swing doesn't hang from a chain. Instead, it sits on more stacks of cinderblocks, making a bench seat.

As I'm debating whether the porch is fit to hold three people at once, gravel crunches stealthily behind me. I spin around, then gasp at the pain in my ankle. There's no one there.

But the unmistakable sound of a footstep in the gravel still rings in my ears. A sneaking footstep, someone trying to be quiet. I know, because I've tried to sneak along gravel driveways a time or two myself.

"Who's there?" I ask, my voice coming out sharp rather than firm.

A breath of warm air sweeps across my neck, and I almost scream. I spin around again, only to collide with a bare, furry chest. This time, I do scream. Strong arms circle me, and a hand clamps over my mouth. His skin smells like animal, sharp and pungent.

"Now, we don't want to alarm anyone, do we, little girl?" he asks. His deep voice carries a strong southern accent and a hint of teasing. In the silvery moonlight, I can make out enough of his features to know I've never seen him before, though something about him does seem vaguely familiar. He doesn't look like one of the were-wolves, though, and they never smell like sweaty animals.

I struggle against him, but he only smirks down at me.

"Don't worry, I'm not here to hurt you," he says. "I'm just here to talk to the joke who lives here. Though if you wanted, we could have a little fun while we wait."

I scream against his palm, scraping my teeth against it, trying to bite him. But my lips only smash against his callouses. He laughs, amusement dancing in his dark eyes.

"Our business here is with Owen," a voice says behind me. "Who are you?"

I make a sound behind the first guy's hand.

"It's a fair question," he says. "If I let go of your mouth, you ain't going to scream, are you?"

I shake my head.

"Good, because I wouldn't want to have to hurt such a pretty girl," he says. "But I will if you scream."

The second he takes his hand off my mouth, I scream. It's cut short by the shock of a blow. My head rocks back, my teeth smashing together. I gasp for breath, trying to force myself to calm down. Mother slapped me around plenty over the past few years. But I've never been punched. I can't seem to recover from the reeling pain of it, echoing up and down my body. All I can do is open and close my mouth to make sure my jaw isn't broken.

"Don't say I didn't warn you," the guy says, turning my body so my back is to him. He grips my wrists behind my back. Through the blur of tears in my eyes, I can see the second guy. While the one who holds me is brawny, the other is wiry. His eyes sparkle with a cold cruelty. They

9

are both naked, so I'm guessing they're shifters who arrived in animal form.

Where the hell is my dad?

"Who are you?" the smaller one asks again. His voice is also strongly accented, but it has a sharp, nasally twang.

"I—I'm not anyone," I choke out, stalling for time. If I can't have a mountain lion protecting me, I'd settle for a witch. Just about anyone can do more damage than a human girl with a sprained ankle.

"You ain't a quick learner, that's for sure," the one holding me says.

"Here's how this works," the smaller one says. "I ask you a question, and you answer, or you get hit. You can understand a simple rule like that, can't you?"

I nod, choking down my terror. As scared as I was of the wolves, I knew them. I knew how and when they'd hurt me. I curse myself for ever leaving their valley. But if I can stall these guys, keep them talking, Mrs. Nguyen will see me out the window. She'll warn Dad, and he'll come eat them.

"Good girl," the skinny guy says, stepping closer and running the backs of his fingers down my cheek. "You must be a werewolf, dressed up fancy as you are. What are you doing all the way over here in the shifter valley with the likes of Owen?"

"I know he likes 'em young and pretty, but damn," says the one behind me, one of his hands still gripping my wrists like a handcuff.

"I'm his *daughter,*" I say, spitting the words out with all the revulsion I feel at hearing his comment.

For a second, they don't speak. Their eyes meet over my head, but I can't read the expression in their eyes.

"Is that right?" the skinny one asks at last.

"Guess that means I'm your second cousin," the deep voice of the other says behind me. "Too bad. I like blondes."

"Second cousin's not too close," the smaller guy says with a leering smile. "Ain't that what they call *kissing cousins*?"

All my life, I dreamed of having a mother. Then I found out I had a mother, and she totally sucked. I dreamed of having a big, extended family with lots of cousins, aunts, uncles, and grandparents. Now that I've met my cousin, I'm going to have to amend that wish, too.

Suddenly Harmon's words flash through my mind, and hope surges through me. As angry as it makes me to say the words, I force them out. "I belong to a wolf," I say quickly. "To Harmon. The Alpha."

"Is that right?" the smaller guy asks. "Because I think you'd make a real nice bargaining chip if you belonged to your daddy."

"But I don't."

Just then, the screen door bangs behind me. The shifter holding my hands pivots, twisting me around so I'm still in front of him, facing the house now. My ankle throbs in pain when I have to set my foot down to catch myself from falling, but no one notices my cry of pain.

"If it ain't Owen," the smaller guy says with a sneer. "*Your Highness*."

"The man of the hour," my cousin says.

"What do you want?" Dad asks. His flannel shirt is

rumpled above a pair of khaki shorts, and he's still bare-foot. I suddenly want nothing more than to curl up in his arms and cry, let him explain all this away, make my life good again. He could always do that. But he looks different now. He's thinner, carrying only twenty extra pounds or so, and his beard is straggly and greying instead of neatly trimmed. I want to ask him what happened, but I don't know if I could stand to hear the answer. I saw the shed where they kept him.

"You know what we want," my cousin says.

"I can't say I do," Dad grumbles, scratching his head. His hair has also grown longer and is badly in need of a shampoo and a trim and a comb.

"Then let me spell it out for you. We want the old hag back."

"I don't know anything about a hag."

"Fair enough," the skinny guy says. "We'll make you a deal. You keep the witch, and we keep your daughter. When you give us back the witch, we'll give your daughter back."

Dad eyes me, and my blood runs hotter than lava. "What are you talking about?" I scream. "Dad, make them let me go."

"Ah, didn't Daddy tell you?" my cousin asks. "He loves that witch. Oh, I know she's an old crone now, but she borrows bodies all over the Three Valleys. Ain't that right, Owen? You been shacking up with that witch for years."

"What is he talking about?" I ask Dad.

"What, you didn't want your daughter to know?" the other shifter sneers. "That witch is going to be pissed when she hears you're ashamed of her."

Just then, something big crashes in the leaves across the road. The boys both sniff the air. Dad listens, his eyes narrowing.

"I don't have your witch," he says. "I don't know anything about her. Now give me my daughter, and you can go on your witch hunt."

I hear footsteps behind me and twist around in time to see a dark shape charging towards the porch. I shrink away as it passes, but the thick smell of it clogs my nostrils, making my eyes water. A second later, it leaps onto the porch, and in the light of the full moon, I see it clearly. It's a bear, blood smearing its muzzle, a jagged hole torn in its shoulder, patches of fur torn off.

Efrain.

The sight of him sends my mind into a panic. With a growl, he charges Dad, slamming him to the ground.

A scream tears from my throat, and I throw myself towards the porch. My cousin's grip slips, and I fall to my hands and knees. All this time, I dreamed of my dad being alive. Only tonight, I found out that he was. They can't kill him now. He is my savior, the one who's going to get us out of here, back to the real world, where people were people all the time, not animals. I scramble forward as a bobcat streaks by, leaping onto my father's prostrate body. Why isn't he shifting? Why isn't he fighting?

The bear that is Efrain throws back its head and roars into the air. And then I see why Dad isn't fighting. His face is slack, either dead or unconscious.

"Take me," I scream, throwing myself under Efrain, between him and my father. His shaggy fur is coarse and matted, and the smell of him nearly knocks me to the ground.

Gravel crunches in the driveway, but I don't turn to see who has arrived. I cover my father's unmoving body with my own, shielding him from Efrain's bloody teeth. "Leave him alone," I scream. "Take me instead. Don't kill him. Please."

Suddenly, a body thuds against Efrain. Twisting my head around, I see dozens of wolves streaming into the driveway, along the side of Dad's truck. Shifters are emerging from beside Dad's house, bears and bobcats, bucks and boars.

Not this again.

Efrain dives into a knot of wolves, throwing one with his massive paw. My cousin has disappeared into an animal form, though I don't know which one. For a moment, I'm left unguarded. I jump up off Dad and grab his arm, heaving with all my strength. His body barely moves. Gripping his wrist, I try again, dragging him towards the door. If I can just get him inside and bolt the doors. Maybe he has a basement or somewhere safe to hide until he wakes up.

A racoon leaps onto the porch, hissing and diving for me. Its claws slash into my dress. I kick it as hard as I can, and it falls back, but the pain in my ankle is so severe I can't hold in a scream. The sound joins the howls and snarls and roars ripping through the air around me. Sobbing through my own pain, I throw open the screen door. Grabbing Dad's wrists again, I throw all my weight back, dragging him to the doorway this time. But my scream caught Efrain's attention, and his big head swings around.

I scream again, this time in fear. All I want is to jump inside the house and slam the door and lock it. But I can't leave Dad defenseless. As Efrain bounds towards the porch, I throw my body over Dad's again. Suddenly, something sweeps over me, something so terrifyingly familiar that I can't help but laugh. My body lurches as my muscles bunch and cramp and contract, the beginning of one of my fits. I've had these fits all my life, muscle spasms and blackouts and nightmares.

But now is not the time to suddenly start hallucinating and pass out. Hysterical giggles flood from my mouth as tears drip from my eyes. I hunker down over Dad, praying he will wake up before it's too late, before we're both dead. But he remains motionless, and a second later, something hits me with the force of a club. For a moment, I'm stunned senseless, and all I feel is the weightlessness of flying through the air.

I'm a bird, I think crazily. And then I slam into a tree, and my head thuds against the trunk, and the world goes dark.

I've been staring up at a dirty window for what feels like hours. Half-awake and half consumed by the throbbing pain in my head, I stir when I hear a muffled scraping sound. I thought I was alone in this cold, damp place of pain, so the noise startles me, sends my heart racing inside my aching ribcage. The scuffling sound repeats, and I cut my eyes in that direction, pulled from the haze of agony for the first time since I woke. This room is not the cluttered attic where I've spent the past two years, where I belong. It's dim, cavernous, and dank with the smell of mildew and damp earth.

With some effort, I push myself up to sitting, wincing like I'm an old woman instead of sixteen. My head throbs with each beat of my heart, an ache so big I think I'll have to lie back down. But another sound stops me, this one a high whimpering sound. My fingers flex against the floor, not the wooden planks of my mother's attic but hard packed soil. No steel chimney rises from floor to ceiling here, making me sweat with heat in the winter and even more now that it's springtime. Here, my pale skin prickles with a clammy chill that my light cardigan can't dispel.

The scuffling sound draws my attention once more. With an optimism I shouldn't still possess after spending the last two and a half years as a prisoner in my mother's attic, I think at once that it must be Mrs. Nguyen, my old babysitter. She also happens to be a mouse and my guardian angel. I grope across the dirt floor for the glass lantern in which she was trapped the last time I saw her. If I was going to choose a spirit animal to watch over me, I would have chosen something big and fierce like a tiger, not a tiny grey mouse who could be imprisoned in a jar. But that choice was not mine to make.

Testing out each muscle as I move, I clamber onto hands and knees.

"Yvonne?" I whisper. "Is that you, Mrs. Nguyen?"

No answering scuffle.

But wait. I did see her after that. We rode on the back of a mountain lion who was also my dad. The thought is so ridiculous I know it can't be true. But after missing Dad painfully for the past years, I can't stop the hope that it was real. "Dad?" I try.

I crawl forward, jerking to a halt when I kneel on my skirt. If I can find the lantern, I won't be alone. Even if she's not inside it, I could still light the lantern. I wouldn't mind a little light or warmth.

I attempt to stand, but a shock of pain pulses through my ankle when I put weight on it, and I fall back to all fours. Outside, thunder rumbles somewhere far away. Far above. Blindly, I move forward, exploring what must be someone's basement. I whisper Dad's name, my voice tremulous. "Owen?"

In response, I hear what is definitely a sigh. My skin prickles. That was no mouse.

I'm not alone down here.

But I've seen too much in the past two years, since

17

coming to live in a community of werewolves, to be relieved. True, it might be someone I want to see—my identical twin, or Mrs. Nguyen in human form, or the father I thought was dead until last night. If it's him, we could get out of here together.

Or it could be an angry werewolf who wants me dead. Or one of the violent, lawless, shapeshifting heathens from the neighboring community. The odds are not in my favor.

Remembering last night, I shiver at the image of a mountain lion towering over Harmon, who had looked like such a huge wolf until that moment. And then, a bear towering over my father. I almost lose my nerve and retreat to my corner under the window. If that is in here with me, I don't want to provoke it.

But another soft, pathetic whimper stops me from turning back and hiding. I have been hiding for two years. True, Mother didn't let me out of the house much. But I could have fought harder. I could have found a way. Like I will find a way out of here, a way back to my father and the normal, sane life we lived in the real world, before he died and I was sent to live in this nightmare.

He's not dead, I remind myself. He's alive. After only hours with him, I was ripped away again. But now that I know he's out there, I will find him. I will find a path back to my real life, where I had friends, a family who loved me, a future. A place where a boy could love me without believing I'm my twin. A place where hope exists.

When my fingers at last find warmth, I'm so shocked I jerk my hand back. It's an animal, all right, but I don't know which one. I want to run away, out of this shadowy basement. I want to curl up behind the potato bin and pray it doesn't know I'm here. But what if it's Dad, injured?

Again, I reach for it, searching until my fingers sink into soft fur. I can feel it breathing. My hands begin to explore over damp, matted fur, a ribcage, down the thick coat, the hip. I'm certain it's a wolf now, or a dog, but I'm not sure if that's safer than a shifter. It depends on the wolf. It's not as safe as a mouse, that's for sure.

Suddenly, my fingers aren't touching fur. They are touching skin—human skin. I almost scream as I fall back, away from the wolf and the human intertwined in this corner of shadow and darkness. A scenario forms in my overactive mind in seconds. A wolf must have attacked a human, and the human injured the wolf, which I heard whining. Or perhaps the wolf was eating the human to regain strength. That's what happens in the horror movies my best friend used to sneak from her brother's room to watch while her parents slept. Or is it vampires that gain strength by feeding on humans? Do werewolves drink blood? Eat human flesh?

Is this the shed where they kept Dad prisoner? If he's here with me now…

My heart constricts painfully. All the fear and pain of losing him, the anger at learning so many of his stories were lies, it all comes rushing back. Last night, when Mrs. Nguyen told me he was alive, I didn't have time to think it over. I was trying to escape, to find him.

When I found him, everything happened so fast I had no time to think.

Escape the wolves. Save Mrs. Nguyen. Escape the shifters.

He wouldn't stop to answer my questions, and now, I've lost my chance to make sense of it all. Anger rises in me like a tidal wave. All that time, locked in solitude in Mother's attic, and he was *alive?* If he'd told me the truth all my life, I would have known that he was alive when I found his body. I would have known he was in trouble, and I could have helped.

Instead, he lied to me. He let me find his body and believe he was dead. He let the state ship me off to a cruel mother with her rules and her locks and her stinging blows. Mother, who made me believe that since I wasn't a wolf, I was nothing. The anger swells. I don't care who this wolf is, all tangled up with a human. The human might be my father. I give that human leg a shove, the thought that it might not be attached occurring to me only when it's too late to take it back.

Instead of tumbling away, the leg is drawn back. A howl of pain, a snarl, and sharp fangs clamp onto my hand. I scream in shock and terror. The wolf's jaws unfasten from my hand, and I scramble back, hardly feeling the volley of fire shooting from my ankle up my leg. The new, fiercer pain in my hand is too immediate. I scramble back to my corner under the dim light of the window. Through the smudged, dirty window set high above, I can see only grey sky. Down here, I can see more —the punctured holes in my hand, the blood streaming out in rivulets like the rain on the pane above.

I press my hand to my middle, curl around it, and let the tears come. Even my sister, when she was injured as a wolf and I had to care for her, never bit me. It hurts worse than I imagined it would. But at least it didn't take my hand off.

When the tears are gone, I sit up and work to tear off strips of the tulle gown I wore to Harmon's ill-fated coronation. I wrap my hand until it's fat with the stuff. Then I touch the tender knot on my head where I hit the tree. The ache of it is unending, a constant drain on my energy, a distraction from my thoughts of escape, as if only half of me is here and the rest is huddling inside somewhere, stunned senseless by the pain.

Another whimper comes from the back of this basement dungeon, but I'm not making that mistake again. I try to ignore its suffering and my own, to listen to the noises overhead and determine whether they are thunder or footsteps. And if it is human footsteps, are they the violent outlaws who my mother has taught me to fear, or the wolves, who experience has taught me to fear? Which is worse? And what are their plans for me?

The next morning, I wake to the smell of food, a sweet, rich scent that sends me back to my life before this place, to Sunday afternoons in the kitchen with Dad. I push to sitting and grasp my heavy, pounding head for a minute, breathing through the pain. It's not as bad as yesterday, but still makes me sway when I stand. My swollen ankle throbs as I hobble forward a few steps, checking the shadowy corner where the vicious wolf lay. I can only hope that it didn't get rabies from one of the shapeshifters.

This morning dawns brighter than the stormy day before, and I can make out more of the basement. A large freezer sits against one wall, but I'm not about to look in there. Everyone knows what happens to the girl who goes snooping around and finds out all her kidnappers' secrets. I hop forward a few more steps, keeping my weight off my injured foot. The damp, musty smell has stopped up my nose, but I can taste the dank air down here. It is definitely not the shed where Dad was held prisoner.

The floors and walls are packed dirt, with a recess below the window where a few dusty old pots are wedged. The room is larger than it felt when I was crawling around in it yesterday. I scan the ceiling for an opening and find shadowy, exposed beams held up by upright supports that look like peeled tree trunks, greyed with age. A few large wooden crates are built against one wall. They're big enough to hide a human…or a wolf.

I shiver and pull my sister's filthy sweater tighter around myself as I take another step, searching the shadows beyond the wooden boxes. That's where the wolf was, but even with the increased light today, I'll have to go closer to see if it's there, and I'm not about to make that mistake again. Instead, I look for a door. If there's a way in, there's a way out. At last, I make out a rectangular shape in one corner that must be a door, though it's shorter than any door meant for humans. I wonder for a second if shifters can open doors in their animal form. I don't like that thought.

I hobble towards the door anyway, the growling in my stomach urging me forward. When I step onto an uneven spot in the pitted floor, I lurch forward, grasping at one of the pillars to stop my weight from falling onto my bad ankle. While I'm catching my breath, I hear rustling in the darkest recesses of the basement, where yesterday the wolf bit me. Since I didn't hear screaming in the night, I can only assume it hasn't eaten its human companion. Or, if it has, the human was already dead.

It's so dark that I almost miss the rickety ladder leading up to another door, this one human sized. It's right above the injured wolf, though, so I skirt around to the little door at ground level. I say a quick prayer, close my eyes, and grip the rusted iron handle. With breath held, I give a tug.

Nothing.

Of course they're not just going to leave it unlocked, to let a prisoner walk out. I didn't expect to find it unlocked. I told myself not to get my hopes up. Still, my body sags with the loss of even that slim chance. With a sigh, I hobble back across the room, avoiding the sight of the injured wolf. I sink down in my spot beneath the window and try to ignore the soft whining when it begins a while later. At last, I can't bear to sit still any longer.

I push myself to my feet and search the room with my eyes. When I find nothing new, I hop over to the freezer. I'm already a prisoner. They're going to do whatever they want to me. Looking in the freezer is not going to change my fate. I heave the lid up and am greeted by a blast of freezing steam. Inside, white paper packages in various sizes fill the well of the freezer, each labeled in red letters.

Ribs

Roast

Shoulder

Hamburger

I can only hope this meat comes from an animal. With a sigh, I close the lid and move on to the first wooden bin. Inside, I find a small mountain of round, dirty potatoes. In the second bin, I find a body.

I scream. The pain in my ankle forgotten, I race for the ladder and scramble up the crooked, wobbly steps. I don't stop until I reach the top rung. Grasping the knob, I turn it as hard as I can. Unlike the loose knob of my mother's attic, this one is brushed steel and firmly set into the door. When it doesn't give, I continue wrenching at it, sure that by the force of terror alone, I will rip it from its mooring, rip the door right off the hinges. When the knob becomes slick from my sweating palms, I begin pounding at the door, screaming to be let out.

At last, voice gone, I sink down on the ladder, clutching it with shaking arms, my hands too raw to hold onto the rough wood. The pain in my ankle returns with renewed sharpness from the time I spent standing on the ladder, ignoring it. A shuddering, broken sob escapes me.

"Finally," a garbled voice rasps below me. "That racket was giving me a headache."

Startled, I suck in the next sob and swallow it. I had forgotten that I'm not alone. That there's another person here—a live person.

"Sorry," I whisper. I'm stuck here. If I go down, that wolf will have full access to my legs. Gingerly, I wrap my throbbing, burning hands around the ladder and peer down, ready to ask the guy if it's safe. But the words stop in my throat, and another scream burbles up inside me, welling with my growing horror.

It's not a man. It's not a wolf. It's a repulsive, deformed monster. One muscular human leg protrudes from the narrow haunches of a wolf's flanks. Wolf ribs, a rounded human shoulder, a human arm with a massive, hairy paw on one side, a wolf's leg on the other side to the elbow, where it becomes human again. A ridge of fur on the back of the neck, behind which, his skin is peeled back from bloody, raw muscle. One bloody, shredded ear is so mangled I can't tell if it's wolf or human.

And the face is one out of a nightmare—a human mouth and chin, a flattened black wolf nose in the position of a human nose, two white-blue eyes surrounded by black fur and a sloping, wolf's forehead.

I want to scream, but I can't. My voice is choked off by horror, a gagging sensation fighting to disgorge my revulsion from my empty stomach. If it weren't bad enough that I'm trapped here with a dead body, now I'm here with a mangled, hideous monster. A monster who already hated me when he was human.

"Oh, just come down already," Harmon snarls. "I'm not going to bite you."

I squeeze my eyes shut, but the image of the twisted, grotesque body is etched into my mind. "You did before," I manage.

"I'm sorry," he growls. "I was out of my mind. But just stay up there until you fall off if you'd rather." He shifts to turn his back to me, then lets out a gruff yipping sound and collapses at the effort. The long, ragged gash bisects his back, a lighter band in the midnight black of his fur. I don't want to see his injuries, but I can't stop staring. My father did that to him. Is this my punishment?

"What's the matter, you've never seen blood before?" he snarls.

I turn away, my heart lurching uncomfortably against my ribs. I didn't know he was watching me. Probably because humans don't have eyes on the sides of their heads. I shudder at the image of that deformed face. And then it hits me. He doesn't know. He is a wounded animal, and the way he looks is probably the last thing on his mind. He thinks I was horrified by his injuries, not his hideous appearance.

I scold myself for being shallow. It shouldn't matter that he's repulsive. He's hurt. I should help him. But I don't want to, and not only because he bit me.

I don't want to help him because I don't want to go anywhere near him. He's dangerous and disgusting and he despises me. Not only did my father attack him, but I basically killed his father, and then came within seconds of tricking him into marrying me, though that was never my intention. But he must see it that way. That's why he chased me into the forest last night. To kill me.

With shaking steps, I begin my descent. I owe him nothing. He got us both into this. If he had just let me go, none of this would be happening.

A hollow thudding sound draws me out of my slumber to consciousness. I sit up, heart pounding in my chest. Something very near is scraping and scrabbling. In one of the bins. I cover my mouth to hold back a gasp.

Another thud, and the lid of one of the vegetable bins flies open. This time, I do make a sound. Just a little shriek, but it's enough to rouse Harmon. He lifts his hideous head and sniffs the air with his strange nose. Out of the bin, Mrs. Nguyen's head and shoulders appear. I almost scream again, because that's the dead body I saw, though it was lying face down and I couldn't be sure. With her befuddled expression and dirt-streaked face and disheveled hair, she looks like a zombie out of a scary movie.

"Here I am," she says with her old granny smile. "I was beginning to think I'd lost this body. Which wouldn't be so bad, mind you, if I could find another one lying around unoccupied."

"Mirror," Harmon mutters.

She turns to him, and an ugly expression morphs her features into someone I don't recognize. I've never seen such contempt on her benign old face, or even thought her capable of it. A sneering, cruel smile twists her wrin-

28

kled lips. "Look at you now," she says. "Not too proud to marry my daughter now, are you?"

Harmon growls low in his throat.

"Didn't your people ever teach you not to offend the wrong person?" she says in a gloating voice. "Guess what, *pretty boy*. I'm the wrong person to offend."

Harmon growls again, then lays his head down on his paws and looks up at her mournfully. And even though he's been nothing but horrible to me, something inside me pulls tight at seeing his sad dog eyes.

Mrs. Nguyen apparently does not feel the same. "You could have united the tribes, just like your father always wanted," she says. "Ever since the last time it didn't work. And this time, we'd all be united. Wouldn't that be nice?"

Harmon lets out a soft whine.

"But no. You were too proud to accept a compromise. You had to have your pick, didn't you? I guess my daughter isn't good enough for your Alpha." She glares at him a second, and then says, in a taunting voice, "What kind of king will you be now, Prince Harmon? Your father is dead, and no one will follow a beast like you. Now you're paying for that stubborn pride the same way the wolves always do. I guess what they say is true. You can't teach an old dog new tricks. I hoped a young pup like you would be different. But I guess you can't teach a new dog, either."

"Leave him alone," I say softly. "He's injured."

"Oh, the poor thing," she sneers. "You think he's as helpless as you, Stella? Ha. He's faking it. Can't you see that?"

I want to argue, to tell her I've seen his injuries, and

they are very real and very severe. But how do I know that? Everyone here lies, and he's just another liar. I can't trust any of them. I don't even know if I can trust her. Where was she last night when the shifters attacked me and Dad? Hiding safely inside his house after he went to all that trouble to rescue her?

"Can you get me out?" I ask, deciding that's more important than whether or not she's a coward. "Please, I have to find my dad again. We can still get out of here. We can go back to our old lives."

"I'd love to, but I can't fight anyone in this shabby old body. If I could, I wouldn't be here with you."

"But—but can't you…" I stop, realizing she's right. She can't turn into a mouse and run back and tell Elidi about me. She's a different kind of shifter, one who hops from body to body instead of morphing from human to animal. She can't walk out of here any more than we can. She's a prisoner, too, at least in body.

But she can escape, in her strange way.

"I can't hang around in this dungeon with you, Stella," she says. "They know that's what I did, what I am. They don't like witches. That's why they threw me in this bin like a piece of garbage. They're waiting for me to come back to this body. If they find me here, they'll kill it before I can get out."

"But what about Dad?"

She glances over at Harmon, who lies with eyes closed, his chin still on his paws. Still, she turns fully so only I can see her face. "I'll be back," she mouths, then puts a finger to her lips. Out loud, she says, "I'm sorry, Stella. I can't help you right now. Find a way out of here, and we'll save your father."

With that, she lies down in her bin and pulls the lid closed. I shiver, a cold draft from the lid blowing across my bare ankles. Harmon's head snaps up and he lets out a single menacing snarl. For a second, I think she must have taken the form of a mouse here in the basement, and a bolt of terror goes through me. If he eats her as a mouse, will she die?

But then he lowers his head and closes his eyes again. I lay back, comforted by the thought that I will have an ally in this place. Unlike when I was in in Mother's attic, I'll have someone on my side. Maybe she won't be here all the time, but I know she'll come back to help me. Just like she did at my mother's.

I can only hope it won't take her two more years.

I sleep fitfully, hunger pangs twisting my guts even in sleep. A particularly cruel one brings me back to the surface of consciousness. All the damp and dank smells of the basement have disappeared behind the sweet, spicy smell of cinnamon. I sit up, searching for the source, sure that this is the most inhumane torture a person could endure.

And then I see the basket swinging gently over Harmon's head. I scramble to my feet, then cry out at the torch of pain that ignites my leg. It's getting worse, not better.

It can't stop me from getting to the food, though, even if I have to hop on one foot to get there. Touching my toe to the floor makes my ankle scream in agony. But the only thing that can stop me is the injured, sleeping wolf-boy directly under the food. I stop when I'm a few paces away. His side rises and falls, rises and falls. A two-inch gap in his black fur shows me what I saw from afar earlier. The skin is pulled back, exposing angry red muscle. I fight back the horror and focus on the basket of food instead. I'll have to reach over his head to get it, pull it towards me and untie it from the cord attached to the handle, while balancing on one foot, without waking him.

My stomach twists spitefully inside me as I eye the

basket, which has stopped swinging and begun to turn lazily. My eyes follow the path of the cord, up to the top of the ladder, where it's hooked over the rough wood. If I can get up the ladder, I can pull the basket up and have whatever is inside. But I'm not sure I can climb without adrenaline pumping through my blood. Even the thought of Mrs. Nguyen's abandoned body lying in a bin of vegetables across the room doesn't curb my appetite.

I take another hop towards the ladder, lose my balance, and pinwheel my arms wildly. I lurch forward, then back, and at last, I have to touch my injured foot to the floor to keep from pitching face first onto the creature sleeping under the ladder. Pain explodes through my foot, and I bite down on my tongue to keep from sobbing. After a few deep breaths, I am ready to go again. But I don't know how I can climb a ladder with one foot. Somehow, I'm going to have to do it, dragging myself up with my arms alone.

That, or starve.

I bend my knee, preparing for the next hop, when Harmon heaves a sigh and lets out a small whine. I squeeze my eyes shut, ball my hands into fists, praying for a little bit of luck just this one time. I'm overdue for it. When Harmon doesn't jump up and ask me what the hell I'm doing, I let myself relax and focus on the ladder again. Three more steps.

I bend my knee, hop forward, hold my arms out for balance. Harmon snuffles in his sleep, whimpers again. I force my eyes away from that deep, bloody swath of exposed muscle. Food is more important right now. My stomach roars in agreement.

I take another hop, sway dangerously, and find my center of gravity. One more step. I reach for the ladder.

With a burst of speed I didn't think he possessed, Harmon shoots forward, snapping and snarling. I shriek and dive away, forgetting my ankle until I try to take a running step on it. My body lurches forward and I slam against the cold dirt floor, the breath knocked out of me. Mind blank with fear, I scramble away from this mad wolf creature on elbows and knees. When his sharp wolf's teeth don't sink into my flesh, I stop, curl into a ball on my side, and grasp my leg. Sobs of pain wrack my body.

When at last I'm out of tears, I uncurl from the fetal position and take stock of the situation. Meeting my eyes, Harmon gives me a mournful gaze, but I shrink back in horror. He has a boy's mouth full of wolf's teeth. Pushing up onto his front paws—or, paw and hand, to be precise—his shoulders jut out at odd angles. The mostly human arm is longer than the wolf's leg, which gives him a crooked, off-kilter appearance.

But he's still in there, the human boy I knew.

"You're going to eat in front of me, and watch me starve?" I ask, pushing myself into a sitting position. Harmon shifts awkwardly, attempting to rise onto all four feet. The long human leg kicks out, scrabbling at the dirt, and he cants to one side as he attempts to pull it under him like a wolf's foot. Failing at this, he topples sideways. It's too horrific to laugh.

While he's occupied by his own pain, I scoot towards the ladder again. He hangs his head, breathing hard, and I feel so sorry for him that I almost offer to help. But when I open my mouth, my empty stomach answers for me.

Harmon lifts his head and gives me a sorrowful look with those big pale eyes. Then he eyes the basket, exactly the way a dog eyes food it can't have. Big, begging puppy dog eyes.

But this puppy is going to wolf down our food and let me die.

I search the basement shadows for something, anything, I can use. At last, I spot a broom in the corner beside the little, child-sized door. I ease myself that way, lifting my weight with my hands and crab-walking sideways on my good foot while the other one sticks up in the air. I must look ridiculous. But I don't care. Compared to Harmon…well, there's no comparison. He's a monstrosity.

More determined than ever, I make it to the broom. I stop and rest for a minute, but luckily, when I was trapped in my mother's house I built beds and shelves and tables and fences. My arms are strong.

I scoot forward and hook my good foot around the handle of the broom, knocking it right onto my head. I barely feel the bump where the handle smacks my forehead. All I want is to get that food before Harmon figures out how to use his new, freakish body to get it. On the way back across the basement, I have to stop and prop the broom back in my lap several times, and when I get back, my arms have started shaking at the effort. But it will be worth it when I get the food.

Using the broom as a cane, I climb to my feet. Harmon lies under the basket, his chin resting on his two mismatched hands, a dog's pose. "I'm going to get the food," I say. "If you try to attack me, I will hit you with this."

Harmon's mouth quirks up into a smirk, and something inside me twists as painfully as the hunger. That once teasing, beautiful mouth now belongs to an abomination, something out of a horror movie. That mouth I kissed just days ago. The thought turns my stomach now. I clutch the broom tighter.

"Okay?" I say. "I'll share with you. I promise."

He lets out a low growl, and I hop forward, using the broom for balance. If he waits until I'm fishing the basket from above him to attack me, he'll have an opening to my most vulnerable parts, full access to rip my guts out. I'd really like to come to an understanding before I do this.

"Are you going to attack me?" I ask.

He growls again. But so does my stomach. Keeping a close watch on him, I reach out with the head of the broom, fishing for the cord. I catch it and slide the broom down onto the handle of the basket. It's rectangular, with rounded corners and a wooden lid and handle. When I pull it closer, though, it slips off the head of the broom and swings wildly. Harmon attempts to jump to his feet, but he lurches to one side and goes sprawling, letting out a tortured howl.

I almost fall, but I catch my balance by dropping the broom head to the floor as a brace. While Harmon is still dragging himself towards standing, I thrust the broom head through the handle of the swinging basket. With a heave, I bring it to me and grab the handle just as the broom slips out. Harmon lunges forward again, and I bring the broom down hard with the momentum it already had from slipping free of the basket. It barely misses Harmon's head, and hits the floor in time to keep me from sprawling on top of him.

He bares his teeth, but he doesn't go after me. I wonder if he knows he's part human, part wolf. I wonder if he has a fully functioning human brain, or if he's flickering back and forth between the two. I wonder if he's lucid enough to realize he spoke to me in human language, that he's not all animal. But mostly, I wonder what is in the warm basket in my arms that smells like Christmas morning, trips to the mall with my best friend, rainy Sundays in the kitchen with flour dusting every surface and a huge grin on Dad's face when he opened the oven and smoke didn't billow out.

I scramble backwards, out of Harmon's reach. But I can't wait long enough to reach my spot under the window that has become my territory, just like the one under the ladder is Harmon's, through no fault of our own but because that's where we awoke in this prison. Greedily, I pull aside the handle, which is on a tiny hinge, and throw open the flaps of the lid. Inside, a warm, steamy layer of wrinkled cloth separates me from the food. With trembling fingers, I lift the cloth, sure that I'll find some trick inside—a scented candle, a warm crumb, nothing at all.

Instead, the basket is full of lumpy, fragrant swirls, the ridges oozing with dark, sticky sweetness. I pull out one of the cinnamon rolls and shove half of it into my mouth at once, closing my eyes and whimpering with relief. Not just food, but amazing food, the best thing I've ever tasted. My stomach rages for more. I shove in the other half, stuffing my cheeks so full I can hardly chew. I haven't eaten in days.

And there is plenty. When I finish the first one, I reach for another, savoring this one a little more, taking time to really chew. They're homemade, coarse and dark, the crust chewy and rough. Sticky syrup oozes between each layer, and raisins nestle into the soft, warm bread inside. I'm licking my fingers clean when I catch sight of Harmon lying under his ladder, curled up with his back to me. Defeated.

I won. But there's no thrill in beating such a pathetic creature. Suddenly, guilt washes over me. I should use these for bargaining with him, making him agree not to hurt me, to let me use the ladder. But I can't.

Holding one cinnamon roll in each hand, I crawl on my elbows towards him. When I'm within reach, I stop. He hasn't moved. My stomach drops when I let my eyes move to that gaping slash in his back, skin peeled back, the black fur matted around it with what must be blood. In the dark basement, I can't see a color difference between blood and fur. But I can see how badly he's wounded, and I know that my father is the one who attacked him.

Defending me, I remind myself. *Harmon would have killed me if my father hadn't intervened.*

"Harmon?" I whisper. Maybe it's stupid to put myself within his reach again, but I can't bring myself to be self-ish. "I brought you some food. Please don't bite me."

He doesn't move. If he bled to death while I stuffed my face, I'm to blame. But I don't know how I could have helped, either. I'm not a doctor, and he needs more than a cinnamon roll. Suddenly, my broken ankle seems like a scratch in comparison. I've been so distracted by that pain that I barely noticed his. I can't imagine what kind of agony he's in. No wonder he snapped at me.

"Here," I say, scooting forward so he won't have to move. I extend a cinnamon roll above his head, not wanting to set it on the dirt. My hand is shaking as he lifts his head, but I don't pull back. He sniffs, then raises his hideous face to look at me. I try not to flinch, in case he can smell my fear. Or in case his thoughts are more human, and he sees my revulsion.

He pushes at my hand with his short wolf nose, then draws back, his head sagging. "It's okay," I say. "You need to eat, too. I won't look." I turn my face away, not wanting to see him eating with his human lips and sharp wolf fangs, his stubby flat dog nose. After a second, he takes a bite. I wince every time he presses down into my hand for more, sure he's going to bite me.

But soon, I'm distracted from that fear by the sensation of his lips on my palm. I know I should be thinking of him like a dog, but he's not a dog. He's a boy. And his lips are soft and warm every time they brush against my skin. When he's finished, his face presses into my hand for just a second, and suddenly, I'm sure he's going to lick me, like a dog. My heart skips a beat when his hot breath fills my palm. But he turns his face away without a word.

I let out a breath and back away slowly, suddenly awkward. Once again, he's a disgusting monster, an animal who bit me. But I can't stop feeling weird about how easy it was to forget that, even when he was eating out of my hand. I leave him another cinnamon roll and retreat to my corner, where, my stomach full at last, I fall into a deep, exhausted sleep.

6.

When I wake again, the basket is still next to me. The first thing I do is check to make sure no one has stolen my food. Four cinnamon rolls remain, now cold but still tempting. I break off half of one and chew it slowly. My head is clearer now, and the pain is mostly gone. I check my hand, where Harmon bit me, and am happy to see scabs forming over the punctures, and no redness or swelling.

Now that my mind is clear, I begin to question the past few days. Maybe I imagined it all—the eclipse, my father, Mrs. Nguyen's visit. But no. That's how I ended up here. At the very least, I should double check that she's alive and begin to formulate a plan to get out and find my father again.

Someone brought the food, lowered it down from above. Which means someone unlocked and opened the door above the ladder. Which means there is a way out. I don't have anything to negotiate with, but they must want something. I just have to figure out what it is, and then figure out how to give it to them.

Since Harmon is in here with me, I can be pretty certain of who my captors are. It doesn't bring much comfort. No matter their faults, at least the wolf pack didn't throw me in a dark basement with a dying wolf and let me starve for days. From what I know about shifters, which admittedly isn't much, I'd rather be in the wolves' custody.

Still, there's a certain power in knowing even this much. If I know who my enemies are, maybe I can find out what they want. If they're trying to negotiate my release with the wolves, though, I could be in for a long imprisonment. The wolves don't want me back.

But they'll want Harmon. He's their Alpha now, after all.

I turn to the corner of the basement and squint into the darkness, trying to make out his form under the ladder. If I ally myself with him, maybe they'll take us both as a package deal, and he won't leave me here to rot. After all, he told me to say I belonged to him. As much as the thought makes me bristle with indignation, it might matter to these people.

In the darkness of the basement, I can't see him. I listen, straining my ears for the sound of his breathing. Suddenly, my heart begins to hammer against my ribs. I can't hear him breathing. What if he's dead?

Picking up the broom, I part the straw that makes the head and prop it under my arm like a crutch. Holding onto the handle and bracing the end on the floor, I hop towards Harmon's territory. Part of me doesn't want to see him lying there, dead. But I can't seem to stop myself from investigating. Not knowing is worse than finding out the truth.

When I come within sight of his spot, it looks impossibly flat. I move closer, straining to see what I already know isn't there. The spot under the ladder is empty, except for a twisted blanket pushed against the wall and a bloodstain in the dirt.

I sink down onto the floor and stare at the empty space. As bad as this basement was with him in it, now that he's gone, I know that I'd rather share this dungeon with a monster than face it alone.

I'm still sitting on the cold dirt floor when I hear him howl, somewhere in another room. I shiver and sit up straight, listening. Then it comes again, a yipping howl of pain. I wince. Listening to him howl, followed by a loud, shrill whine, I know he's in pain. As awful as he can be, I never wanted him to hurt.

I think of that big red gash on his back, and I wonder if they're poking it, torturing him. I crawl back to my corner and wait, heart hammering, for them to come for me. Instead, whatever they are doing to him goes on and on, until I think I'll go crazy having to listen to it. I can't imagine what he's going through right now. And I don't want to.

If they kill him, I'll never get out. The wolves won't bargain to get me back. They'll be glad to be rid of me. I can't stop thinking about how creepy all the shifters I've met have been—from the suggestive comments Efrain made and the way he looked at me, to the things my cousin and that other guy said. They treated me like a bargaining chip, and if I didn't turn out to be as valuable as they expected, they'd find some other twisted use for me.

I shiver and wrap my arms around myself, huddling into my corner. Without my mother to protect me by locking me in her attic, I have no chance. I'm completely alone and in the hands of a bunch of animals who live by their own rules. Or no rules, if the wolves are to be believed.

When the howls subside at last, and only a quiet whimper drifts into the room, a soft, feminine voice speaks. I strain to hear what she's saying, but I can't make out her words.

"Can you undo it?" Harmon asks, his voice hoarse and still garbled as he speaks past his new teeth.

The answer is so soft I can't hear it. Frustrated, I move towards the tiny door, trying to hear the other side of the conversation.

"I didn't do anything," Harmon growls. "She wanted to Choose my mate."

I'm still hovering near the tiny door when it swings open. Stifling a cry, I stumble back against the wall. On all fours, Harmon lurches through the opening on his crooked legs. Watching him walk is worse than anything, that one human leg so repulsive suddenly, when attached to the wrong body. But when he enters the room, his middle is swathed in a wide, white bandage. I can't tell if that's all that holds in his guts now, or if it's a bandage.

Swallowing hard, I force down my questions and close my fingers around the handle of my broom. Pathetic as it may be, it's my only weapon.

Without so much as a glance in my direction, Harmon paws his blanket from the knot against the wall, spreads it out, and collapses onto it. And still no one has come through the door. When I'm sure no one is going to, I begin to creep towards Harmon. In the dark, his white bandage moves slowly up and down as he breathes. At last,

I reach him, and whisper a question into the darkness. He doesn't answer.

I place a hand on his side, tentatively, and a shudder passes across his skin. But he doesn't stir. I sit over him, in the near-dark, waiting for him to wake up so I can ask him what happened. But after a while, I grow drowsy. It's not Harmon now, but an injured animal. So I lie down beside him, not against him but close enough that I can sleep with my hand still resting on him. If they come to take him away, this time I'll know it. If he wakes in pain, I'll know it.

I sleep fitfully, half of my mind on alert for someone to come in or for Harmon to wake. Finally, near dawn, I sleep for a few hours. When I wake, Harmon has turned to face me. His eyes are open, watching me, their paleness almost glowing in the dimly lit room. Still drowsy, I lie there, returning his gaze, neither of us moving, for what seems like forever.

Finally, awareness sinks in. I'm lying next to a boy. A boy who wanted to kill me the night we were captured. A boy who already hated me because I almost killed his father, and because my father almost killed him. A boy who is now a beastly human-wolf hybrid who bit me just days ago.

A boy who kissed me like I was the only girl on earth.

"What you doin' there, Stella?" he whispers.

"Nothing." I sit up quickly, then gasp at the pain in my ankle when it touches the floor. Biting down on my lip until the throbbing subsides, I manage not to cry in front of him.

"What's wrong?" Harmon asks, his eyes still intent on me.

"Nothing," I say again, bracing my hands on the floor to scoot away. "Just my ankle."

He reaches for my hand as if to stop me, then pauses, staring at his wolf paw like it's not his own. He sets it down on the dirt and studies his mismatched paws. One is wolf, the other is a deformity. Long human fingers, wolf claws, fur.

While he's temporarily occupied with figuring out what he is, I take the opportunity to scoot away. I don't know how he'll react to the realization that he's no longer the sexy, strutting guy he was in his own pack. Now he's not only a prisoner, he's a monstrous thing, a *creature*. I should feel sorry for him, that he's lost everything. But for the moment, I only think of how little sympathy he and the wolves had for me when I arrived in their valley after losing everything.

7.

I've lost track of the days since I've been here, sleeping and waking at odd times in the dark basement. But after what must be a week, I'm going crazy sitting around doing nothing. In my mother's attic, I was always cleaning, or building something, or she let me out to help around the house or in the backyard. When I had nothing else to do, I could always read.

While Harmon lies motionless under the ladder, recovering from whatever was done to him, I push myself upright with the help of the broom and hobble around the room. Outside, the sun is shining, but it barely makes it through the dirt-streaked window. Still, my eyes have grown accustomed to the gloom over the past week.

I hobble to the wooden bins that line the wall beside the freezer. Since the last time she visited, I've been waiting for Mrs. Nguyen to return as promised. But I have been too preoccupied with other things—pain, hunger, fear—to dwell on it. It has lurked in the back of my mind, though, a nagging voice wondering if this is yet another trick. No one is trustworthy here. Whether it's my mother, who threw me in her attic instead of welcoming me into the family, or a father who didn't jump to my rescue the moment he saw that I was in danger.

Using the edge of the bins for balance, I hop down to

the one I think holds the body. With a quick glance at the door to make sure no one is coming, I grip the heavy wooden lid and lift. Inside, a mountain of dusty potatoes greets me. She's gone.

My pulse quickens as I lower the lid, feeling guiltier now than I did before opening the lid. How did they get a human body out without my noticing? I don't sleep that deeply. Maybe I have the wrong bin. I hop to the next bin and grip the edge of the wooden lid.

"Curiosity killed the cat."

I spin around, my heart slamming against my throat so hard I can barely swallow.

Harmon has pushed himself up on his one human elbow. His mouth twists into a smirk, grotesque on his half-human face.

It gives me a certain courage that I wouldn't have if he was still the gorgeous boy I met three years ago. "Don't you want to know if she's still here?" I ask. "Or where we are? How to get out?"

"I know where we are."

"So do I," I say. "We're in a dungeon, and there's a body in one of these bins. And if they'd just throw her into a bin of potatoes and leave her for dead, what do you think they'll do to us?"

He just sits there, not blinking, watching me like I'm a child having a tantrum. "I think we'll be okay," he says at last.

"What's wrong with you?" I ask, throwing up my hands. "Don't you want to get out of here? Don't you want to be able to go lead your pack, and be able to eat whatever you want, and use a real bathroom instead of a bucket, and wear something besides this stupid dress." I tear at the puffy, bedraggled skirt as I speak.

"Of course I want to get out," he says bitterly. "But when is that going to happen? Look at me." He holds up his hands. "I don't even know what I am."

"Then why are you so calm?"

"Because what you're doing, freaking out, is not helping."

"Easy for you to say." I turn back to the bins. "You're the Alpha now, right? They'll negotiate to get you back. The pack can't function without its leader. But what am I? A freak for not being a freak? They don't want me back."

"Stella…"

"Don't patronize me," I snap, and wrench open the next bin.

And even though I knew she was here, even though I saw her before, it still startles me. I let out a little shriek and drop the lid.

Harmon chuckles.

I spin around to face him, fury swelling inside me. "Just because you're some werewolf freak and probably eat dead bodies doesn't mean it's normal," I hiss. "The only dead body I've ever seen is my father. There. Does that make you happy?"

The smile drops from his face, but he keeps staring at me with those inscrutable blue eyes. "She's not dead."

"How do you know? She could die any time, and we'd never know. We'd lose our only hope of getting out of here. Do you even know who this is? Mrs. Nguyen, my babysitter. You know her?"

"I know…of her."

I throw open the lid to the bin and gesture at her body. "Then why don't you tell me all about her, since you know so much. How about you start with what she has to do with all this magical weirdness around here. Or maybe we could start with the important stuff first, like why they threw her in a bin of potatoes—."

"Onions."

I stop ranting long enough to take a breath. "What?"

"They're not potatoes," he says. "They're onions."

"Onions, whatever," I explode. "That's not the point. I'm sick of being kept in the dark. Why won't anyone tell me anything? I know your secrets, Harmon. You're a were-wolf. Big freaking deal. I'm over it. So just tell me what's going on, so we can figure out how to get out of here before they throw us in the onion bin with her. Because like I said, if they'll toss another shifter in the basement and forget about her, or I don't know, maybe they threw her in with the food because they're planning to eat her? So what are they going to do with us?"

Harmon pushes himself up, wincing, and seems to be trying to figure out how to sit with his mismatched legs. It occurs to me suddenly that he might have an actual tail. The thought makes me shudder in revulsion.

"She's not a shifter," he says.

I throw up my hands in exasperation. "Well, whatever you want to call her. A form shifter, a skin walker, a were-mouse, a projectionist, a person who takes the form of an animal. Sorry I'm not up to speed on your terminology."

"She's not a shapeshifter," he says.

"Fine," I say through clenched teeth. "A witch. Does it really matter?" I turn my attention to the body lying in the bin, still wearing so much camo it looks like she's joined the army and is setting off on her first mission. Nothing is impossible anymore.

"It's somewhat important, if we're putting labels on things," he says.

"Well, I saw her turn into a mouse," I say. "So she's a shifter to me."

"Really? You saw her body change from human to mouse?"

"She left her body, and turned into a mouse."

"Yeah," he says, lying back down with a grimace. "That's what sorcerer's do. Shifters don't leave their bodies. They transition into something else. Like us." He lifts his half-human hand and flexes it, staring up at it like he doesn't recognize it.

"A mirror," I say, remembering what she told me.

"What?"

"A mirror. That's what she is."

"No," he says with exaggerated patience. "A mirror is when she does it to a human and refuses to give the body back, thereby killing the rightful owner, and then she pretends to be that person. That's a mirror."

"Right." I look back at her body and a shiver goes through me. I remember standing over my father's body, shaking him, unable to wake him. Running next door to Mrs. Nguyen, crying. I remember her calling Dr. Golden and coming over to look at my father. Telling me he was dead.

A lump swells in my throat, and I reach out to touch her cheek. She held me while I cried. She went to the funeral with me.

But then I pull back, a fresh wave of fury ripping through me. She let me go on believing he was dead, even when she saw it destroying me. Did they bury his body and then dig it up once I was gone? I understand that my father couldn't come home because he was trapped, but she knew all along that he wasn't dead. She could have told me the truth, or at least tipped me off somehow. Instead, she watched me suffer and did nothing. If even the mothball-scented cat lady next door can betray me, who can I trust?

A scraping sound draws my attention, and I turn back to see the little door in the corner of the basement opening.

"Now *she's* a shifter," Harmon says.

Before I can ask what he means, a figure appears, stooping to come through the door before straightening. In the dimness, I can't make out more than the shape of a woman, her hair in two long braids. A memory tugs at me, but it doesn't fully form until she strides over to me with a bag in one hand. Up close, she looks just like…

"Dr. Golden?" I whisper, unable to believe what my brain is telling me.

"I hear you're having a problem with your ankle." Though she must be in her mid-forties, her soft, childlike voice makes her seem young. The same voice I heard through the walls the other day, when Harmon was screaming.

"Who—what are you doing here?" I blurt out, shrinking away from her.

"I'm here to look at your ankle," she says. "Can you walk?"

"Uh…kind of," I say, glancing at Harmon. "But why are you here? Is my dad here? Is he okay?"

It's her turn to glance at Harmon. "We'll worry about that later."

"No," I say. "I want to know. I don't care if Harmon knows. Why won't anyone tell me anything?"

"Just let her look at your ankle," Harmon growls from under the ladder. "She's a doctor in just about every culture."

Ignoring him, Dr. Golden gives me an encouraging smile. It's hard to imagine her inflicting pain on anyone. "Have a seat, and I'll make sure it's not broken."

After a second, I relent. I hobble back to my spot under the window and sink down in relief. While Dr. Golden gently prods at my ankle, flexes my foot, and asks me when it hurts, my mind goes back to the moment when she walked in.

She's a shifter.

That's what Harmon said.

"Is…is Emmy here?" I ask, not daring to hope that my best friend from my old life will appear next. If my dad is here, and Mrs. Nguyen is here, and Dr. Golden is here, couldn't she be here, too? Maybe she's a fairy princess. It wouldn't be any more unlikely than the rest of this nightmare.

"Who?" Dr. Golden asks, not looking up from my ankle. She sets my foot down and opens her bag, which looks like an old-fashioned doctor's kit. I flinch at the sight of a scalpel. That could make someone howl like Harmon did.

"Emmy," I say to distract myself from visions of her

slicing open my ankle without anesthetic. "My best friend."

"I don't know that person," she says.

I sink back in disappointment. Of course not.

"So what about my dad?"

She leans forward and lowers her voice so I can barely hear her. "I'll see what I can find out." Then she stands and says in a normal voice, "It's sprained, maybe fractured. I'll get a brace on it and it'll take care of itself. Try not to put weight on it."

I sneak a glance at Harmon, wondering why she doesn't want him to know if my dad's alive. Wondering why I'm always the last to know everything.

"Is anything else hurting?" Dr. Golden asks. "I can give you a further exam, if you need one."

"No, I'm fine," I say. "Can you get us out of here?"

"That's a nasty bruise," she says, crouching down again. She touches my sore cheek. In the time I've been here, I haven't once thought about how I look. For all I know, I'm as hideous as Harmon.

I allow Dr. Golden to move my head back and forth, answer her questions about whether my neck is sore. "You really shouldn't be sleeping on the floor," she says.

"Yeah, thanks, I'll book a room at the Hilton tonight."

She pats my knee. "I think you'll be okay," she says. "At least your lovely sense of humor is still intact."

I wrack my brain for memories of her, for all the times I've gone to see her. Dad called her the witch doctor, which is a bit ironic now that I know there actually are witches. She gave me tea for the blackouts and migraines and nightmares I developed after falling down a flight of stairs. I try to remember that incident, but like usual, it's veiled in darkness.

"Wait," I say, grabbing her hand when she goes to stand again.

"Where's your necklace?" she asks, her gaze falling to my neck.

My hand goes to my throat, but the necklace is gone. The last time I saw it, Dad was slipping it into Mrs. Nguyen's pocket. "You remember my necklace?"

"Of course," she says. "I was there when your father bought it."

While I'm still mulling this over, she stands and walks out, leaving the little door standing wide open. I look at Harmon. He looks at me.

I wonder where that door leads. He's been out there, so he knows. But I don't. And I don't have time to ask him. I feel a little bad making a run for it and leaving him. But they won't kill him. They can't. He's too important. I'm not important, which makes me expendable. And before they can realize that, I've got to get out of here.

Besides, Harmon's injuries are too severe. It's bad enough that I have to limp and hop the whole way to the little door. If I had to help Harmon, we wouldn't make it ten feet past the door. I duck through the opening and knock my head on a dirt ceiling. I'm in a little tunnel, no taller than the door. It ends about ten feet ahead, but my ankle is not going to cooperate. I drop onto hands and knees and attempt to crawl through, which is made incredibly difficult by the long skirt of my sister's gown, which I'm still wearing.

When I make it to the end of the tunnel, I crawl out

with relief, only to find myself in a small, cozy room that resembles someone's personal library. A low wooden table and four padded leather chairs with low backs and armrests sit in the center. Two candles burn in the center of the table, along with a vase of tiny white flowers. Beside the door from which I emerged, and on the wall opposite, are bookshelves lined with books. The third wall, beyond the table, contains stacks of dusty board game boxes with broken corners, a shelf of records and an old-fashioned record player, a lamp, a globe, and other odds and ends crammed there for easy storage.

After a cursory glance, my gaze falls on what I'm looking for. Directly opposite the door I emerged from is another doorway, this one normal sized.

I rush to it and dart through, only to find myself in a bedroom. It's dim and damp, but in the light filtering in one tiny window, I can make out a patchwork quilt on the bed. All this time sleeping on the dirt floor, and I could have been here, in a real bed. Instantly, I wonder who has been here. Who sleeps down here, just through a sitting room and a little tunnel to where I am?

Before I can think too much about it, a door swings open and Dr. Golden steps out, wiping her hands on her pants. "Oh, hi, Stella," she says, as if this is perfectly normal. "I didn't know you could walk this far or I would have had you come in here for the exam."

Without a word, I charge. It's not a very powerful charge, since I have to hobble the whole way, but I catch her by surprise and barrel past her, through the door from which she emerged.

I find myself in a windowless bathroom.

I start to laugh, and I can't stop. I laugh until I'm crying, until my sides hurt. I'm stuck here, underground, like a mole. My great escape brought me not freedom but a toilet.

Still, when my hysterics end, I decide I could really use a shower. It's been at least a week, maybe more. Dr. Golden stands in the doorway, looking at me like I'm insane, which might be partially true.

"Can I take a shower?" I ask.

"I don't see why not." She hits the light switch, steps out and closes the door, and I'm alone. I drop my dress and underthings and throw them aside before stepping into the shower stall. My feet are black against the white tile, and the warm water rushing over me feels like life itself is flowing over my body, like I'm a plant being watered by the rain.

Even if Dr. Golden is a shifter, and therefore, allied with my captors, I am grateful to her for now. For this small blessing that suddenly seems so momentous. There is no way out of the bathroom—no second door, no windows—but just being clean makes me feel more human. I hadn't realized how dirty I was, with blood and dirt caked on my knees and ankles, scrapes that by some miracle didn't get infected from the dirt crusted into my scabs, my hair hanging in tangled, greasy clumps.

When I climb out of the shower at last, I stop short. I left my dress and dirty undergarments strewn where they fell. But now they are gone. Sitting on the closed lid of the toilet is a towel and a neatly folded stack of clean clothes. It's a little creepy, but I just hope it was Dr. Golden who came into the bathroom while I was showering, not my creepy cousin or any other shifter guy.

I pull on the pair of jeans, almost groaning with the pleasure of wearing something that's not stiff with dirt. They're not nice new clothes, but I don't care. The jeans are worn soft with age, and the small tear in the knee looks like it ripped naturally instead of for the sake of fashion. I pull on the t-shirt and then the sweatshirt, zipping it up and snuggling into it. They're all a little too big, but so much better than the dress that I'm suddenly and inexplicably tearful with gratitude. The only thing missing are socks and shoes, and I cringe a little when I step out of the bathroom onto the dirt floor of the bedroom in my bare feet.

Dr. Golden is sitting on the bed with her kit all laid out. Immediately, I'm on edge, remembering Harmon's howls. "Will this hurt?" I ask.

"It shouldn't hurt much," she says, patting the bed. She pushes her two long, blonde braids back and gets to work setting my ankle as soon as I sit down. As she works, I look around the tiny, bare bedroom. Besides a bed, there is a small dresser and a side table and a door. At first, I don't dare hope. It must be a closet.

But Dr. Golden didn't come through the door above the ladder. She had to get in somehow.

When she finishes the brace, she has me stand. The brace is unwieldy and cumbersome, and I have to limp around, but it didn't hurt.

She closes her bag and stands.

"What about my dad?" I ask quickly.

"I'll see what I can find out," she says, glancing at the

door. "I haven't seen him. There were so many who were injured in the attack—on both sides. If your father hasn't called me, I can only assume he's fine."

"Can you find out for me?"

She sighs. "You should really talk to Harmon."

"What would he know about my father?"

She looks like she's going to say more, then shakes her head. "Honestly, Stella. I'm just a doctor. I don't play politics."

"Not just a doctor," I point out. "Harmon says you're also a shifter."

For a second, she eyes me, as if waiting for me to say more. When I don't, she nods. "I am a shifter, among other things. My calling is to help people, no matter who or what they are. That comes first."

That gets me. She's the one who felt Dad's pulse, told me he was dead. "Like when you helped Mrs. Nguyen pretend my father was dead?" I ask.

"I'm sorry about that," she says, looking genuinely pained. "I know it doesn't matter, but I told them I didn't want to be in on it. I didn't think it was right. But your father insisted you would be fine once you arrived here. And Yvonne gave your mother's contact information to the state, stayed until you were safely here."

Suddenly, I remember seeing a mountain lion in the woods my first day in the Three Valleys. Was that my dad, making sure I arrived safely? And if it was, why didn't he come and get me then?

"Why didn't he have me sent to him?" I ask.

She looks uncomfortable, but offers me a small smile. "You should talk to him, Stella. I'm sure he had a reason for sending you to your mother. Maybe he thought you could benefit from getting to know your mother."

A snort escapes me. "Have you met my mother?"

She smiles sadly. "I have."

Without another word, she holds up a hand, makes a quick excuse, and walks back towards the tunnel. I want nothing more than to chase after her and trap her here until she explains away all their betrayals. But more than that, I want to lie on this soft bed and sleep for a hundred years. After a minute or two, I start to get that creeped out feeling like I'm in someone else's bedroom, which I am. I rise from the bed. As soon as I hear Harmon and Dr. Golden talking, I jump up and try the door next to the bathroom. Locked.

Of course. Just because they sent a doctor down, and she's nice, doesn't mean they'll let us walk out of here. With a sigh, I hobble back through the library room, and through the tunnel, and push the little door. At first, I think it's locked, but after a few seconds, it gives and swings open.

"Well, look at you," Harmon says from his spot under the ladder. Dr. Golden is kneeling beside him, checking his bandages.

"Yeah, look at me," I say, suddenly feeling a little awkward in my too-big clothes.

"You were just complaining you wanted to get out of that dress."

"I never want to see a dress again," I say, stopping at one of the support poles and leaning against it.

"I didn't think you'd be back," he says, rolling over so Dr. Golden can see his back. She doesn't look up from what she's doing, but I don't want to give anything away in front of a shifter.

"Why wouldn't I be?" I ask carefully.

"You found the shower," he says. "You must have seen the bed."

"Yeah…"

"So you should sleep there."

"Why?"

"Because it's a bed," he says. "And you're sleeping on the floor now."

"Why don't you sleep there?"

"You're a girl," he says. "You should have the bed."

I laugh, then catch myself and stop. Nothing about this is funny. "You're important," I say. "You should have it. Plus, you're injured."

"I'm fine here," he says sharply.

"So am I," I say, pushing away from the pole and hobbling back to my spot. "And besides, I don't know whose bed that is. What if someone comes down to sleep there and finds me. I'd rather be here."

"Right. Because I'm going to be able to protect you so well."

"I don't need protecting," I say. "I have my broom."

Harmon makes a sound that might be a laugh, but it's bitter. "How do I fix this?" he asks Dr. Golden.

"I can't lift another witch's curse," she says. "Let's hope you're okay by the next full moon."

"That's in two weeks," he says. "I don't think I'll be okay by then."

"You have three moons to heal," she says. "That's plenty of time."

His face goes still for a second, his eyes hardening. "Until what?"

"You're a wolf," she says, standing. "You know what."

Even I know what. If they don't transition into their wolf form for three months, they lose the ability forever, something my sisters said is a fate comparable to death.

"I'm sorry," I say when Dr. Golden goes back into the tunnel.

Harmon rises unsteadily to his four feet. He does have a tail. I look away in disgust, trying to hide my expression. But he's not worried about my reaction. He lurches out of the room, leaving the little door open behind him. Just as I relax against the wall, a giant crash sounds in the other room. Harmon howls, but this time, it's not a pained howl but one of rage. I wrap my arms around myself and huddle against the wall, glad he's not in this room as he tears around out there, throwing things and screaming.

I wish he'd stop, though. When the shifters come down and see what he's done to their basement rooms, they're not going to be happy. But I'm not going to go out there into the line of fire.

At last, Harmon wears himself out and limps back into the room, where he flops down under the ladder with his back to me. He must have torn open his wound again, because a spot appears on the clean bandage as I lay there watching him.

"Are you okay?" I whisper after a while.

"No," he says. "I'm not okay. I'm a werewolf who can't turn into a human or a wolf. I'm a monster."

"But it'll get better, right?" I ask. "Maybe when you

transition into one or the other at the next full moon, you'll get…unstuck."

"You wouldn't understand," he says.

"What don't I understand? My sisters told me what it was like. That it's like missing half yourself if you can't transition. But Dr. Golden said you have three months to get better."

"It's not three months," he says quietly. "It's three full moons. And next month, we have a blue moon."

A blue moon. Two full moons in one month.

I sink back to the floor and try to think of something good to say. "That's only a few days less," I say. "The full moons are still twenty-eight days apart."

"And what if this time counts, because I couldn't transition back to human?"

I don't have an answer for that.

The days pass with agonizing slowness. Upon visiting the tiny bathroom the next day, I discover the mirror shattered into a million shards of glass, glittering and crunching underfoot. I don't mention it to Harmon. I try to stay out of his way in the following days, to occupy myself and ignore his presence as he paces the basement, scowling, or trying to figure out his limits, his balance, his strength.

After a few days, the glass on the bathroom floor disappears, but the frame hangs there with a few broken shards stuck in the edges, like a cruel reminder.

But slowly, I stop noticing what Harmon looks like. Over the next weeks, I grow accustomed to my imprisonment. After being Mother's servant for years, I almost feel indulgent when I sit around reading all day. And it's nice to have a toilet again after years of using a bucket. Nice to have a shower without having to first heat the water on a stove. The dresser is full of clean, comfortable clothes, and the shelves are full of books.

Every morning when I wake, there is food in the basket hanging above Harmon. Usually, we sit in silence on the dirt floor, sharing the meal, our backs turned to each other. If it's not exactly gourmet, it's a step up from the food I ate at Mother's. In the evenings, we either eat what's left or find food on the small table in the next room.

Despite the comfort of our prison, I check the doors every day. They are always locked.

One day, as Harmon emerges from the tunnel into the little room, he catches me playing the *Memory Game*.

"Are you playing *Memory* by yourself?" he asks, a note of scorn in his voice.

"Who else am I going to play it with?" I ask when he doesn't stalk off like usual. "You?"

He glowers, which is his usual response. It doesn't bother me so much anymore. I'm used to it. "I may look like a mutant, but I didn't hit my head," he says. "My memory is fine."

"Okay. If you want."

He scoots in opposite me at the table while I politely avert my eyes to avoid embarrassing him as he struggles to do something so ordinary and human.

"Deal me in," he says, but he won't meet my eyes. Despite his surly, bitter attitude about everything, I can't help but feel sorry for him. I'd probably be just as insufferable if I was in his place. "You're staring," he growls.

"Oh—I'm sorry." I sweep the cards off the table and into my lap, then lay them out in rows, face down. This time, I'm the one who can't look at him. "I wasn't staring," I say after a minute.

"I told you, I didn't hit my head," he says. "I'm not stupid, Stella. I know what I look like." His lip curls in disgust. "You pretending otherwise doesn't make me forget. It only reminds me."

"I'm sorry," I say again, laying the last card and

meeting his eyes. "What do you want me to do? If I pretend you're normal, it reminds you. If I'm staring, you snap at me."

"Stop feeling sorry for me," he growls, flipping over two cards—smack-smack!—like he's settling a score. He scowls at them and turns them back over.

"You make that easy," I say, flipping over two more cards.

For just a second, I think I see a smile playing on his boy lips. But instead of answering, he flips over two more cards. I've seen one before, and I try for it when it's my turn, but I get the wrong one. "And you thought I had a bad memory," he says, collecting the matching pair.

"I don't have a bad memory. I just got them mixed up. You're distracting me."

This time, I'm sure the corner of his mouth pulls up for just a second. "Okay," he says, taking his next turn. "Tell me what you remember."

"About…?" I ask, wary of what he's asking.

"About anything," he says, seeming not to notice my cautious answer. "How you got here, or the night it happened, or your life before. I don't really know you, Stella." He looks at me steadily, though I see the flinch in his eyes when my eyes move from his human mouth to his dog eyes, and then away.

"Why would you want to do that?" I ask. "You never bothered before."

"You were in someone's attic. I made an effort."

"You didn't make an effort to get me out."

"Would you have, if you'd seen me in the attic of my house?"

I make my first match despite his distracting line of questions. I remember the thumps I heard coming from his house one night. "No," I admit, flipping over two more cards.

"And why would you? You don't know me, so why would you risk yourself for me?" He makes another match. "I didn't save you. There it is. The truth. Now here we are. So what are we going to do?"

I stop with my hand on a card. "There's no *we* here, Harmon. You made that clear from the day we woke up here."

"I'm sorry I bit you," he says seriously. "I wasn't myself. But now I am." He gives a small, ironic smile and shakes his head. "So let's remedy this. One day, maybe I'll be Alpha and you'll be in the pack. So tell me something. Anything. What else do we have to do?"

I know he's hitching himself to me, the way I thought of doing at first. He wants me to know him so I'll take him with me when I go. I'm the strong one, the healthy one. It would be a huge risk to try to take him with me.

But he's right about one thing. I have nothing else to do but talk. So I tell him.

While we finish the game, I tell him about my life before magic. Before werewolves and shifters and witches. I tell him about Emmy, and how we wanted to be models. To my surprise, it doesn't embarrass me. Now that years separate that girl from this one, I can laugh about it. Those wounds are no longer painful. Time has made my child-hood into scars, my dreams into silly stories. Three years ago, I was a child playing dress-up, as out of touch with reality as a five-year-old saying she wants to be a princess when she grows up.

"Do you miss it?" he asks when I finish.

I shuffle through my stack of matched pairs. "No. I don't let myself think about it anymore."

"Why not?"

"Because it made me sad," I say simply.

"It sounds happy to me."

"It was. That's why it makes me sad. I know I'll never have that now."

"What if you could? Would you go back?"

I give him an incredulous look. "Of course I'd go back. I was happy there. Here, I'm a prisoner and an abomination. In case you've forgotten, your people don't look favorably on identical twins."

"What do you miss most?" he asks, like this is some kind of game.

I sigh. "Emmy. Clothes. Food. Freedom. I don't know, being normal, I guess. Being happy. It's hard to explain."

"I think you did okay."

"It's not one thing," I say. "It's all of it. Having a simple, carefree life. Going to school, boys, friends, makeup, a phone. Those are things from that life. But what I miss most is that life itself."

"And you could only get it back if you lived there again?"

I shrug. "I'll never get it back. I know about werewolves. I've been a prisoner for three years. I'm never going to be normal."

"What if you could have one part of it here," he says. "What part would make you happiest?"

"My dad." I wait, my heart beating, for him to rage against the man who made him into a monster, wounded him so badly he can't transition. I haven't asked him about it once. All this time, for almost a month, I've been waiting for this moment. A moment when he might tell me something real.

"What was he like?" His voice is casual, but I can hear an undercurrent of calculation to that apparent disinterest. He's a liar, like all of them. I have to remember, even when we're talking like friends, that he's not a friend. He's an enemy.

"He was a great dad," I say. "I miss him more than anything. I guess he's the only thing I still miss. It doesn't help to know he's still alive somewhere close by. That there's a possibility I'll see him again. That makes it hard to let go."

He takes the cards and begins to lay them out again. "How do you know he's close by?"

"Mrs. Nguyen told me."

"Witches are notorious for twisting the truth to suit them."

"You're one to talk."

He hesitates and then nods. "You're right."

"She had no reason to lie," I say after a tense moment. "I thought he was dead. She could have let me think that forever."

"You were close to your dad?"

"I thought so." A trace of bitterness creeps into my voice, and I check to see if Harmon noticed. He did. His eyes are intent on me, curious. It strikes me how ridicu-

68

lously doglike he looks, and I have to stop myself from laughing.

"What?" he asks.

"Nothing," I say. "It's just funny, you know? My whole life, I thought I knew my dad so well. And now I find out he had this whole other life. He's a shifter. He married a werewolf. Our neighbor was a witch, and our doctor was a shifter. And he knew it all along. I know he did."

"And that's funny?"

"It's ridiculous that you even exist. It's the stuff of fairy tales, not real life."

"Here I am," he says. "In real life. To me, there is no other world. I can't imagine that world you talk about. I don't know your dad, Stella. If that's what you're hoping I'll tell you. About what kind of person he was, how he led this life you never knew about. I'm older than you, but not by much. I don't remember him from back then, before you left."

"Oh." I look down at the blue design on the backs of all the cards, and suddenly, playing silly kid games is the last thing I want to do.

"But I know something about him," he says.

I swallow hard, my throat aching. Maybe he doesn't know my dad is the one who attacked him at all. "What do you know?" I whisper.

I'm sure as hell not going to tell him.

"I've heard stories about him."

"Really?" I ask. "Why would anyone tell stories about my dad?"

Harmon shifts in his seat and switches around a few cards without looking at them. Apparently he's not in a hurry to play again, either. "What do you know?" he asks at last.

"Nothing," I say before I have time to think through it, to be crafty and get him to reveal information that he thinks I already know. I'm good at that after a few years of using it to find out any scrap of information I could glean while in my mother's attic. "But my sister doesn't even remember him," I add. "So that means my mother is telling the stories? The woman who let him take me away and pretend my whole family was dead, so I'd never know and come back to find her? I'm not sure she's the most impartial storyteller."

"You formed a certain picture of him when you were growing up," Harmon says. "I'm not trying to taint his memory."

"Taint his memory? So it is bad, what my mother said?" I don't know why I'm surprised. She's never had a good word to say about anyone. Still, my anger bubbles at the thought of her lies. He was a good parent, which is galaxies from what she is.

Harmon looks so miserable under my glare, I almost feel sorry for him. But not sorry enough to let him off the hook.

"What did she say?" I demand.

"Your mother never talks about that," he says, sweeping all the cards into a pile before we've even started. He sets his hands on the table, then notices the furry paw and moves them into his lap, where I can't see them.

"Then how do you know?" I ask slowly. All I want to do is reach across the table and shake the information out of him.

"I only know the story," he says. "It was an arranged marriage. And your mother either didn't want it, or didn't agree to it at all."

"How's that my dad's fault?" I ask. "If it's an arranged marriage, and he loved her and she didn't love him, that doesn't make him the bad guy. I feel sorry for him. She's cold and heartless, and she's probably incapable of loving anyone."

A frown creases his forehead as he drops the cards into the box and replaces the lid. "Maybe there's a reason she is that way."

"I was a baby when we left. And as far as I can see, it was the best thing my father could have done for me. At least I have those fourteen years of good memories. If I'd lived with her all my life, I'd have nothing but the memory of being a prisoner in an attic."

"I'm sure it would be different if you'd grown up here."

"Yeah, well, I'm not so confident of that," I say, pushing back from the table. "You can defend my mother all you want, but in my eyes, there's no defense for the way she treated me. If she said something nasty about my dad and you want to believe that, fine. But I know the truth." I step away from the table and walk to the tunnel with my head held high. But I'm glad my back is to him so he can't see the hot tears welling in my eyes. I hurry to my spot under the window, thankful that he doesn't follow me. I don't want him to see me curled up on my blanket, crying like a baby for my daddy.

I sit bolt upright, startled out of a dream about Dad. I haven't dreamed of him much in the last few years, but knowing he's alive has reawakened the memories. Now he comes to me in my sleep almost every night. In this one, it's the day I found him dead, but instead of dying, he's trying to wake me up because I'm going to be late for school.

"Psst. Stella."

My head whips around, even as awareness sinks in. This is not my father's voice. The room is brighter than usual, which means it's late afternoon, when the sun hits the window above me. Mrs. Nguyen is sitting up in her potato bin. Or onion bin.

"Come here," she says, gesturing with one hand. "I've got to stay here. I need to be able to hide if they come down to check."

"Okay, okay, I'm coming." I scrape myself off the floor and shuffle over to her, still half asleep.

"You know what's coming up in just a few days?" she asks, a twinkle in her eyes.

"No, sorry," I say through a yawn. "I've lost all track of time."

"The full moon, dear child."

"Oh." I glance at the empty spot under the ladder.

"It's our chance," Mrs. Nguyen says. "He'll be completely preoccupied with transitioning. Though if you ask me, that's not gonna happen. But he's going to be trying, don't you doubt it for a minute. He's going to be trying from dusk 'til dawn. Which means, my dear, it's the perfect opportunity to sneak out while he's caught up in his own fruitless striving." She gives a smile of great satisfaction, her adorable grandma face as radiant as if she'd just baked a pan of cookies she's especially proud of.

"We're just going to leave him here?" I ask.

"Of course we're going to leave him," she says. "What use is he to us? His own pack won't have him for a leader, not with a face like that. You expect to go out in public with that thing when we leave the Second Valley?"

"No, of course not," I say quickly. "You're right. So what's the plan?"

"It's not to marry him off to my daughter," she says with smug satisfaction. "She wouldn't marry that beast if her life depended on it."

"Can I ask you a question?" I say. "How do you have a daughter who looks like she's my age? I mean, she can't be older than twenty, and you're…"

She grins, her slightly yellowed teeth and wrinkled skin pulling into a picture of grandmotherly pride. "My dear, I told you. I occupy different forms."

"Yes, but you said you didn't kill people to do it."

"I didn't kill Mrs. Nguyen," she says. "I simply took up residency the moment she jumped ship. Think of it like…a squatter. This building wasn't being used, so I'm using it."

"So...she was old and died, and you took her dead body?"

"If the heart is still beating, it's up for grabs," she says merrily.

I try not to shudder at the thought. "So how old are you really?"

"A lady never tells," she says, shaking a finger at me.

"Young enough to have a teenage daughter."

She gives me a wink. "Let's just say, I'm younger than I look."

"Well, I guess that explains how you and Dad had so much to talk about. I always thought that was weird."

"That has nothing to do with age," she says. "We always got along well, your father and I."

"I'm guessing you knew my father before we moved next door."

"Of course," she says. "We call this the Three Valleys. One belongs to shifters, one to werewolves, and one to witches. We both grew up here."

I take in this new information, and though I have a million questions I want to ask her, I decide they can come later. When we're free. Already, I can hear Harmon moving around in the next room. "So how do we get out of here?" I ask. "On the full moon?"

"There are two ways," she says. "The easy way, and the hard way."

"What's the easy way?"

"The easy way, assuming you still have the natural ability your father has, is to do what I do."

"Oh," I say, shrinking back a little. "Leave my body here?"

"You think I like living in this old arthritic trap?" she snaps. "Of course not. You take what you can get. I keep my other body alive and protected, but there's always a chance someone could find it. Or this one, when I have to go back to the other one. You can come back to your body and check on it if you're worried Harmon's going to do something untoward with it." She winks like that's a great joke.

"He wouldn't do that," I say. Harmon may be a lot of things, but he's not *that* bad.

"If you say so," she says, her eyes still twinkling merrily.

I narrow my eyes. "How can I come check on my body?"

She sighs. "You'll understand when you do it. You have a natural tie to your body. It snaps you back when you get close."

"What if I leave my body here, and someone moves it? What if they give it back to my mother? Or…" I shudder, imagining my dad waking up in a coffin, buried in the ground. "Or bury it."

"No one here is going to do that," she says. "They know about projecting. They'll know you're not dead."

"What if I can't find my way back?"

"It's up to you to decide if it's worth that risk. How badly do you want to get out of this place?"

In the next room, a hollow clunk sounds. A book being replaced on the bookshelf.

"What if I can't do it?" I whisper urgently.

"You can."

"How do you know?"

"Your father is the strongest natural projector I've ever known, and I've spent my life practicing and studying it. He could still beat me today if we battled for a body. And you have his gift."

"How do you know? Does my sister have it, too?"

"I don't know about your sister, but I know you do."

I grip the edge of the bin so I won't shake the answers out of her. "How do you know?" I ask again through clenched teeth.

"Because you've done it before."

I pull back, my eyes widening. How does she know? And why don't I know? Is that what happens when I have the nightmares, when I dream I'm someone else, something else? I've woken in a fog of pain, semi-conscious, and seen things. A deer's feet, bound together with course rope. Was I inside a deer's body, and my father tied me up so I wouldn't run off somewhere and get lost? Can a person project without trying, without knowing?

"When?" I ask. "What did I project into?"

Mrs. Nguyen lies back in her bin and shifts on the onions as a scraping sounds in the tunnel. "Lots of things," she says. "Your father can tell you all of them, if you need the list."

"What?" I whisper, too loud, so loud Harmon must hear me. The scuff of his crippled gait sounds again in the dirt tunnel, his foot scrabbling against the walls and floor. The image of it still curdles my stomach, but not as much as what Mrs. Nguyen just said.

She puts a finger to her lips. "I'll be back on the full moon," she says in the softest whisper imaginable. Then she closes her eyes and gestures for me to close the lid.

I don't want to. I want to scream at her, at all of them, for keeping me in the dark about everything. But from the stillness in her body, I can tell she's already gone.

"Is she dead yet?" Harmon asks behind me, just as I've finished closing her in.

"No," I say, my heart hammering so loudly I'm sure he can hear it with his wolf ear. Does he know she's been here? Can he sense it? Is that why he snarled the first time she left, because he could feel her departure?

He's looking at me strangely. Isn't he? It's hard to tell with his grotesque face. I can't look at it too long. Especially now. I just want to be alone to think. But he's always here.

"Hey, about the other day," he says. "I was pretty hard on your father. I can see why you got defensive."

"I didn't."

"I think it's great that you were close to him when you were growing up. It sounds like you had a really great childhood."

"Is that your attempt at an apology? Because it's pretty lame."

He smiles, and for a second, I think he's going to make some snarky comeback. But my eyes slide away from his. They're too far apart below that unnaturally sloping forehead, above the almost-human mouth. I swallow hard, my eyes fixed on the top of the ladder. Without a word, he moves towards his blanket, his human leg crouching under his mostly wolf body, lurching unevenly as he goes. "Maybe I was a little jealous," he says, not looking at me.

I snort at that. "Why? Your father is basically the president around here. My dad is a botany professor who thinks it's okay to wear socks with sandals."

"What's wrong with wearing socks and sandals?"

"If you don't know, I can't even answer that."

"Well, maybe I don't understand that one. But believe it or not, you don't have the market cornered on cold parents. I do understand that."

"Your dad is cold?" I remember Zechariah's small, hard eyes, and the scars on Harmon's chest his father left when he defied him. But then I remember watching from the window as Harmon dutifully walked with him, abandoning even his friends on his big coronation night, to help his injured father along.

"How do you know it's not my mother?"

"You said cold parents. If it was your mom, too, wouldn't you have said *cold mothers?*"

"Clever kitty," he says, settling under the ladder.

"So," I say after a minute. "What is your dad like? When he's at home, I mean. Not when he's being the president."

Harmon shrugs his narrow wolf shoulders. "He's a good Alpha. He's done a lot of good for us, and tried to form alliances with some of the other people around here."

"The shifters."

"Everyone in Three Valleys. It's hard with the shifters, because they don't have a leader." He glances at me and then away. "So they're a bit lawless."

"I know."

He grimaces. "I'm sorry."

"Not your fault."

"I should have protected you," he growls. "That's why

I followed you that night. I didn't want them to capture you. But they did, anyway, and I ended up like this." He holds up his hands, his lip curling in disgust at the sight of his own body.

I swallow hard, my chest tight. "I'm sorry," I whisper.

"It's fine," he snaps. "My father was a great leader. Everyone says so. So now you know all about him."

"But...?"

His voice softens. "One day, when I have kids, I hope they say the same about me. But I also hope they say I'm a great dad."

"Like my dad and your dad combined," I say, smiling tentatively at him from where I'm leaning against the wooden bins.

He doesn't return my smile. "Stella...I meant what I said. I want you to be part of the pack. I wouldn't let them lock you in the attic again. You'd be one of us."

"That's...nice." A twinge of guilt goes through me when I remember Mrs. Nguyen's words. I won't be here much longer. But he doesn't have to know that. She also said he was a liar, that everything he said was a lie. So I can't trust his word, anyway. And if he's lying to me, why shouldn't I do the same?

"Do you know what it means to be part of the pack?" Harmon asks.

Instead of returning to my spot, I move closer to him and lean on one of the support poles, a peeled tree trunk of some sort. "Kind of."

"It's more than just words," he says. "When a wolf makes a promise, when I tell you you'll be part of any pack I lead, I mean it. We take our word very seriously."

His moon-pale eyes are intense, almost glowing out of the dimness again. I wish I'd sat near the window. The light outside has faded, but I'm sure he can see the lies on me, can smell the scheming. That's why he's saying all this.

"Okay."

"A wolf must have full loyalty to the pack. That's why, the other day, I defended your mother. She's part of the pack, which means she's…she's a part of me. We have to put the pack first, always. That's why I'll never be Alpha if I can't transition." He glances at the window, his eyes searching the deepening blue of the sky, as if searching for the moon that will soon tell his fate.

"I respect that," I say. "But I'm not a wolf, Harmon. I'm not part of your pack. You should understand that. My loyalty is to my father, not your pack. No matter what he's done, no matter what he didn't tell me, he's my father. Nothing will ever erase that."

"That's fair," he says. "I won't force you to join our pack. But when I'm Alpha, and I officially invite you, you'll have to choose whether to stay or leave. You can't stay and not join. We all work together. That's pack life."

I pick at a hangnail on my thumb. It seems too much of a coincidence for him to say all this now. He must have heard me talking to Mrs. Nguyen, and now he's testing me. And what if she doesn't come back on the full moon? What if something happens, and she's trapped in her other body? I'll be stuck here. Harmon will transition, and then he'll be back to normal. Injured, but an injured human. He'll be able to lead his pack. And I'll be stuck here forever.

But if I tell him yes now, he'll take me with him. If

what he's saying is true, he'll have to save me. No wolf left behind. All for one, one for all. If I agree, pretend I want to join him, he'll get me out. It's not as good as Mrs. Nguyen's offer, but it's a backup plan. I'm not a wolf. My promise doesn't mean anything. All it means is that I've hitched myself to a more desirable bargaining chip. Whatever they trade for Harmon, they'll have to throw me in, too.

I push away from the pole and stand straight like a soldier about to salute. "Okay," I say. "I'm in."

10

The next day, we sit at the table in the little room, with a deck of cards spread out in a jumble in front of us. Harmon has been suspiciously nice since I agreed to be an honorary member of his wolf cult.

"I have three questions for you," Harmon says, a smile tugging at his dark lips. It seems unfair that boys always get naturally dark lips and long lashes. Girls, on the other hand...well, let's just say that now that I don't wear makeup, it would be very difficult to tell that I have eyelashes at all. At least I don't have half a wolf's head.

"Okay," I say. "Shoot."

"One, do you have any queens."

"Go fish."

He draws a card from the pool on the table and smiles. "Two, if you had a loaded gun right now, would you shoot someone?"

"Wow, that's an abrupt change of subject."

"Would you?"

"No. Do you have any sevens?"

"Go fish. What if it would get you out of here?"

I pick up a card and make a set of fours on the table in front of me. Now I know where the line of questioning is going, so I have to tread carefully. Harmon has been getting himself stronger, learning to balance on his deformed body, pushing himself to work out and gain muscle. It's not for nothing. He's been thinking of escape plans, too. Of course he has. Maybe that's the reason behind his offer yesterday. He needs to know I'm going to work for it, too, that we're a team.

"Depends on who I had to shoot," I say with a smile.

"Would it matter?"

I shrug. "I guess not."

"What if you had to shoot me? Or what if you got out? Would you want revenge on your mother for keeping you locked up?"

"No," I say, frowning at my hand. "Ask me."

"Do you have any twos?"

I hand over a pair.

"What about the people up there?" he asks, his eyes flicking up towards the ceiling.

"If I had to shoot someone to get out, and they were trying to keep me in…yeah, I probably would shoot them. But I'm not going to go on a shooting rampage once I get out, trying to kill them all. I'm not a psycho, Harmon. I don't want to kill anyone. Even if I had to shoot someone to get away, I wouldn't try to kill them."

"Hm. Your turn."

"Was that the wrong answer?"

"No," he says evenly. "What do you need, kitty cat?"

"Ummm….aces."

"Go fish. Ready for the third question?"

I pick up another seven, my third. "Okay."

He stares at me until I look up from my cards. Then he leans forward, his paw-hands on the edge of the table. "What does pizza taste like?"

I laugh before I can stop myself. Harmon's eyes stay trained on me, those pale blue circles intent and curious. "Wait, you're serious? You've never had pizza?"

"No. What's it like?"

I sigh and lean back in my plush seat. "Like a slice of reality," I say. "Cheesy and salty and…fun. It's not even about the taste. It's about staying up until midnight with your best friend waiting for delivery on Saturday night. It's about eating in the dark with your hands, sitting on the living room floor wrapped in a sleeping bag, watching a scary movie. Laughing about the awkward—or cute—delivery boy when he leaves. It's about…life. You know?"

For a second, I forgot where I was, who I was talking to. He's watching me speak, a strange expression on his face.

"What?" I ask, suddenly embarrassed.

"Do you have any sevens?" he asks with a wicked grin, showing off his sharp teeth.

"You suck," I tell him, handing over my three sevens. He makes a set on the table.

Suddenly, a whiff of something catches my attention. It's not pizza. It's roses. My eyes fly to the window above the table, the one at ground level. It's small, probably too small for my hips to squeeze through. But it's open, slanting inwards at a forty-five-degree angle. It felt different in the room today, like spring had somehow crept in. More light, more air, more hope. I thought it was Harmon's cheerful demeanor. Now I know. Someone opened the window for us.

Harmon is still watching me intently. For just a

second, he's a hungry dog, following his master's every move with his eyes, waiting for food.

"Did you open that?" I ask.

"Maybe."

"How'd you reach it?"

His eyes flick to my chair.

"What's out there?"

"Want me to lift you up to see?"

I hesitate a long moment. "You can't lift me. You'll hurt yourself."

"I can lift you."

"No, it's fine. It doesn't matter. It will just make it worse that we're stuck in here. Besides, the window isn't big enough to climb out." Not for a human. I remember Mrs. Nguyen's promise. She will come back, and we'll escape as something else. A mouse could slip out of there in a second. Even a cat could fit through.

"I can lift you," Harmon says again.

"You should save your strength. When's the full moon?"

"Tomorrow," he says, glowering at his cards as if he'd like to murder them.

"Oh. Sorry. I didn't know it was so soon."

"Well, it is."

"Can we just play?"

He starts to arrange his cards, but he only has one mostly human hand, with the addition of fur, and one that's almost entirely a paw. His cards suddenly tumble from his hand, cascading across the table and fluttering to the floor. With a snarl of frustration, he tries to get up, but he's off balance, trying to stand on two legs when he still walks on four. He tumbles from the chair and lands on the floor with a thud. Without missing a beat, he rolls to his feet, dragging his human leg behind him as he lurches into the tunnel, cursing a blue streak the whole way. I hear him reach the basement room, scream with fury, and snap something wooden.

I'm pretty sure it was my broom. At least he waited until my ankle was better before destroying my crutch.

I go to the bookshelf and take down an old copy of *The Great Gatsby*. It's a nice book, with a leather binding and gold foil printing on the ridged spine. For a second, I let myself indulge in the memory of watching the movie for the tenth time with Emmy. Then I settle into one of the soft chairs, put my feet up, and start reading. I barely even hear Harmon tearing around in the next room, throwing things and cursing.

11

All the next day, Harmon is quiet and moody. He paces the basement like a caged animal, lurching along, his human leg crouched under his body, looking obscenely naked compared to the rest of his fur-covered body. When he finally goes into the other room, I'm relieved. I nap, then return to the sitting room to read more of the book. The window is open again, the scent of roses on the fresh spring air.

Finally, in the evening, the door in the other room scrapes open. I've seen our captor a handful of times now—one of them. I know there are more, because I hear their footsteps overhead, the muffled voices as they talk and eat and live their free lives. The woman who feeds us is nondescript and middle aged. She always opens the door a crack and peers through, then, when she sees no one on the ladder, thrusts a basket through and closes the door. Sometimes, if we're sleeping, she lowers it down to us. But usually she leaves it at the top, now that I'm well enough to climb up and get it.

Tonight, I find the basket on the top rung of the ladder when I come through the tunnel. A familiar scent drifts down as I climb the ladder. But it can't be. Since I've been here, I've eaten soup, beans, casseroles. It's pretty much the same fare I ate at my mother's but better. Sometimes a lot better—homemade bread with butter and honey, beef jerky, cookies. But as excited as I am to carry the warm basket down the ladder, unease creeps along my spine.

"Harmon," I call, ducking into the tunnel. "Harmon?"

I emerge into the room and set the basket on the table and peek inside to make sure. "Harmon!"

He steps in from the bedroom, looking a little winded. He must have been working out again, preparing for tonight.

"You're not going to believe this," I say, opening the basket and peeling back the cloth lining.

He peers inside.

"It's pizza."

"I see that."

"Oh," I say, a little let down. "I thought you didn't know what pizza was."

"I know what it is," he says. "I've just never had it."

He keeps staring into the basket, and I wonder if he's having the same apprehension I am. "It's not delivery," I say. "But it looks pretty good. Probably a frozen one from the store, but not one of the super cheap dollar pizzas. This is a good one."

"What's delivery?"

"You know, when they bring you a pizza."

"Looks to me like it was delivered."

"No, I mean from the pizza place," I say, holding back my laughter. He's so innocent and naïve in some ways, it's kind of cute. But I don't want him to think I'm laughing at him.

"What's the pizza place? The place that makes them?"

"Exactly," I say. "Well, a lot of places. And they drive to your house and bring you a pizza."

"Why?"

This time I do laugh. "So you can eat it, silly."

"Like a neighborly visit," he says, smiling. "Where you bring some food and have dinner together."

"No," I say, stifling more laughter. "They don't eat with you. They bring a pizza, and you pay for it, and they leave."

"That sounds strange," he says, but to my relief, he doesn't seem offended. Instead, he clambers up into the chair he always takes, on the far side of the table. I sit on the side towards our room.

I'd never admit it to anyone, but this place is not so bad. We have everything we need, and though Harmon isn't exactly Prince Charming, he's not terrible company. It's a hell of a lot better than being alone.

"You said you eat this with your hands?" he asks, looking doubtful. I know he doesn't like to eat in front of me, that it embarrasses him. Before tonight, we've never eaten together at the table. He eats under the ladder, turning his back to me so I can't see his clumsiness.

"Yes," I say, reaching into the basket and carefully lifting it out. It's still on the cardboard backing that frozen pizza comes on, the one that goes in the oven with the pizza. Aside from that, nothing. No forks or plates, and no knives, not even a plastic one.

"Normally, you'd have it sliced in triangles," I say. "But I guess we're just going to have to tear it apart with our hands." I rip off an uneven piece and, seeing Harmon's expression, I hand it across to him. He takes it without a word. When I've sat down opposite him, I take a big bite, thinking I'll let some cheese hang down my chin or something, so he doesn't feel too bad eating in front of me. But as soon as I take a bite, I forget all about Harmon.

I'm at a pool party in sixth grade, everyone running out of the pool when the girl's mom pushed open the screen door and came out back carrying a stack of pizza boxes. I'm at Mrs. Nguyen's, sitting on the couch beside her, watching TV and pushing cats away with my feet while I hold a slice of pizza and try to tear through the overdone crust with my teeth. I'm at a movie with Emmy and her boyfriend, giggling at my pepperoni burps while she shushes me because she wants her boyfriend to think she's mature. We're alone at my house the last summer we had together, picking bits of brown cheese off a blackened crust, trying to salvage whatever edible parts we could.

"This is your favorite food?" Harmon asks as I reach to rip off another hunk of it. He's only eaten half of his. At least I didn't have to pretend to be messy to make him feel better. I just scarfed down pizza faster than a boy. And I totally don't care.

"Yup," I say through a mouthful of my next piece.

"It's kind of like this is my last meal," Harmon says, staring down at his slice.

"You know what a last meal is, but you don't know what pizza is."

"I know what it is," he corrects me again.

"And?"

"It's okay."

"Okay?" I ask, then slump in my chair, chewing slowly. "Yeah, you're right. Tepid pizza from a box isn't the same. When we get out of here, we'll get a real pizza."

He sets down his pizza and forces his eyes to mine. "Stella, listen…"

"We're getting out," I say. "And if your people won't have you for a leader, I'll take you with me. It's kind of crappy that they haven't come to get you, don't you think? I mean, even if you are injured and you can't be their leader, they could at least negotiate to get you back. Or do they have some policy about bargaining with kidnappers?"

"Everyone is doing what's right for the pack," he says, picking up his pizza again. "The pack's second-in-command will make sure of it. Our job isn't to question that. It's to think of what's best for everyone, regardless of our selfish whims."

"Well, I'm not a wolf," I remind him. "I still have selfish whims. Speaking of, don't you think it's a little weird that we were talking about this literally yesterday, and today pizza shows up in our dinner bucket?"

Harmon drops his half-eaten slice, and his eyes fix on the window above. A shudder goes through his body like a wave, and he braces his hands on the table until it's gone. "I'm going to go lie down," he says quietly, staring at his hand as if he can will it to turn human again.

"Oh—okay."

He stumbles from his chair, draws his human leg under him, and lurches towards the tunnel.

"Do you need anything?" I ask as he steps inside, his tail disappearing behind him.

"No," he calls back sharply.

The pizza is not nearly as appetizing once the memories dissipate and my taste buds adjust to this new, old taste. Now it's just lame, cardboard-flavored pizza with rubbery cheese on top. I nibble at the crust a while, managing to finish my piece. Then I wrap up the leftovers. Dad was a cold-pizza-for-breakfast guy, but I never saw the appeal. Still, it's a change from the healthy, homecooked meals. Sometimes, you just need junk food.

Outside, twilight is falling. I read for a few minutes, until the light filtering through the window is too dim. Thunder rumbles somewhere across the mountains. Glancing at both doors to make sure I'm alone, I push the chair over to the bookshelf, the one with games and random junk on it. Above it, the wedge of freedom beckons. I don't care if rain comes in and everything gets wet.

I want to smell that clean, wet air that comes up from the earth when it rains, as if the forest, the world, is breathing. I want to reach my arms out the window, let the raindrops run down my skin, soaking me until my shirt clings to me the way it only does in the rain. I want to let my fingertips dance with raindrops, with the wind and the tiny white petals I see plastered to the windowpanes in the morning.

And oddly, I want to go and get Harmon, to make him stand up in the chair next to me, to reach his fingers towards freedom with me.

I climb down and duck into the tunnel. It's completely dark inside, and I have to feel my way along. For a second, I think he's locked me out. But when I give the door a healthy shove, it creaks open. Harmon is lying under the ladder, like usual. I sneak a quick peek at the vegetable bin, but the lid is still down. I don't know how I'm going to have a conversation with Mrs. Nguyen while Harmon lies right here.

But who cares if he hears us plotting? By then, he'll know I was lying, that I never intended to join his pack. If she has a way out, I'll take it. I'll be free tomorrow, and he'll be left in this dungeon alone.

It isn't so bad here, I remind myself. *He'll be fine.*

"There's a storm blowing in," I say, taking a step closer to him. It feels wrong not to say goodbye. It's not like he's ever going to replace Emmy, but we're not enemies anymore, either.

His eyes roll up towards me, and all I see is the animal in him. A scared puppy.

I take a step closer. "Are you okay?"

"No," he says. "This is it, Stella. What if I can't do it?"

"You can," I say, moving to join him now that I know he's not going to go all savage wolf again, like he did the first day. I kneel beside him, sitting back on my heels. "You will. You've been working hard. You're strong."

He grimaces, and we both turn towards the window, where flickers of lightning have begun to show as it grows dark outside. When I turn back, he has that dazed look in his eyes, like he's concentrating very hard on something.

"It's not working," he whispers.

"Give it time," I say. "You have all night."

"Will you stay with me?" The arrogant boy is gone, the proud Alpha, the angry wolf who throws tantrums, all the

93

airs he puts on, that everyone puts on. It's just him, the real him, and it breaks my heart.

It breaks my heart that he trusts me so much, that he would show me himself at his most vulnerable, when I don't deserve that trust. When I'm using him at best, deserting him at worst. So I take his hand, and I do the kindest thing I can think of. I lie.

"For a while," I say, linking my fingers through his. The fur between his fingers is softer than I'd imagined, downy and white. He closes his eyes, and I watch the room grow darker, darker, and the lightning flash brighter, so frequent it's like a strobe light outside. Thunder rumbles distantly, but the bin stays closed.

Another shudder goes through Harmon's body, this one stronger, and I think for a second he's dry heaving. His fingers tighten around mine, his body tense. Something wet snaps inside his body, and I want to heave, too. But he lets out a hoarse cry of pain, and then I forget about being disgusted by what's happening to him, by how his human leg is so long and thick and naked, and his wolf body is so doglike, and his face is so unnatural and bizarre. I stroke his hand, and I tell him he's going to get through this and everything will be okay.

"What if I don't?" he asks, his voice muffled by his blanket, where he's buried his face.

"You will," I say. "You won't die from transitioning." In truth, I have no idea if he could or not. I only know that he's in pain, and it's my job to give him hope.

"What if this is the curse?" he asks. "Dr. Golden said a witch laid a curse on me but she couldn't tell me what it would do. What if it kills me when I transition?"

"It won't."

He doesn't answer, too caught up in the pain of his body rearranging itself. I stroke his fur and try to be strong, to swallow my tears.

"Talk to me," he says when that round of shudders subsides. "Tell me something."

"About what?"

"It doesn't matter," he says. "Just talk. Please."

So I tell him more about life in Oklahoma City. I talk about my teachers, about school and selfies and the bands I liked. I talk until my voice is wearing thin, and the thunder is closer, louder. Rain begins to fall. Something rustles in the onion bin.

Why didn't we come up with a signal, a way for me to tell Mrs. Nguyen it's safe?

She must figure it out herself, because the lid doesn't open. I keep talking. I tell Harmon about getting left in Bricktown by Emmy's boyfriend and having to call our parents to rescue us. About middle school dances, and sleepovers, and movie theaters, and fashion magazines. "It's silly," I say. "I wanted to be a model." I've never told anyone that except him. And each time I tell him, it seems sillier, farther removed from reality.

Harmon's voice is raspy and dreamlike. "You should be a model."

"You should get some sleep," I say.

"You should, too." He's still now, not seizing up every few minutes, and I haven't heard any bones rearranging inside him for a while. His head rests in my lap, and my fingers absently stroke his silky, pointed ear, his soft fore-head, the thick coat on the back of his neck. It's past midnight, and the rain has slowed to an occasional drip off the roof onto the ground outside the window, where I can hear the wet plunk as each drop falls into the puddles under the eaves. The thunder is gone, the lightning with it. I can't see anything in the darkness. But I know whatever magic he was hoping for didn't happen tonight.

# 12.

At last, Harmon goes still in my lap. Once in a while, an involuntary shiver wracks his body as he sleeps, but it's more like nerves firing than his joints and ligaments popping. I'm so tired I don't know how I'm still upright, too tired to even lie down and go to sleep.

I startle to alertness when the lid to the onion bin lifts with a groan. "Stella?" Mrs. Nguyen whispers.

"I'm here."

"Is he a wolf?"

"No. Why?"

"Because it's harder to get past a wolf than a human," she says. I hear her groaning and grunting, and onions shifting in the bin.

Harmon stirs in his sleep, nestling against my belly.

"I'm not going."

The movement stops. An onion rolls against the side of the bin, thumping against the wood. "What?" Mrs. Nguyen asks.

Harmon growls in his sleep.

"Let me put a sleep charm on him," she whispers, crouching beside him. She places a hand on his side, and I feel his fur bristle. Rushing to get the words out, she lays the spell on before he can wake completely.

"May this creature stay asleep

Slumbering in the deep.
His eyes will close, he will not wake
Until this spell the caster breaks."

She draws her hand back and stands. "He won't wake now," she says gleefully. "Stop this nonsense and let's get going. Your father is waiting."

"I'm not going without Harmon."

"What are you talking about? This is your chances. Are you really going to be so stupid as to stay in prison because of that…that thing?"

I stroke the soft fur on Harmon's forehead and ears, down to the thicker, coarser fur on his back. "He's not a thing," I say. "He's still the same person. And if he had a chance to get out of here, he'd take me with him."

"You want us to carry him out the front door? Do you think they'd let us do that?"

"Then we'll wait until he's well enough to do the projecting thing, too. You said anyone can do it, even an ordinary human. Which means he can."

"It could take years to teach him," she says. "You've already done it."

"I don't remember how," I say. "It could take me years to remember."

"Don't be a fool," she scolds. "I have been a fool for love, and you know how it ended? Living in this saggy old lard-bag half the time."

"I'm not in love."

She scoffs. "You're not? Then why aren't you coming with me?"

"Because…because I can't just leave him here. He's alone, and he's going to be…" I can't even describe how he's going to be tomorrow. Devastated doesn't cover it. When he finds out he can't switch back, he's going to need me. I touch his cheek, run my finger across his very human lips.

No, that's stupid. He doesn't need me. In fact, it will be easier for him to go home without me. Suddenly, a cold chill creeps up my spine. At the eclipse, the shifters were butchering the wolves. Who knows if Harmon even has anyone left to go back to. What if they haven't negotiated for our freedom because there's no one left in the pack? I can't just leave Harmon here alone, with no hope.

My sisters once told me a story of a werewolf who couldn't transition, so he ate poison. What's to stop Harmon from doing the same? He's not just a werewolf, he's a monster. A monster who has lost a lot more than the ability to change from a human to a wolf. He's lost who he was when he was healthy and good-looking. The boy with all the promise in the world in front of him. He could have Chosen any girl, and she would have been over the moon. He was going to lead his pack, do great things.

Now he's grateful for the company of a plain human. And up until this moment, I've been kind of awful to him.

Mrs. Nguyen waits quietly while I figure things out. At last, I shake my head. "I can't do it."

"What about your father?" she asks. "Don't you want to see him?"

"Of course I do," I say. "Where is he?"

"He's at home," she says again.

I swallow hard, my resolve to stay with Harmon crumbling. "In Oklahoma?"

"No, silly, he's at his house in the shifter valley. And

you'll never see him as long as you stay here with this brute," she says. "If you don't come, you'll regret it. Things are not always what they seem. You know this by now, my dear. How many more times do you have to learn that lesson the hard way before you take it to heart? This boy may seem pitiful to you, but he's here by choice. He could have married my daughter. He could have united the Three Valleys, but he chose not to. He could do many things differently."

"Are you leaving?" I ask, afraid of the finality in her voice.

"I told your father I would come for you, and I have. But now you're choosing to stay with that animal, and if I can't convince you otherwise, you have no need for me."

Panic tightens my chest. If she leaves, I'm stuck here. She's my ticket out—alone.

"I do need you," I whisper.

"In truth, Stella, I hate being this disgusting old dead thing. But I did it for your father. Now it's time for me to let go of these old bones for good. You're sixteen now. If you're old enough to choose not to listen to me, then you're old enough to take care of yourself."

I want to laugh at that, to tell her she's crazy. What do I know? I've been living in an attic for years, perpetually stuck at the age I was when I arrived and my life became suspended, waiting for freedom. Three years have passed, but if anything, I'm less able to take care of myself than I was when I arrived. Since then, I've been broken.

"But I'm not," I protest. "Please don't leave."

"You don't need me," she says. "You have him."

"Don't make me choose between you."

"I think you've already chosen, dear."

"No," I say. "It's not like that. I'll come find you as soon as we get out. Where are you going? How will I find you?"

She strokes my hair, her face turned down towards me in the darkness. "Look around you, child. Open your eyes, but don't believe everything they show you. Listen. But don't believe every word you hear, especially from the lips of those who tell you what you wish to hear. Above all, feel. When something doesn't feel quite right, it's because it isn't. If you can remember all that, I've done my duty."

With that, she turns and steps back to the onion bin and climbs inside.

"Wait," I say. "What about Dad?"

"Your father is fine," she says, shaking her head. "He's always been a survivor."

Dad? Seriously? Does she know my dad? He can't survive a week without football, a day without comfortable socks, or a dinner without a beer.

"But is he okay?"

With an affirming nod, Mrs. Nguyen lies down in the onion bin and drops the lid. "Keep your eyes open," she says, her voice echoing inside the wooden box. "I'm not going to do the work for you. If you wanted that, you would have come with me. Now you're on your own. Figure it out."

Stung, I turn back to Harmon. Did I just give up my chance to leave for this creature, this mutant? My chance for freedom, to see my father and get some straight answers? I bury my fingers in his thick black fur and tug. He makes a sound somewhere between a growl and a groan, but it doesn't sound angry. It sounds like someone who doesn't want to wake up. Curling my fingers into his fur, I pull harder.

"Hey," I say, yanking once more.

"I'm moving, I'm moving," he says, rolling away from me.

"No," I say, reaching out to poke his shoulder. "I want some answers."

"Right now?"

"Yes, right now."

He sighs. "What's your question?"

I don't even know where to start. "Okay," I say slowly. "Are we, like, married in werewolf land or something like that?"

"Did we have a wedding I don't know about?"

"No."

"Then we aren't married. Is that what you're worried about?" He makes an incredulous sound. "You think you're stuck with me? That's not the way it works, Stella."

"Then how does it work?"

"What?"

"All of it. The werewolf stuff. You said you'd invite me to your pack. So how does it work? I'm not just going to blindly say yes, Harmon. Tell me what I'd have to do. What it's like."

He shifts restlessly in the dark. "Haven't you lived here for three years? I know you weren't part of it, but you lived with three wolves. You saw how it worked."

"No," I say. "I really didn't. I barely saw anyone, and my mother wouldn't even let me talk to my own sisters."

He's quiet for a minute. When he speaks, his voice is softer. "I'm sorry," he says. "I didn't know it was that bad."

"So you thought I just hid every time you came over? You visited my sisters all the time. Didn't you ever wonder where I was?"

"Your mother always had a reason. You were busy, or you weren't feeling well… And then after you found out about us, she told us you were terrified and didn't want anything to do with us."

"Yeah, well, she was lying." My voice breaks on the last word.

He reaches out and tugs at my knee. "Hey, come here. Don't cry."

"I'm not crying," I snap, but my voice is choked by the tightness in my throat.

"Stella…come here." He pulls at me again, until I relent and lie down next to him on the blanket. He throws another blanket over us, but leaves enough distance between us that only our knees touch when I curl up on my side, facing him. My throat is tight, but I'm not sure if it's his nearness or the conversation. I'm suddenly very aware of our closeness, our aloneness, my vulnerability in this basement with this boy-wolf. No matter how injured and deformed he is, he could overpower me in a second if he wanted to.

"I knew your mother wanted to keep you hidden," he says. "I didn't understand why she didn't make an effort to have you assimilated after you found out. There was nothing to hide after that. I never knew she kept you from your own sisters."

"Well, she did."

103

He's quiet a moment. "The truth is, everyone is a little freaked out of you," he says at last. "You're not a wolf, but look just like your sister. And people here, they know what you can do, Stella. It scares them."

"What do you mean, *what I can do*?"

His voice drops. "Projecting."

"That's why they look at me like I'm a giant freak? Mrs. Nguyen said anyone can do that."

"Maybe, but we don't do it. It's dangerous. They're not looking at you like you're a freak. They're looking at you like you're a loaded gun."

"Have you ever done it?"

"No," he says, sounding slightly horrified. "I'd never want to. The only wolf I know who's ever done it is…your mother. And I've never asked her about it. It would be rude to ask about something like that. I'm sure she doesn't like thinking about it. It would be like if you asked me intimate questions about losing my father."

"My mother did it? Seriously? Mrs. Rules did something forbidden?"

"Yeah, she did," he says. "And she got stuck out of her body. The only reason she's alive is that a witch put a spell over her to preserve her body until she found her way back. In return for the spell, we had to give the witches access to the trees in a huge part of our valley. That's why we have enchanted trees here."

I shudder, suddenly relieved I didn't agree to leave with Mrs. Nguyen. I came so close tonight. If I'd left my body here, who knows when I'd have found it. But then I remember that she said I did it before, and I must have found my way back then. Even Harmon knows I did. Apparently, everyone knows more about me than I do.

"Do you remember me?" I ask. "From before I left. I lived here when I was a baby, right? And you're two years older. Do you remember if I really did it, or did people just say that?"

He reaches out and touches my cheek with cold, human fingertips. "I don't remember you doing it," he says. "I wasn't there. I was five when you left. I sort of remember you being around. And we grew up knowing why you left. There aren't really secrets for us."

"Except what it's like to project."

"If I wanted to know, I could ask your mother. If I asked, she'd tell me."

"So if I joined the pack, and I asked her, she'd have to tell me?"

He hesitates. "I'm not sure," he admits at last. "It's not really a rule. We don't have a lot of those. It's just…that's how things are."

"So she'd tell me?"

"I don't know," he says. "Your mother, she's…"

"Mean?"

"She's had experiences no one else has. It sets her apart a little."

"Because she projected?"

"That's one thing," he says. "And she married someone who wasn't a wolf. That doesn't really happen around here."

I have to work up the nerve to ask the next question. "Is that why…you didn't want to marry that girl?"

"Witches, they'll marry anyone," he says with a note of scorn. "They can have unlimited mates at the same time. When they get tired of one, they release him. It's not like that for us. When we Choose someone, it's not something to take lightly. It's a choice you make once, and it lasts forever."

"I thought you didn't have rules," I tease, trying to lighten the mood a little.

"It's not a rule," he says. "It's a law of nature. That's how we are. If you Choose badly, that's unfortunate. But you don't get to Choose again. You've given that person your word, your heart, your matehood... I don't know if there's a word for it outside wolves. But you're bound to that person. Forever."

"Would you have married her if you knew she was a witch, not a shifter?" I ask. It's easier to talk to him in the dark, where he seems so human.

He chuckles softly. "No. But I might have rejected her more politely. You don't want to get mixed up with witches. And you definitely don't want to offend them."

"Mrs. Nguyen seems pretty harmless." But a shiver runs up my back when I recall her abruptness when she left. What if I offended her by choosing to stay? She said I chose Harmon over her. Is that an insult?

"Oh, it's all gravy if you're on their good side," he says. "In fact, I'd like to unite our people with theirs, too, not just the shifters. They aren't bad people as a whole. But marry one? They're polyamorous and matriarchal. Their lifestyle is basically the exact opposite of wolves'. It would be hard to reconcile ourselves to the marriage. I can't imagine either of us would be happy."

"Girls can't be pack leaders?"

"No."

"Why not?"

"That's not how wolves are in nature. Why would it be so for us?"

"Hmm. So girls can't be leaders, and you only get one chance at love, and if you screw it up, you're...well, screwed." I pause to think it over. "Sorry to disappoint you, but you're really not selling me on the whole were-wolf thing."

"Women are every bit as important as men," he says.

"Then why can't they be pack leaders?" I challenge.

"Don't get all offended. I didn't say you'd be a second-class citizen. I said you couldn't be Alpha. Which you couldn't be anyway, because you're not a werewolf."

For a while, we lie in silence. Harmon's breathing goes deep again, but I can't fall asleep. I replay every part of the conversation I can remember, trying to keep everything straight, treasuring the most basic information. For so long, I've been in the dark. Finally, someone is answering my questions. I can't help but think of the tentative friend-ship I formed with Harmon before I threw an ax at his father's head. I really shouldn't have done that. If I hadn't, we'd have remained friends, and he might have told me all this a long time ago.

But that's not what happened. I lost his friendship, and I was chained in my mother's attic for attacking the Alpha.

My mother. Thoughts of her churn in my mind. I hate her, and yet...she fascinates me. I want to know her. In some twisted way, I still want her to love me. God, I'm pathetic. But she's my mom.

My mom, who was once a rebel, who dared to go against the werewolf code and marry an outsider. She didn't just accept the werewolf way because that's how things had always been done. She wanted more for herself. Not that it worked out very well for her in the end, but I still admire her for having enough grit to go against the norm—even if she did end up loveless, divorced, shamed, and saddled with three daughters.

No wonder she's bitter.

13.

Eventually, around dawn, I fall asleep. When I wake, the slant of the sun streaming in the window tells me it's early afternoon. I sit up, trying to figure out what's different. And then I see the window. Someone has washed it, so the sun doesn't have to struggle through a layer of splashed up dirt and mud. Throwing off Harmon's blanket, I look around for him, but he's not in the basement room.

I stumble to my feet and find my way through the tunnel, the sitting room, and into the bedroom before I find Harmon. He's sitting on the far side of the bed, slumped over, with his back to me. Still half asleep, I visit the bathroom and then groggily shower, trying to wake up after oversleeping. When I get out of the shower, I notice the cardboard box on the counter. Every few days, I find a folded stack of freshly laundered clothes on the counter next to the sink, the same clothes I've worn from the dresser—ill-fitting jeans, t-shirts, sometimes a sweatshirt. Never a box.

Suddenly as excited as if it were Christmas morning, I grab the box off the counter. As I tear off the shipping tape, I realize how weird it is to think of Christmas. It's been so long since I celebrated anything. I don't even keep track of my birthday in a definite way. Last fall, when I turned sixteen, I didn't even realize it was my birthday until a few days later, when I saw the calendar downstairs in my mother's house.

Inside the box, I pull away the crumpled brown paper to find clothes. Real clothes. New clothes. My fingers tremble as I kneel on the floor beside the box and take out a shirt as carefully as if it were made of ash, halfway terrified it will fall apart in my hands. I must be dreaming. This can't be real.

I'm being silly, though. There's no point in having new clothes now. I'm in a freaking basement. Still, my throat refuses to cooperate when I try to swallow, and it takes several attempts before I succeed. I hold up the shirt against my body. It might actually fit. Real clothes, meant for me.

I stand and drop the shirt over my head. It feels strange to wear anything other than a faded, baggy t-shirt. Besides the one night I wore my sister's dress, and the week afterwards when I had nothing else so I kept wearing it even though it was covered in mud and blood and who knows what else, I haven't worn anything remotely cute in three years. And even though I'm not sure this is my style, or that I even have a style anymore, I know it's cuter than anything I've worn in ages.

The lavender fabric is light and airy and soft, with little fringy threads hanging from the hem. It's stretchy, but not too tight. I find a pair of cropped, skinny jeans and pull them on, relishing the way they hug my slight curves. Then I stand there, looking down at myself, feeling so ridiculous. I look like I'm going to the mall. I dig into the box, but there's nothing ugly and baggy in it.

A pair of cute pajamas, dark wash jeans, denim shorts,

a few more shirts, a package of new underwear—hallelujah. I tear through it all like a starving person. I try on everything, leave it lying in heaps all over the floor, like I'm back home, trying on clothes at Emmy's house. For the first time, I wish Harmon hadn't broken the mirror.

Thinking of him brings me back from my clothing madness. I look at the mess I've made, leaving my new clothes all over the gross floor. Suddenly guilty, I grab everything and shove it back in the box, my heart hammering. What if these clothes aren't for me? And I just put them all on, assuming they were mine. Why would someone get me nice clothes? I close the box, searching for a return address, but it's just a generic Amazon box. I dig through it again, looking for a gift receipt, but all I find is a packing slip.

Oh well. They fit, and I'm wearing them.

I pick up the box and pad back to the basement on my bare feet. Harmon is sitting at the table in the little den, but I don't look at him as I pass. I'm afraid he'll say something about the clothes, and I don't know how to react to that. But I can't stay in the basement room all day. I'm too excited. So I duck back through the tunnel, trying to act normal as I face Harmon.

"You look nice," he says, thrusting a tiny vase at me. Spilling from the top is a cluster of tiny white roses.

"Oh," I say, taking it without thinking. But all I can look at is him. I have to fight back a scream. I thought he hadn't changed last night. He's not human, but he has changed. One of his arms is entirely human now, and the other one is somewhere between wolf and human instead of all wolf. His chest juts out on the wolf side, like the narrow chest of a dog, while the other side is flatter and more human shaped, but covered in a thin layer of black fur bisected by scars. And he's wearing clothes now—a pair of jeans rolled up on his more wolf side, with his paw hanging out the bottom and the shape of his leg obviously not right for human clothes.

I try to swallow, feeling sick. I don't want to look at his face, but I can't help it. That's changed, too. His chin is more square now, more human, and patches on his neck and face are bare of fur. But it doesn't make him look better. His ear is still a wolf's ear, the good one. The other, now uncovered from the bandage Dr. Golden put on it, hangs down at an odd angle, and while it is the shape of a wolf's ear, it is grossly naked of fur. One of his eyes is now slightly elongated, like a human eye, while the other is still fully wolf. And his head is a different shape, his forehead not sloped so much, his eyes off center as the wolf one stays closer to the side of his head while the more human one has moved closer to the center.

Overall, he's more human, but no more disfigured and repulsive. His features have rearranged themselves into an even more grotesque picture, if that is possible.

"I know what I look like," he says, slamming his fist down on the table. I jump a mile, shame sweeping through me. Harmon lurches from the table, and the familiar mix of pity and awkwardness swirls through me as he cants to one side, trying to get his balance. Now he has to learn to use his body all over again. It would have been better if he'd stayed the way he was. Because at this rate, he's not going to be fully one or the other in two more months. He hasn't changed that much.

We spend the day in different rooms, avoiding each other. That evening, I'm lost in my book when he comes shuffling in, so I don't look up.

He stands there a good minute, then says,

"Love has gone and left me, and the neighbors knock and borrow,

And life goes on forever like the gnawing of a mouse,

And tomorrow and tomorrow and tomorrow and tomorrow…"

He stops when I just stare at him. "Your book," he says, looking slightly irritated and slightly embarrassed.

"You read girl poetry?"

"I read poetry," he says, scowling. "Why do you look so shocked?"

"Because you're a boy who doesn't even have to go to school, which means you memorize poetry for fun."

"I wasn't always a disgusting brute," he says, then stalks off into the bedroom. A second later, the bathroom door slams.

Since it doesn't seem like he'll be thanking me for staying with him last night, I continue reading. Once we get used to his new hideousness, it will be easier. I'll forget what he used to look like, and what he looks like now. He'll just be Harmon. And for a moment here or there, he'll forget it, too, and he won't be this insufferable monster. We'll just be two people trapped in a basement. God, I'm tired of being trapped in a stinking basement.

14

For a few days, I give Harmon his space. He lies under the ladder more now than he has in weeks. I don't know if he's in pain or hiding his new face, or both. But it's funny what a few new clothes can do. It's crazy that something so inconsequential—what are new clothes to someone in prison?—can motivate me, but for some reason, it does. Wearing normal clothes makes me want to be normal again. It gives me something that I'm sure whoever bought them for me never meant to give.

Unless it was Mrs. Nguyen, as I suspect it was. I don't know how she did it, but she knows how much I loved clothes and fashion in my old life. It would be just like her to do something that she knew would get me going. No one else here knows about my old life except Dad, and if he was free to buy clothes, he'd be free to find me. From what I know, he's probably as stuck as I am.

After a few more days of pacing around while Harmon lies under the ladder, hardly moving, I can't take it anymore. Our roles are reversed now. He used to pace restlessly while I lay under the window. I don't know how he could stand it. It begins to irritate me beyond measure to see him lying there day after day.

A week after the full moon, when I set his breakfast

down beside him, I sit down on the floor instead of eating in the sitting room.

He gives me a baleful look and pulls his plate towards him with his wolf paw.

"We need to get out of here," I say, taking my plate into my lap. "When are you going to be ready?"

"I'm ready," he grumbles.

"Then why haven't we tried to leave?" I ask. "I waited for the full moon so you could change. But you didn't. I'm sorry, it's unfortunate, but I'm not going to rot in here forever because you don't want to show your face. They're not just going to leave us down here feeding us eggs and biscuits and buying us clothes forever."

"Then leave," he snaps.

"What is wrong with you?" I snap back, losing my patience. "We've been here over a month. I'm sick of this. We need to get out of here before they do whatever they're going to do to us. Why don't you want to leave?"

"I want to get out of here as badly as you do," he says, turning his flashing blue eyes on me. "But I can't just leave."

I throw up my hands. "Why not? We haven't even tried."

"I just...I can't," he says, turning back to his food. After a second, he pushes the plate away and lies down with his furry black back turned. The bandage on it is old and dirty now, but Dr. Golden hasn't visited since before the full moon.

"Well, I'm leaving," I say, my throat suddenly tight. I put my own plate back in the basket. "I thought we were in this together, Harmon."

"What gave you that idea?"

I swallow hard. "You asked me to be part of the pack. What happened to that? What happened to all that stuff about wolves being noble and taking care of each other? Was that all lies? I thought wolves didn't lie."

"You didn't want to be part of the pack."

"I gave up a chance to escape for you," I say quietly. "Isn't that what a pack member would do? Put the pack first, above myself?"

He doesn't even stir at that revelation. He remains lying with his back to me, his voice sharp with bitterness. "I never asked you to do that."

"Mrs. Nguyen asked me to go with her while you were sleeping, and I said no. I thought we were a team."

"Well, I guess that wasn't a very good decision. If that's what you wanted, you should have left."

I ball my hands into fists, wanting to strike him with all the anger and frustration building inside me. "Stop feeling sorry for yourself, get up, and let's go," I growl.

At last, he rolls towards me. "Feeling sorry for myself? Yeah, I am. But guess what? There's no pack in the world who will follow a leader who can't transition. I'm not a werewolf anymore. I'm nothing. I'm a mutant freak that a shifter can't even look at without her face twisting up like she's holding back vomit. So if I don't care to get out of here, forgive me. But there's nowhere any better than this. Don't you get that, Stella? It doesn't matter where I am. It matters *what* I am. And there's nothing out there for a person like me."

"Then stop being selfish," I say, unable to keep my lip from trembling as tears fight to free themselves from my eyes. "You said you'd put the pack first. And if I'm part of your pack, and I want to get out, you should put that before your own needs. Just like I put you first when Mrs. Nguyen asked."

"I don't have a pack to lead," he says, lying down with his back to me again. "I said if I became Alpha, I'd invite you. But I'm never going to lead anyone. So you're free from that decision. Go do whatever you want to do, Stella. Be a model. Eat pizza. Have your fun, happy life. I'm where I belong."

"Come with me. If you don't have a pack, then you don't have to do what's good for anyone else. But you can still be noble and all the things you say wolves are." A tear trickles down my cheek, and I reach out and touch his shoulder. "I'll be your pack."

"You're not a wolf."

I jump to my feet and swipe at my tears. "And neither are you. But I guess it's good to know how the wolf thing really works. I'll figure out how to get out of here myself, and you can stay here and rot, because it's best for the pack that abandoned you. That's not the kind of pack I'd ever want to be a part of, anyway."

Harmon doesn't stir when I run back to my corner, choking back tears, and begin to shove all my new clothes into an old shirt to take with me. When I'm finished packing, I head for the ladder, ignoring Harmon's motionless form. If he doesn't want to get out, I can't make him. But I'm getting out of here.

I wait at the top of the ladder for hours. Harmon gets up and goes into the other room after a while. My determination doesn't waver. Eventually, someone comes to bring us food. When the door opens, I'm ready. I dive through, knocking the door wide open. As we tumble to the floor together, the woman screams like I've never heard anyone scream before. The terrified shriek that tears from her throat lances my eardrums as I scramble off her, crawling blindly forwards. As I stumble to my feet, I have a second to take in my surroundings—I'm in a huge wooden lodge with a fireplace surrounded by comfortable chairs and couches.

But I don't care about the house. I care about the door straight in front of me, across the open floor. As I take a step forward, the woman's hand clamps around my ankle. Her banshee shrieks echo through the cavernous space with the vaulted ceiling. I stumble forward a few steps, dragging her along with me, before I lose my balance and fall. On all fours, I struggle onwards, kicking to shake her loose, ignoring the new flare of pain darting up my leg from the ankle that has only just healed.

Before I'm halfway across the room, the front door flies open and two men charge through. I'm sure I've seen them before, but I don't have time to place them. One of them grabs me around the waist and hauls me up, lifting me off my feet. The woman's grip slips from my ankle as the man turns back towards the basement door, still standing open. I scream and kick as, in two steps, he erases the distance I fought so hard for. I lash out at his legs, striking them with my heels and clawing at his thick arm around my middle.

From below, in the basement, Harmon gives a sharp protest. But it's too late. The man flings me through the door. My body hurtles forward, and I slam into Harmon.

Together, we crash to the basement floor below. For a second, I'm too stunned to register anything, even pain. I roll off Harmon, who is lying in a heap under me. An ominously still heap.

"Harmon?" I grab his shoulder and shake him. He is heavy as death, as my father was when I found him that day. "Harmon," I scream, crouching over him. My eyes move up to the door, where the man stands silhouetted against the light from above. "Help him," I scream. "He's not moving, please, help us."

Without a word, the man closes the door.

"Harmon," I scream again, unable to find the volume control on my own voice. I swallow hard and try to calm down. Like he said before, freaking out isn't going to solve anything. I cradle his head, search for the spot where it must have hit the wooden support pole nearest the ladder, or maybe the ladder itself, or the packed dirt floor.

Please don't let his neck be broken, I pray as I search for bumps.

His eyelids flutter, and suddenly, his beautiful frost-blue eyes are staring straight into mine. "Well hello to you, too," he says, his voice slightly hoarse.

I release his head, which drops to the floor with a thud. He closes his eyes and draws a breath, his face scrunched in pain.

"I'm sorry," I blurt, reaching for his head again, then pulling back. "I'm sorry, you startled me. I didn't mean to…I wasn't thinking. I didn't do that on purpose."

"Remind me what happened?"

Before I can answer, the little door to the tunnel grinds open, and Dr. Golden appears, bag in hand, and rushes over. She kneels beside Harmon, not bothering to acknowledge me at all. I back away, but I don't know what to do with myself, so I hover while she examines his head and neck.

She swings around to look at me at last. "What happened?"

"It wasn't her fault," Harmon says pushing himself up. I watch his face, noting the wince of pain when he sits. I know his face now, as strange as it is, know every twitch and tell. I know he doesn't complain even when he's hurting, but I know how to spot it, in the tension of his jaw, the twitch in his cheek, the careful breathing and the grimace when he moves.

"Does anything hurt?" Dr. Golden asks.

"Why don't you ask *them* what happened?" Harmon says bitterly. "Or better yet, tell them not to throw a girl down a ladder."

"She fell on you?"

"I was halfway up," Harmon says.

I imagine how hard that must have been, for him to climb the ladder after me. Is that why he didn't want to come, because he didn't want me to see that he couldn't do it without struggle, didn't want to slow me down? Whatever his reasons, he must have changed his mind. He was following me out. Which means that once she leaves, we can start plotting our escape. This time, we'll make it. We'll have two people, and a plan.

Or that's what I keep thinking when she takes him into the other room to examine him. I keep thinking it until he comes back with his arm in a cast and tells me it's broken.

15.

A few nights later, I wake in the dark to the sound of yelling overhead. I sit up, straining to make out the words. Angry footsteps stomp across the floor above us. Someone shouts something about a leader.

"Harmon?" I whisper urgently. "Are you awake?"

"I'm awake."

"I think they're here for you. Maybe they're getting us out."

He doesn't answer.

"Can you hear what they're saying?" I ask, not wanting to come right out and inquire whether his naked wolf ear still works, whether his disfigured ears can hear better than mine. Wolves have better hearing than humans, after all.

"Well enough," he says quietly.

I get up and tiptoe across the room to him, my blanket wrapped around me. I crouch beside him. "Are they getting us out?"

"They're talking about my arm," he says.

Suddenly, an inhuman scream cuts through the angry voices. I freeze, an icy chill racing across my skin. "What was that?" I whisper.

"It's just someone who was injured that night. They'll get the doctor."

"How do you know?"

"I just do. Come here," he says, tugging on my blanket. "Don't be scared."

"I am scared," I say. "How can you not be scared? What if that was my dad? What's going to happen to us?"

"We're going to do the only thing we can do," he says. "We're going to lie here and wait to see what happens next."

I want to argue. There must be something we can do. But I don't know what it is, and the awful scream echoes through the basement again, as if it's coming from the earth itself. A shiver wracks my body, and I sink down next to Harmon and huddle against him, hugging myself. He curls around me, his arm slipping over me, his elbow cradling mine. After a second, his hand covers the back of mine and he laces his fingers into mine and squeezes.

The scream comes a third time, and I shiver as running footsteps pound the ceiling overhead. Harmon holds me hard, his forehead pressed to the back of my neck.

"How come you're so good at making me feel better, and I can't make you feel better when you're scared?" I whisper.

"Because I'm a big bad wolf, and I don't get scared."

I elbow him. "Shut up. I'm serious."

"When you've broken as many hearts as I have, you learn how to comfort a crying girl."

"Oh, right. I'm sure that's it."

And though his voice says he's kidding, I remember the way they looked at him the night of his coronation. He was a beautiful prince that night, and all the girls wanted him. I wanted him.

"So exactly how many of these girls were there?" I ask after a while.

"What do you mean?"

"You know what I mean," I say, nudging him. "You already know my history. What's yours?"

"I really don't know what you mean."

I can't tell if he's kidding, and suddenly, I'm very aware of his warm body pressed up against mine through a few layers of blankets. We're so alone. We've been alone together for over a month now, but tonight he's a boy to me, not a creature.

"I mean, have you hooked up with all the girls here?"

"Oh," he says, sounding surprised. "I...I don't really know. It's different from what they show on TV. It's not the same for us."

"What's it like, then?"

"I don't know," he says slowly. "What's it like for you? It's a big deal, right?"

"Well...yeah."

"It's not for us. Once you Choose, that's a big deal. And there's no more playing around with other people."

"What if someone cheats?"

"You mean after they're mated? No, that doesn't happen."

"No one's ever cheated, in the history of werewolves."

"No."

Urgent voices interrupt our conversation, and we lie in silence, straining to hear. Harmon holds me hard, his nose pressing into the nape of my neck. And just like that, I'm reminded of his weird nose, his gruesome face, and my body stiffens. I can't help it. I wish I didn't care what he looked like. I've always been shallow, and even like this, in a dirt dungeon, I can't shed that part of me.

"Don't think about it," he says. "Tell me something happy. That's how you make me feel better. When you talk about that, and your voice sounds all shiny and your face gets all soft and peaceful."

"Um, okay," I say, pulling away from him to shift onto my back. I tell him about prom, and how I never got to go, but how his coronation was kind of like that, but with importance. And that maybe if we get out of here, we'll be able to do something silly and meaningless, like prom. Harmon listens without interrupting. When I finish, he says, "I thought you never wanted to wear a dress again."

"I think I could make an exception for prom," I say, smiling in the dark. When I stop talking, the silence closes in around us. No more voices, no more footsteps. No more screaming. As I crawl back to my spot under the window, disappointment creeps in. I'm relieved it's over, but some perverse part of me is sorry that nothing happened, because even something that started out horribly could lead to escape. If nothing ever happens, we'll never get out. I just need an opening, one small slip, and I can try again.

16

I'm in the middle of reading *Much Ado About Nothing* when I realize I haven't seen Harmon out from under the ladder in days. He doesn't work out anymore, trying to get stronger. He just lies there, waiting to die. His body is barely more human than before the full moon, and his arm is now broken. But that doesn't mean we both have to give up. Dropping my book on the table, I duck through the tunnel into our dirt room.

"Hey," I say. "Come here, I want to show you something."

"What?" he asks without moving from his spot, lying on the blanket with his back to me.

"You have to come in the other room," I say. "It's a surprise."

With a few grumbles, he hobbles to his feet. Now, he can sort of walk upright, though he's stooped and crooked as an old man. As his father, I think, a fresh pang of guilt going through me. It's my fault his father was injured so badly he couldn't shift into a wolf. That's why he had to retire. And the night Harmon took over, he was injured just as badly.

"What?" Harmon asks when he emerges from the tunnel behind me. His fur sticks up on one side of his head, like he slept on it funny.

125

I can't help but smile. "We're going to do a play."

"A what?"

"A play," I say, picking up the Shakespeare volume filled with all his great plays and sonnets.

"A play." Harmon is staring at me, and I have to wet my lips before going on.

"Yeah. I can't do all the parts myself. I'll do the girl parts, and you can do the guy parts."

"No, thanks," he says, turning back towards the basement.

"Wait," I say. "Please? I'm going crazy down here, Harmon. I need to do something. We need to get out of here, and if you won't do that, help me do this. For my sanity."

He pauses for a long time, his back to me, his shoulder canting in the direction of his shorter, wolf leg, his tail still there, hanging out the top of his pants. "I'm sorry, Stella," he says. "Maybe another day. I don't feel like it right now."

"When are you ever going to feel like it?" I ask, raising my voice when he ducks back into the tunnel. "When are you going to feel like getting off your blanket and doing anything? When are you going to stop wallowing and help me get us out of here?"

He doesn't answer. I collapse into a chair and blow out a breath. I thought it would be better after the full moon. When I saw that he was changing, albeit slowly, I figured he'd redouble his efforts. That the little changes would give him hope. For a week or so before the full moon, we were even sort of friends. Now he's cold and distant, hopeless. And I don't know how to reach him.

I pick up Shakespeare, but I have to read the words

over and over, and even then, I can't concentrate on their meaning. I try to focus, to read a line out loud. And that's when I decide I don't need Harmon. I can read by myself.

An hour later, I duck through the tunnel and stand in the middle of the room, feeling like a complete idiot. Like usual, Harmon's back is turned, so he doesn't notice. Holding the book in one hand and a weird lacy hat I found in a box in the other, I begin.

"Act One, Scene One," I say. Harmon doesn't move, so I forge onwards, reading the setting and then starting in on Theseus. "*Now, fair Hippolyta, our nuptial hour draws on apace.*"

"What are you doing?" Harmon asks.

"*Four happy days bring in another moon, but Oh! Methinks, how slow this old moon wanes. She lingers my desires…*"

Harmon rolls over and stares at me as I read, quite dramatically, I must say.

"Why are you yelling Shakespeare at me?"

"I told you I was losing my mind," I say. "But you wouldn't read the play with me. So I'm doing it myself. Now stop asking questions, you're ruining the effect."

Harmon shakes his head and lies down with his back to me again.

I take a deep breath and go on. "*Four days will quickly steep themselves in night; Four nights will quickly dream away the time; and then the moon, like a silver bow new-bent in heaven, shall behold the night…*" When someone exits, I slip behind a support pole, then enter as four different people, which requires skipping back and forth behind the support. But Harmon doesn't see it, so I just go with it.

Harmon sighs and sighs.

After about fifteen minutes, he turns to face me again.

If I felt stupid before, reading to his back, I can hardly go on now. I lose my place, and Harmon smirks. I read in a man's voice and he rolls his eyes and shakes his head. I have to pretend to sleep and squeeze flowers on my eyelids as someone else at the same time. Harmon snorts. When I finally read, "Either death or you I'll find immediately," and duck into the tunnel to end Act Two, I'm kind of hoping death will find me immediately.

But I won't let him win. I refuse to let his sulking and mockery kill me. I'll pretend I don't even hear his flat, sarcastic applause. After a few deep breaths, I step back out and announce proudly that Bottom, Snout and Starveling are entering. I ignore his snickering as I deliver such gems as, *"What sayest thou, bully Bottom?"*

But he can't keep it up as long as I can. I read, and read, and read. I do all the voices. I lie on the floor, I jump to my feet, I crouch over the invisible person where I was lying. I put on the hat, I take off the hat, I hold up invisible lanterns. I stab myself with a broom handle and die… repeatedly. I lose my place, skip lines, repeat lines, have to stop in the middle of my song and dance routine to find the next line.

Harmon isn't laughing anymore, though. I've outlasted him. He sits on his blanket, watching me intently. I can't tell if this is part of his plot to throw me off, but I go on, anyway. I go on until the last lines, when I approach Harmon where he sits, and hold out my hands, palms down.

"Give me your hands, if you be friends, and Robin shall restore amends."

For a second, I think he's going to scoff at my outstretched hands and turn away. But after a beat, he puts his hands under mine, palms up. He closes his big hand around mine, and I close my fingers around his paw. And then I just stand there, the silence in the basement suddenly stupendous. I need more lines. I don't know what to say now that I don't have them.

Harmon tugs at my hands, and I sink to my knees beside him. "Stella," he says softly. "That was…amazing. I'm amazed. Speechless, in fact. And you…" He gives my hands a little shake. "Are completely mad."

"I warned you."

And then he laughs, and I laugh, a bit hysterically. "I can't believe you did that," he says, shaking his head. His eyes move over my face, my eyes, my cheeks, my lips. My lips. My lips.

Something trembles along my spine, settles in my lower belly.

I pull my hands away and stand. "I should put this stuff up," I say, gathering the book and the hat.

"Yeah," he says. "Definitely. Here, let me help." He stands and shambles over to me, taking the props from my hands without looking at me.

Something weird just happened, weirder than me doing a one-man Shakespeare play in a dirt room prison. While he puts up the things, I straighten the basement. The broom handle, the head of the broom, some onions I used, a t-shirt I danced with as if it were a partner. I try to think about something besides Harmon, like how those men the other day seemed familiar, and how Mrs. Nguyen's body disappeared. I don't know if it is some of the magic or if someone snuck down here and removed it while I was in the shower one day. The thought makes me shiver.

"You got something," Harmon says, returning from the other room with a box. It's like the other one, the one my clothes came in.

"Where did this come from?" I ask, taking the box.

Harmon shrugs and returns to his blanket, but he sits watching me instead of lying down like usual. Slowly, I sit down with the package. When I pull back the tape, my stomach is heavy and thick instead of weightless with excitement. I remove the crumpled paper inside and lift out a garment wrapped in clear plastic. It's some kind of dress, a pale eggshell color. My throat tight, I work to swallow.

"Is this a wedding dress?" I ask. My mind goes back to the night of his failed coronation. The night of the attack, when we were thrown in here. And I remember my sister saying that she didn't want him to Choose her, that she wouldn't have a choice if he did.

"Why are you asking me?"

"I don't know," I say, slowly peeling the plastic down off it. The silky fabric cascades over my arm. I sigh with relief when I see that it's not a wedding dress—too short and poofy. I turn it around and hold it up. "Wow. This is nice."

"Let's see you in it," Harmon says, smiling like a kid playing dress-up. Which I guess is kind of what we are, except I'm the one dressing up. He's already in his *Wild Thing* costume.

I duck out of the room and through the other rooms to the bathroom. Still, I can't shake the weird feeling as I pull it on and smooth it down over my hips, again wishing Harmon hadn't broken all the mirrors.

"That is nice," he says when I return to the basement room. I stand there, curling my toes against the grainy dirt floor.

"I have to tell you something," I say, darting in and dropping to my knees beside him. "It's going to sound crazier than me reading a play all by myself."

"Okay."

I lower my voice to a whisper and lean in. "I think we're being watched."

"Really?" Harmon asks, pulling back to look around.

I grab his shoulder and pull him back to me. "Stop being obvious," I whisper. "I think they have cameras somewhere in here."

"They don't have cameras," he says with a little laugh.

"Thanks for blowing our cover," I say, climbing to my feet. "You didn't have to tell them we knew."

"Stella, come on. There's no cameras."

"Then how did they know I was just talking about a prom dress the other day? And then there was the pizza, and the times I talked about new clothes, and *voila!* New clothes." I grab the poofy, knee-length skirt and shake it to illustrate my point.

"Maybe they're trying to take good care of you."

"Yeah, right," I say, searching the ceiling for glints of a lens. "Easy for you to say. You're not the one they're probably watching undress." I remember the time I got out of the shower and my clothes were right there, and I wrap my arms around myself.

"Right," Harmon says bitterly. "Because no one would ever want to look at me."

"I didn't mean it like that," I say. "But you're a boy."

"No, it's fine," he says. "You're right. I'm going to have to get used to it. This is how I look now. No one's ever going to want to look at me unless they absolutely have to. Like you."

I curse myself under my breath. I almost had him, almost got him out of his stupid hidey hole under the ladder. But now he's lying back down, turning away.

"Don't make me get out the Shakespeare," I threaten. "I only read one play. There's, like, twenty in there."

"I'll read one with you later," he says, pulling the blanket over himself.

17.

A week later, I wake with a start, my name ringing in my ears. "Harmon?" I whisper, pushing myself up.

"I'm right here," he says, his voice close.

I grope across the gritty floor, searching in the darkness. "What are you doing?"

"I want to show you something."

"What?"

"Just come," he says, his human hand finding mine. He stands, pulling me to my feet. Chill, damp air settles around my bare legs, and the day comes back to me. I'm wearing the pale prom dress that came last week. We read *The Tempest* over the past three days, one act each day. Harmon has come out from under the ladder every day. But he hasn't had an idea, had anything to show me, since the day we arrived. The excitement coursing through him finds its way from his hand to mine, curls up my arm. This is something. Something new. Big.

It's not the kind of excitement that might lead him to punch a shifter in the face and run for it, but it's something. I'll take it.

He squeezes my hand and pulls me through the tunnel, then stops. "Okay, put this on," he says, handing me something I can't quite make out in the dark. "Or let me."

133

"What is it?"

"Turn around."

He drops a cloth over my eyes, pulling it tight and tying it behind my head. "Okay, this is weird," I say. "I feel like I belong in some kind of kinky kidnap movie."

"Maybe just the kidnap part," he says. "Now seriously. Don't take it off. Okay?"

"No promises."

He takes my hand and laces his fingers through mine. His hand isn't furry now, but totally human. And so big it swallows mine as he guides me forward. At last, I hear a door open, and his arm snakes around my waist. I reach for the blindfold, but he catches my hand with his paw. "Not yet." I shuffle forwards. "Now step up."

Suddenly, my stomach is shaking. My legs are shaking as I take another step up, and then another. "Are we getting out?" I whisper, my eyes suddenly damp behind the blindfold.

"Just wait. You'll see."

We step up and up and up. At last, he stops, and I reach for the blindfold again. Again, he stops my hand. A door scrapes. Dust tickles my nose. And then I feel it.

Air. Real air, from outside. It's damp, but not in the stale way the basement is damp. It's damp with dew, with mist, with fog and the smell of rain on the air. It's thick and chilly as it caresses my cheek, as solid as fingers. I can hear frogs singing somewhere close by. I can smell the roses.

"Just a few more steps," Harmon says, but this time, I don't let him stop me. I reach up and tear off the blindfold.

The night is bright around us, nothing like the dark basement. The blades of grass shine with the blue moonlight reflecting off their wet surfaces. Each tiny white rose glows as brightly as if the moon has fallen from the sky and fractured into a hundred thousand pieces, each one stuck in the thorns. I step forwards, my bare feet thirsting for the dew clinging to the cold grass. I have to fight the urge to throw myself into the thorny bushes, to roll in them and anchor myself to their thorns so I can never be dragged back to that dungeon.

"What—what is this?" I ask, finding my voice at last.

"They're multiflora roses," he says, as if that answers my question, as if that's what I wanted to know. He reaches out and carefully selects a thin stalk, twists the green tendril-like branch until it tears free. With a smile, he hands me the sprig. I breathe in the sweet smell, closing my eyes. The moonlight caresses my skin like a hand, so heavy after so much time in the dark. When I open my eyes, Harmon is watching me, his face inscrutable. My heart catches, and for one wild second, I can't breathe. I can't swallow. I can't look away from his hungry gaze.

He drops his eyes and turns away, and the spell is broken. A twinge of disappointment flickers inside me, but I push it away. What am I thinking? Just because he kissed me once, when he thought I was Elidi, doesn't mean he'd ever want to kiss me again. Not the way he did that time. And why would I want to kiss him anyway?

"Come on," he says, pulling me forwards. We step onto a narrow path through the bushes, overhung with heavy, flower-laden branches but passable still. Under my feet, the tiny white petals that have fallen are soft as silk.

Harmon leads me forwards, ducking under heavy branches, following the winding path through the briars. At last, we stop. Across a wide strip of tangled brambles, I can make out a crumbling cottage, its stone walls intact but the doors and windows gone.

"Has your mother told you about this place?"

I'm snapped back to reality like I've been caught daydreaming and had a bucket of ice water thrown in my face. "My mother? No. What is it?"

"It's this old cottage," he says. "Your mother grew up here, too, you know."

"No, I don't know," I say. "Just assume that I never know anything."

"Why are you getting mad?"

"Let's just go," I say. "We're outside." I'm not dreaming this, no matter how dreamlike and sedating the sweet roses are.

"You want to go back already?"

The sprig of delicate white roses and wicked green thorns drops from my fingers to the ground. "No, I don't want to go back. I want to get out of here. Let's go. Now. No one caught us, Harmon. We need to run, not stand around smelling flowers."

I grab his paw and pull him through the maze of winding paths, ignoring the hesitance in his step. When we finally reach the entrance to the briar patch, he pulls away. "What's wrong?" I ask. "Why aren't you excited about this?"

"I'm not going anywhere," he says quietly.

"What do you mean you're not going? You got us out. We're free."

He shakes his head, his eyes fixed on the millions of star-like roses lighting up the night as much as the half-moon overhead.

"Harmon, this is our only chance. You found a way through that door. They won't leave it unlocked again."

A frown furrows his brow, but he just shakes his head. "I'm going back in, Stella. I'm not leaving. I can't. I belong here."

I open my mouth to argue, but then I stop. Slowly, I turn to look at the house. And even though I've never seen it from the back, I know. Even though I never knew so many roses existed, even though I've never seen anything like this, and it is incredible, I can't see it anymore. All I see is Harmon, his odd face with the sloping forehead and the fur where human hair should be.

"You're not leaving," I repeat, backing away. "You didn't want to leave because these aren't shifters. They're your people. You were never a prisoner. This is your house."

18

Harmon can't answer. He can't even look at me. My mind reels with everything I should have known, should have seen. The way he never wanted to escape, never talked about it or tried. The way the doctor came to take care of him. The familiarity of the men who threw me back into the basement when I tried to escape. Harmon's lack of concern over whether the wolves would come for us. The way the clothes and food showed up when I talked about them.

Before he can come up with an inexcusable excuse, I turn and run. It doesn't matter who imprisoned me. I'm free now.

"Stella," he calls sharply, but I don't stop. I race across the narrow stretch of grass, across a wide, worn footpath, and into the shadowy forest. As soon as I'm under the trees, the moonlight disappears. I'm in the Enchanted Forest, where trees snatch people up, give them false hope, and thirst for their blood. But what choice do I have? It's this or a basement prison.

I continue forward, arms outstretched. Suddenly the eerie, ominous feeling of the forest at night closes in on me. With a shiver, I step forward. My toe rams into a rock, and I fight back a yelp of pain. But I don't have time to stop and nurse it, so I step forward again. Five steps later, I bark my shin on a fallen branch. Next, my legs get tangled in a thorny vine, the barbs biting into my bare skin.

A warm arm circles me from behind, and I scream and throw an elbow into his gut. This is not a strong, capable man, like the one who threw me down the stairs. This is an injured half-human creature, twisted and deformed and hateful. I have a chance.

With all the force of my anger, I stomp my heel down on the bridge of his foot. I feel a sickening snapping under my heel, and this time, he's the one who cries out.

"Stop it," he growls through clenched teeth. I dig my nails deep into the flesh of his forearm, the one across my middle, and draw a deep breath. I scream into the black forest, send my ear-punishing shrieks echoing and bouncing off trees, a sound with the sharpness of fangs and the depth of betrayal.

But no one comes to help me. They knew I was trapped in my mother's attic all those years. Why suddenly care that I'm trapped in someone's basement? What's the difference to them? They must know I've been there all along. Like always, I'm the only one who didn't know. I thought he was my friend. I thought he was actually giving me real answers at last.

With renewed fury, I throw my elbow into his gut. "You liar," I scream as we stumble forward, both of us trying to throw the other off balance while keeping our own footing.

"I didn't lie," Harmon says, squeezing me harder, so I can barely breathe.

"You lied about lying!" I yell, crushing his foot with my heel again.

With a loud curse, he releases me, and I go sprawling. A sapling crunches under my weight, its splintered end jabbing into my flesh and tearing skin. I scramble forward, trying to ignore the pain. Just as I gain my footing, Harmon crashes down on me. I scream and kick at the ground, flailing under him. I dig my fingers into the leaves, scrabbling for something solid to hold onto, but all I find are loose rocks and dead twigs.

"I didn't lie," he growls, wrestling to get my arms under control without being able to grip anything with his wolf paw. "If you'd stop a minute, I'd tell you what happened."

"You mean you'd tell me more lies?" I say, my voice harsh and bitter as my mother's. Harmon grabs my shoulder with his good hand and in one motion flips me flat on my back. Before I can roll away, he grabs both my wrists in his big hand and pulls my arms over my head, letting his full weight pin me to the ground. His twisted, grotesque face looms over mine, illuminated by the moonlight streaming through a break in the canopy.

"Stop fighting," he barks in my face. "You're not going anywhere." He may not be fully human, but he's still bigger than me. I writhe to free myself, but it's no use.

"Let me go."

"There's nowhere to go, Stella. It's not safe out there. The trees would rip you apart in two minutes flat."

"Out there?" I ask incredulously. "You locked me in a basement for two months and pretended to be there with me. You weren't a prisoner. You're the warden. My prison guard. Is that what you were doing when you listened to my plans for escape? Planning how to stop me? Or were you just using me for your own amusement, laughing at dumb, naïve Stella who's never been out of her attic long enough to realize she was five houses down from her mother the whole time?"

"I wasn't laughing at you," he says. "And I never lied about it. You assumed."

"And you let me," I burst out, struggling furiously again. "Just because you didn't technically lie, that doesn't mean you deceived me any less."

"You're right."

"So what was the point in all that?" I ask, ripping one hand free of his at last. I punch at his shoulder, his head. "Why not just let me go home?"

"It wasn't my decision." He grunts when the heel of my hand smashes into his lips, then snatches my hand and shoves it between our bodies, holding my wrists in one hand and sandwiching them between us.

"Oh, no, of course not," I say, still wriggling to free my hands. "It's not like you're the Alpha and you can do whatever you want."

"I can't," he says sharply. "I have to do what's best for the pack. If that means sleeping in a cold basement so they don't have to see me like this, until they can find a real leader, that's what I'll do. And if it means keeping you there when you're too stubborn to see the dangers out here, then I'll do that, too."

"I'm not in your stupid pack," I scream in his face.

"That's the problem," he growls. "If you were, you'd stay for the good of the whole."

"Oh, poor Harmon. Sorry to be so difficult."

"I'm sorry, too," he says. "But you're not leaving, Stella. It's too dangerous. *You're* too dangerous."

I go still under him, the reality of his words sinking in. "So I'm going to be your prisoner for the rest of my life?"

"No," he says. "You can join the pack."

"What a noble thing to offer, Master Harmon. Join or be a prisoner. Hmm. Fair choice."

"I thought you'd see reason," he says with a small smile.

"Right, like that's going to happen. Why would I believe a word you say?"

"Because I give you my word, and I don't take that lightly."

"Yeah, you gave me the whole spiel about wolves not lying," I say. "Too bad it was a lie, so I can never trust a word that comes out of your mouth again."

For a long moment, his eyes search my face. Finally, he slides his hand from between us, freeing my hands. "That is too bad." He rolls off me and lays on his back, staring up at the leaves shifting overhead. Around us, the eerie rise and fall of frog song begins again after falling silent during the commotion. I gather up my energy, moving slowly so as not to draw Harmon's attention. But just as I'm about to roll over and spring to my feet, his hand shoots out and clamps down on my arm. "Don't make me chase you again."

"Why? Afraid you can't catch me anymore, now that you don't have the unfair advantage of turning into a predator?"

"Oh, I'll catch you all right," he says. "As long as you

142

can run, I can catch you. I'd just rather not go traipsing around the Enchanted Forest all night."

"Is that supposed to scare me?"

"Yes," he says, sitting up. "Speaking of which, we should probably go back."

"The Enchanted Forest sounds better to me."

"Come on," he says, standing and holding out a hand. I stare at it, wanting to rip it right off his body. How can he act like this is all normal and okay? That I'm supposed to just accept it and move on as if it's nothing more than an unfortunate blip on the radar. It's not. I thought we shared something, even if it was something as awful as imprisonment, pain, and the madness-inducing boredom of the basement. But we don't. Mrs. Nguyen tried to warn me. *Keep your eyes open. Don't believe everything you hear.*

Now, I can't run. Like he said, he'll catch me. And just because he doesn't have wolf teeth doesn't mean he won't hurt me. When a twig snaps nearby, I startle. After one more second, I take his hand and let him pull me up.

There's a full moon in another week. I should have gone at the last one, like Mrs. Nguyen said. Instead, I chose Harmon.

I won't make that mistake again.

But for now, I will play nice. I will pretend, lie, and deceive as well as he does.

With each step I take, my feet grow heavier and heavier, as if collecting more and more weight as I go. I try to memorize each tree, each landmark, but there are no landmarks and the trees look like trees, nothing more.

"You know, I'm glad you found out," Harmon says, herding me along in front of him. "I was hoping you would. I never meant to lie to you, Stella. It's just...by the time I realized what you thought, it was too late to correct you."

"Yeah, you tried so hard. Too bad I'm too stupid to understand."

"Well, you know now. That's the important part. I don't like secrets. Now we're on more even ground."

I stomp through the leaves, ignoring the rocks biting into the soles of my feet. "Oh, you mean master and slave? That's more equal than when I thought we were both prisoners?"

"Slave? Really? What work did I make you do?"

"You're right. Being a prisoner is so much better than being a slave." I just need an opening, a break in the woods, so I can run. But who am I kidding? I need more than a gap in the trees. I need a wide-open road, or possibly a racetrack, and a pair of running shoes. A gun with silver bullets might come in handy, too.

"I'm sorry, I don't see how I've treated you so badly," Harmon says. "You saw a doctor. You were fed. You had clothes. Books. Games. I shared everything I have with you. And I offered you the bed. It's not my fault you were too stubborn to take it."

Tonight was my chance, and I blew it. I didn't plan and plot what to do once I got out of the basement. Like usual, I ran as blindly as an animal. And I was caught like one.

"Oh, how noble of you," I say, holding onto the anger so I won't break down in tears at the thought of returning to that basement. "You didn't beat and starve your prisoner. I'm still a prisoner, Harmon. I don't care about stupid pizza and dresses. I want to be free."

At long last, I step out onto the wide, beaten path that separates the woods from the grass in his backyard. Harmon stops, catching my elbow. "I'm sorry, Stella. I really am. That's the one thing I can't give you." He looks so sincere that I almost believe him. But I know better now.

I turn away. My shoulders sag as I start across the strip of grass between the path and the house. It seems to shrink to only a few steps, and before I can memorize the damp, green feel of living grass beneath my feet, we've reached the back porch of the house, where the door still stands open.

"We can stay out longer, if you want," Harmon says quietly, his fingers resting on my back for a second. "If you're not too cold."

I shiver, but answer honestly. "I never want to go back in."

Harmon sits on the edge of the wooden porch and pats the spot beside him. I slump onto it. I can't believe this is it. That this will be my whole life. I've dreaded the thought, but no one has ever come out and told me that's how it would be. Not even my mother took away my hope.

"What's so bad about this enchanted forest?" I ask after a minute.

Harmon finishes unbuttoning his flannel shirt, peels it off, and wraps it around my shoulders. Without putting my arms into the sleeves, I hold it closed around me, absorbing the warmth. It smells like a boy, not a dog.

"It used to belong to us," Harmon says. "To the pack, I mean. This whole valley and the forest in it was ours." He stops speaking, and I watch him carefully as he formulates what to say next. Is that his cue, his tell? Stopping to make up more lies?

"And?"

"And now it belongs to the witches," he says. "The trees, not the whole valley. Our Alpha traded them for the spell to protect your mother."

"Why do they enchant the trees?"

He shrugs. "I guess they don't want them in their valley. The witches and all the other creatures live in the First Valley."

"Creatures?" I ask, huddling into the shirt.

"You know. Fairies, imps, nymphs, trolls." He glances at me. "Wraiths."

"Okay," I say, laughing at little. It's so ridiculous. But no more ridiculous than werewolves. "And angels and vampires, unicorns and dragons?"

"Don't be silly," he says with a grin. "They don't live around here."

"So…all those things you mentioned. They're dangerous? I mean, if I'm going to live here forever, shouldn't I know these things?"

"Most of those things aren't dangerous to us," he says. "Sometimes mischievous. But the wraiths are the real reason the witches wanted the forest."

"That's a ghost, right?"

"A malicious ghost," he says. "The witches have a binding spell. They trap the evil spirits in the trees of the Enchanted Forest."

"So the trees are evil," I say, nodding. I've always felt an eerie presence in the woods here, as if they were reaching out to snatch me up and devour me. Now I know why.

"The trees aren't evil," he says. "But some have evil spirits bound to them."

I imagine being one of those spirits, bound inside a tree trunk prison. The wolves probably consider me evil. And Mrs. Nguyen. Anyone who mirrors another person. If I died, would they stick me in a tree for eternity? If I thought the basement dungeon was bad, being trapped in a tree sounds like literal hell.

"So your dad let witches put evil spirits in your trees, in exchange for a spell to protect my mom?" As I ask the question, I hear the faint echo of my sane, normal self, the one who lived in the real world until a few years ago, telling me that's the most absurd sentence I've ever spoken. But a series of images flashes into my mind—Zechariah helping my mother carry home her share of the apple harvest, laughing with her under the pavilion, coming over to talk to her when I found out about them. Did he Choose my mother, but she Chose my father instead?

Everything feels suddenly dreamlike. The intoxicating scent of wet grass and roses. The silvery moonlight falling across the glittering grass, the fairy-sized flowers with their petals like stars, the undulating trill of frogs and insects in the forest, the cool, damp air hugging my legs and the boy's shirt pulled on over a frivolous, fun prom dress.

For the first time in years, I find myself trying to wake up from this dream so I can call Emmy and tell her about it. It used to be a straight nightmare. Now it's some kind of bizarro, funhouse nightmare, which is even more horrible in that it's not that horrible. Life in the basement is boring and pointless, but it's also easy. If I've ever been spoiled in my life, it's now, when all I do is sit around reading, trying on my new clothes, and playing card games.

"My father didn't make the bargain with the witches," Harmon says. "Uriah did."

"Am I supposed to know who that is?"

Harmon turns to me slowly, with a strange look on his face. "Yes."

I sigh. "Well, I don't. So just get it over with. Laugh at me. When you're done making me feel stupid, go ahead and tell me who it is."

"Uriah was your grandfather, Stella."

"My grandfather." I try to remember what people have said about him before. I know I've heard him mentioned. Harmon is watching me, waiting for a reaction.

Finally, slowly puzzling it out as I speak, I ask, "My grandfather gave the witches access to your forest? Which means…he was the Alpha. So my grandfather was…your grandfather. We're cousins?"

"No," Harmon says quickly. "That's not how wolves choose their Alphas. It has nothing to do with bloodlines. That's how shifters do it. That's how they ended up without a leader. We select someone based on their dominance, usually when they are very young. I was raised to lead the pack. My father…" He breaks off and swallows, and I hear a clicking sound in his throat. "My father wasn't Alpha until I was five or so. The elders had seen the mark in my hair and determined that I was the wolf of the prophecy. That's why Zechariah was selected for Alpha. Because I was destined to lead. Not the other way around."

"I don't get it."

"My father took over the pack from your grandfather, Stella."

"Oh." I sit with that knowledge for a minute. My father isn't a wolf, but my mother is. My mother, proud and cruel and yes, regal on occasion. It makes sense. I can see it now, the shamed daughter of the king, a princess stripped of her title for rebelling.

"So in some weird way, I'm like...wolf royalty?"

He smiles. "We don't really call it that. Although, now that you mention it, I wouldn't mind if you called me *Your Majesty* every now and then."

"Yeah, you keep on hoping for that," I say. "In the meantime, tell me how my mother, the Alpha's daughter, ended up married to an ordinary shifter, by arranged marriage, if that's even true. Not really sure how much to believe you."

"I'll tell you what," Harmon says, standing carefully on his injured foot. "Why don't I let someone who knows the whole story tell you. That way, you don't have to doubt whether it's true."

I stand, too. I don't want to go back in there, but I'm cold even with his shirt on. "You should probably see Dr. Golden about that foot," I say, following him to the door in the side of the house. "I think I felt something break."

"Trust me, I felt it, too."

"I'd say sorry, but you deserved it."

"What's another broken bone? I've got so many I lost

count." He opens the door, and the smell of damp earth wafts out, the smell of the basement where we've spent the last two months. At least he stayed down there with me instead of leaving me down there to go mad alone.

"Maybe you shouldn't have locked me up," I say, not wanting to step back into that black pit. "Then you'd have two less broken bones."

"Has anyone ever told you that you're sadistic?"

"No. Mostly people told me I was pretty."

I expect him to laugh, but instead, his voice goes quiet and serious. "You are pretty."

"So…you're taking me to see your dad, right? The Alpha who can answer my questions about the last Alpha?"

"Stella," he says, his paw reaching out to cradle my elbow. He stands there, blocking my way in, and waits until I meet his gaze. "You're beautiful."

"Thank you," I say, reaching for my throat automatically, for the necklace that's no longer there. My comfort for the past ten years is gone, and I have nothing to hold onto in moments of discomfort or awkwardness.

Harmon may think I'm beautiful, but he must not trust me any more than I trust him, because he doesn't go in first and let me slam the door and run. He gestures for me to go ahead, and then steps back and waits for me to enter.

"I'm going," I mutter, taking a last deep breath of fresh air. Holding the door frame for balance, I step down into the darkness of the basement. This entrance has stairs instead of a crooked ladder. They groan under my weight as I step down, and down, and down. Harmon closes the door, and we're plunged into pitch blackness. I feel my way slowly down the next step, one hand on the dirt wall beside me for balance.

"Why is your dad down here?" I ask. "Is he injured, too?"

"My father's dead."

I stop, and he stumbles against me. I pitch forward, but his warm hand closes around my arm, steadying me. "What? Why didn't you tell me?"

"When?"

"I don't know, how about when you found out?"

"It's nothing you need to worry about."

"You mean, you didn't want me to know when you found out, because you wanted me to think we were trapped by the shifters."

He doesn't say anything.

"You know, for someone who calls them shifty shifters, you're not much better."

"I got it," he snaps. "You think I lied to you, you'll never trust me again. Let's just go."

"What are we doing, then?" I ask, taking another step and another, until my feet settle on the familiar gritty dirt floor. "I thought you were taking me to see someone who could answer my questions."

"I will," he says. "I want you to see *your* father."

I emerge from the door into the bedroom and turn back to Harmon. "Why are we back here?" I ask. "Where's my dad? What did you do to him?"

"He's fine," Harmon says, standing in the doorway, leaning heavily on the knob. "And you'll get to see him. But not tonight."

I close my eyes and take a deep breath. I should have expected this. "Let me guess. You're holding him prisoner, too. Is that who was screaming that night?"

"Stella, no," he says, sounding horrified. "A lot of wolves were injured that night. I told you what that was. And your father…"

"What about him?" I snap, exasperated by all the vague answers. "Can you please just tell me the truth for once in your life?"

"He's with his people," Harmon says. "The night of the attack, I was injured, but I sent part of the pack after you. I'm sorry I couldn't come for you myself."

"You sent them to bring me back here to be your prisoner?"

"To make sure you were safe," he says. "If you were safe at your father's, they would have left you there. But the shifters had you, and…they had other plans for you.

We got your father, and he said they'd give you to us if we turned him over to them. So we did."

Dizzy, I reach out to steady myself on the doorframe. "You gave them my father?"

"He's fine," Harmon says through clenched teeth. "He's the one who offered to trade. He's living at his house in the Third Valley. You don't have to believe me. I'll show you tomorrow. But tonight, I'm going to see the doctor. You can do whatever you want down here." He pauses, then turns back to me. "And Stella? I'm sorry."

With that, he steps back and closes the door. I throw myself at it, trying to turn the knob before it locks, but I'm too late. I hear the deadbolt clunk into place, and I slide down the door and rest my forehead on my knees. Behind the door, I hear Harmon's uneven footfalls on the wooden stairs. I refuse to feel guilty for injuring him.

But I do, anyway.

After a while, I return to my spot under the window. I have a lot to think about. Most of all, how I'm going to get out of here, find my dad, and leave once and for all. I can't stop returning to that one question—why hasn't my dad come to get me? Harmon must be lying about him living at his house. He'd come for me if he could.

I should have gone with Mrs. Nguyen. I think over her words. She told me not to trust Harmon, but I didn't listen. Now I know she was saying those things for a reason. I replay what she said before she left. Look around. See what's there, but don't trust my eyes. Don't trust anyone or anything. The wolves say they're honest, but if I've learned anything here, it's that they are all liars. And I am always alone.

20

The next few days are strange. Harmon lies under the ladder on his blanket, with a new cast on his foot. It's hard not to feel sorry for him. Just when he gets out of one bandage, another one appears somewhere else. His father died. He can't take his rightful place as Alpha.

But when I start to feel guilty, I scold myself out of it. I know better than to believe his sad act. He's here by choice. He could be up there, being waited on hand and foot by all the cute wolf girls who would at least pretend he's not hideous. They'd probably still flirt and beg to be his wife. Pride alone keeps him down here.

As for me, I have other obstacles to consider. I no longer sit around reading, occupying my time and waiting for something to happen. Filling my time and escaping the mind-dissolving boredom only appealed when I couldn't find a way out. Now that I know I'm Harmon's prisoner, everything is different.

I realize as I settle into the bed the night after Harmon's confession that I am not afraid of him anymore. I'm not scared of what might happen if I try to escape, because I know Harmon won't hurt me. The thought doesn't sit easy with me, but there it is. From that night on, I sleep in the bedroom, leaving Harmon to wallow in despair in the gloomy basement. The bedroom is damp and musty, too, with the same small window at ground level that the other rooms have. But I don't have to share the space with Harmon. I only see him when he shuffles through to use the bathroom, his head down, his eyes fixed on the floor. Good. At least he's feeling guilty about what he did. He deserves it.

When he's not in the room, I take to filing the splintered end of the broom handle against the rough sandstones that make up the wall beside the bed. It's the one stone wall in the basement, on the far end of all the rooms. I'm guessing it's aligned with the wall of the house above and needs fortification. I'm using it as a grinder to sharpen a stake. Emmy would have rolled her eyes and told me stakes are for vampires. But as I don't expect a gun loaded with silver bullets to magically fall into my hands, I'll have to make do.

At the very least, it will slow them down. These wolves seem as vulnerable to injury as regular humans. Which means I can sharpen a wooden broom handle and impale someone. I can use the fork I squirreled away last night to jab someone in the eye. If Harmon is going to keep me in prison, I'm going to have to start thinking like an inmate. I conjure scenes from long-forgotten movies and TV shows, drawing on them for inspiration. Harmon has no idea what I'm capable of.

Now that I know my enemy, I can fight him. I have all the advantages. Harmon thinks I'm going to passively accept my fate like I have the last two months. The last two years. He thinks it's fine to let me use silverware. He's no prison warden. He's a slacker, as trusting of me as I was of him before I learned the truth. To him, it's as if it makes no difference, as if the only thing that has changed is my knowledge of it. But everything has changed.

Finally, after a week of plotting, the day arrives. The day of the second full moon. As Harmon stalks into the bathroom, I hide my broom handle between the wall and the mattress, smiling to myself. Maybe I should have gone with Mrs. Nguyen, learned how to be a witch. I've already got a broomstick.

And it will have to do, because I don't get a chance to work on it all day. Harmon paces the basement and the sitting room all morning, and I'm too nervous to risk him walking in and finding me with a weapon. In the afternoon, he appears in the bedroom doorway. "Do you want to go outside?"

"I thought you were the dog here," I say, swinging my legs off the bed.

Harmon looks confused. Of course. No one here has pets, so he wouldn't know about taking the dog outside.

"Never mind," I say.

"I'm going to go walk the paths in the rose garden. Do you want to come?"

I want to go so bad my toes curl in anticipation of the soft grass underfoot. But I feel a trap in this, somewhere. I want him to think I'm normal, though, that nothing has changed. If he gave me a chance to get out last week, wouldn't I have done it? Refusing the offer might raise his suspicions. He may not turn the place upside down for the wooden skewer I'm going to drive through his back while he's incapacitated, but he might realize I've finally snapped.

"Sure," I say. "Aren't you afraid people will see us, though?"

"No one goes back there except kids playing on the path."

"And they're too afraid of your face to brave it?"

A muscle in his cheek twitches. "Are you coming or not?"

"Coming." I hop off the bed and beam up into his glowering face.

He turns and stalks to the door, but he can't manage an intimidating gait with his crooked legs. By the time we reach the top of the creaky wooden stairs, I'm fighting a mixture of impatience to get outside and remorse about my plan. Like I told him, I don't actually want to kill anyone, even my jailer. But I will, if it means escape. It's easy to hate him when he's not with me. It's harder when he's here, so human in his monstrosity.

He throws open the door, and I blink against the brightness. When we step outside, though, my eyes adjust quickly. It's not actually very bright. I'm glad I'll be escaping at night. If the sun was shining, I might be completely blinded after spending so long in a shadowy basement.

Harmon takes my hand and leads me towards the rose patch, the tiny white petals bright under the dark clouds. It's one of those stormy days of early summer, the air thick with a heavy warmth, the earth expectant. Deep grey clouds hang low in the sky, looming over us as we step onto the narrow path through the tangled vines.

"I don't know if I'd call this a garden," I say as we duck around a barbed branch hanging in our way. It seems to reach for us as we pass, but we slip by. Harmon didn't say anything about possessed roses.

"That's what my mother called it," he says, leading the way. This time, he lets me walk behind him, but he keeps hold of my hand. "She cut the paths through it so we could walk here and enjoy it. It used to be an impassible patch of thorns."

"Where is your mother?" I ask, glancing around. I realize I've never seen his mother, never heard her spoken of. It's one thing to have a male pack leader, but to have his wife completely obscured by his status is another.

"She's dead." He doesn't slow when he speaks, and his voice has no inflection. But it's a practiced flatness, I can tell. I've grown to know the subtle shifts in his voice, his face, his body language. I really don't want to have to kill him.

"I'm sorry." I wait for him to tell me what happened, but he doesn't. Of course not. No one volunteers information to the outsider. Determined not to let it bother me, I follow him through the green bushes, their thorns stark beneath the solid ceiling of ominous, angry clouds. At last, we reach the end of the path. Before us lies a large rock, the bushes cleared away for a few feet around it.

For a long time, we sit in silence on the stone. Harmon rests his elbows on his knees and stares at the brambles. I work a thorn out of my bare foot.

At last, he says, "You can come out here any time you want."

"As long as I put myself back up when I'm done?"

He frowns down at his hand, kneading his paw as he speaks. "I don't want you to feel like a prisoner."

"I am a prisoner."

"You don't have to be."

"I can go home? To Oklahoma City?"

"No," he admits. "No, you can't do that."

"So I'm free to live here…against my will."

He turns to me. "Why are you so against joining us? We'll take care of you, Stella. I don't understand why you don't want to be part of the community. I'm offering to take you in. For you to live here like anyone else. They're not prisoners. They're members. Why do you insist on seeing it that way?"

"Really? You don't understand why I don't want to join your pack?"

"No," he says. "I honestly don't. You'd belong. We'd accept you as one of us. We're good people. We'll be good to you."

"Like you have been for the past three years? Leaving me in my mother's attic and doing nothing? Or like you have been the last few months, letting me think I'm being held captive by evil shifter kidnappers, when really you're the evil kidnapper?"

"Okay, I admit, I should have told you. And if you want to go home, to your mother's house, I can ask the pack if they're okay with it. I should have done that a long time ago, you're right. I just…" His crooked eyes meet mine, and I have to look away first. Harmon clears his throat, and his voice takes on a businesslike, impersonal edge, so I'm sure that he was going to say something other than what comes out. "I don't know how responsive they will be to me. I've never been their leader. I was injured before I took over."

"So who's running things?"

"Everyone," he says, throwing up his hands. "Everyone but me." He's quiet a minute, glowering at the millions of tiny white roses. Finally he goes on. "Mostly your mother is in charge. As the former Alpha's child and my father's Second, she's equipped to lead. But she doesn't have the necessary bond with the pack to be Alpha."

"And she's a woman."

Harmon sighs. "Why are you so fixated on that? Women aren't second class citizens to us. They're treasured and protected, the same as any other member of the pack. They do equal work and have equal status."

"Except for Alpha."

He's silent for a long moment. "Yes," he admits at last. "That's our tradition. It's never happened before. But I don't see why it couldn't."

"So my mother could be Alpha?"

He thinks this over, frowning down at his hands. "As far as I know, a woman has never wanted to be our Alpha. But if your mother wanted to challenge me for the position…"

"By fighting you? She's old, and a girl, so she has no chance. That sounds fair."

"So you'd expect me to take it easy on her, right? Now you see why it doesn't happen?"

I grumble my displeasure at the unfairness, but Harmon's expression remains stoic. "If she wanted to challenge me now, she'd have the advantage," he says quietly. "Since I haven't been confirmed, and I'm unable to shift, she's acting Alpha. Before my father died…" He breaks off and swallows. "She had a lot of influence on him during the past year, when he was injured. He was confused, and she'd feed him ideas, and he just…went along. She's practically led the pack this last year. The pack trusts her."

I try to wrap my head around that, to see my mother as their leader. My cold, heartless mother putting everyone else first? But then, Zechariah wasn't exactly warm and friendly. It's easier to imagine them moving from him to my mother than from him to Harmon. I wonder what she'll do with me if she's Alpha—certainly not invite me to join the pack.

I remind myself that it doesn't matter. I won't be here then. I'll be somewhere else…maybe Oklahoma, though my childhood dreams have lost their luster. Even college seems like a laughable fantasy now. What am I going to tell people about my high school?

Oh, you danced with your friends and took cheesy pictures at prom? I went to a werewolf coronation which was interrupted by irate shapeshifters, and my crush was brutally attacked by my father, who, FYI, happens to be a mountain lion.

I am not equipped for a career in anything but how to survive in prison, which I'm guessing is not a booming field of study. When I try to imagine the future, it's a big fat nothing.

"So what happens to you?" I ask.

"I stay in the basement until I can shift," he growls. "My aunt has been bringing us food. I don't have anyone else. This is my house until they choose a new leader."

"And in that time, I'm just supposed to be happy to be subjected to the whims of the pack at any given moment? I'm confused about why I should want to be a part of this community now, after being treated the way I have. Especially if my mother is Alpha."

He frowns down at his black paw. I try not to stare at him. I can't keep my eyes from him, but I can't look too long, either. In daylight, his grotesque appearance is magnified, laid bare to see. The black wolf fur sprouting from tan human skin on his neck makes me shudder. His clothes fit him strangely, hanging loose in places they shouldn't and stretching tight in others.

"You're right," he says at last. "But the fact is, I can't change any of that now. All I can do now is offer you this. To live as one of us, not a prisoner. To be part of our pack, and if you don't want to do that, at least a part of the community. You'll have your own house. A share in the community garden. It's not what you want. But it's the best I can do right now. It's all I have to offer, and I'm offering it to you."

"I'm sorry," I say, standing to face him. "It's not enough."

21

We walk the rest of the twisty-turny path through the roses in silence. Harmon walks ahead, his hand in his pocket, his paw hanging loose. If I had my broom handle, I could stab him in the back right now. But I can't stomach the idea. He's not the only one keeping me prisoner. If I kill him, the pack will probably kill me. If I injure him and run, which is my plan, they'll run me down and devour me. If I'm lucky, they'll simply throw me back in the basement and lock the door. But I'll lose Harmon's trust and…friendship.

That's all it is, I remind myself. Even so, the thought—and my accompanying resistance to the idea—is unsettling. Maybe I am his prisoner, but I'm more than that to him. I can see it every time he looks at me. And I don't want him to see me differently than he does, to look at me with hatred and disgust. No matter how I feel about him, I don't want him to despise me.

When we reach the end of the winding path, and step out onto the grass, Harmon turns to me. "Is there anything I can do to make you happy?" he asks.

"Besides letting me go?"

"Yes. Anything."

I square my shoulders. "No. I'll never be happy here."

"Then what would make you happy?" he asks, rocking

a little on his human foot, forwards and back. "If you went back to Oklahoma, what would be different? I asked what you missed, and you said pizza and clothes. I brought you those things. And you're still not happy."

"Maybe it doesn't translate for a wolf," I say slowly. "You're all about obedience, and being one with a pack. I want to be myself. It's nice to feel like part of something, but I also want to be an individual. And here, I can't have either. I'm not part of the pack. Even if I join, I'll never be one of you."

My throat tightens as I speak, and when I meet his eyes, they're so full of sadness and compassion that I have to look away again, swallowing to stop the tears.

"And what would you do once you got home?" he asks.

But it's not like before, when I'd tell him about my old life to pass the time. That's all gone now.

"I'd bring my dad home," I say. "And we'd start over."

"You can't go back in time," he says. "You can't forget what you know. This is who you are now, Stella. You know about us, and that's dangerous."

"I'll never tell a soul," I say, my heart hammering. He is looking at me differently, like a stranger. An outsider. Like he might be considering it. "I promise. My dad lived out there for years, and he never told. I—I'll do anything you want. I'll sign a contract promising."

He smiles a little. "I don't think my people would put much faith in a shifty shifter contract. And look what happened to your father. Something brought him back here."

"He got trapped here."

"Because he came back."

"Fine, you're right, he came back," I say. "But you said you'd take me to see him. When? Are you holding him hostage somewhere, too?"

"I'm going to talk to the pack tomorrow," he says. "After...after everyone's awake. I'll ask about letting you go back. And I'll show you how to see your father tonight."

22

Later that night, I pace the tiny bedroom and the equally tiny sitting room, as nervous as Harmon about what the night will hold. When I hear the door in the other room scrape, I duck through the tunnel. It's too early to make a move. Harmon is sitting under the ladder, with his back to the wall, his eyes closed.

"Do you feel anything yet?" I whisper.

He nods once, then goes back to whatever meditation he's doing. Maybe trying to concentrate on transitioning. I don't know how it works. I return to my spot under the window, where I haven't been in a week. It already feels different, strange. As the light fades outside, Harmon shifts restlessly on his blankets. I think about what he said. That I'm different now, that this is who I am now.

It's true. I can't unsee the things I've seen. My mother, as a wolf, about to rip my throat out. Harmon's father, slammed to the ground like a side of beef. A hatchet, thrown from my hand, hitting his skull. A mountain lion closing its jaws around the throat of the boy I'd just kissed. A wolf pup sailing through the air and landing in a raging fire. Harmon's skin ripped open, the muscles in his back exposed and sliced open. His repulsive, distorted features as he waits, trapped between man and beast, to see if he'll ever be able to claim his rightful place in the pack.

After seeing that, how can I care about the girls on the glossy pages of fashion magazines, about makeup pallets and this season's sandal?

I don't want to spend the rest of my life looking backwards, wondering what might have been, wishing for childhood to come back and capture me. I want adult things, too. When Harmon talks about marriage, about his kids calling him a good dad, I know I want that one day, too. And I know I can't have it while I'm here.

And so, I wait. I listen to Harmon's breathing grow shallow. I hear the first snap of something inside him, and the intake of breath, the hiss as he breathes through his teeth, through the pain. And then I climb the ladder. I pull up the basket and untie it from the thin rope.

I start to saw at it with the butter knife I stole. After a while, my arms are tired and I'm only halfway through.

"What are you doing?" Harmon asks from below.

"Nothing," I say, peering down into the shadowy spot under the ladder. He's lying curled up on his side, shuddering like someone with the flu.

"In the bathroom," he says. "Ask to see your father, and you will."

Sensing a trap, I don't react. Instead, I go back to sawing. Nothing can distract me from my task. At long last, when it's completely dark out, I make it through the rope. Ignoring the grisly popping noises his body makes as he tries to change into a wolf, I descend the ladder. He's not going anywhere tonight.

Outside, the clouds have broken up, and the moon periodically escapes cover and lights the spot below the window where I used to sleep. But in this end of the room, I can barely make out my own hands, clutching the thin rope. I creep towards Harmon, my heart beating hard. He groans softly, and a meaty snapping sound gives away his location. Swallowing the urge to gag, I step closer. At last, I can make out a shadowy mound where he lies under his blanket. As I kneel beside him, his head snaps back, then forwards. A shaft of moonlight falls across the floor, and I can see the cords in his neck standing out, straining. He's breathing hard, his shoulders hunched.

Slowly, I peel back the blanket.

"What are you doing?" he asks again, his voice an uneven groan between shudders.

"It's okay," I say. "Don't worry. Just relax. Here, lift your shoulder a little."

He's the worst prison guard ever. He does exactly what I tell him, and then, I have the rope around him. He's so out of it, I don't think he even knows what I'm doing until he's halfway immobilized. I push away any pity I feel. If he turns into a wolf, he'll be able to chew his way out. But I'm pretty sure that's not happening. The fur on his back is thick and coarse as ever, but he's still talking, which means he's still human.

He barely struggles when I bring his hands behind his back. But when I pull the rope tight, he strains, thick strands of muscle standing out along his arm. I start losing my grip, and panic wells inside me. Now that he knows what I'm doing, he'll never let me get away with it. But before he can pull away, another round of convulsing wracks his body. While he's preoccupied, I yank the rope tight and quickly tie it.

"Stella," he moans, his head lolling towards me. "What did you do to me?"

"You're fine," I say. "You're going to be fine. I told you, just relax and go with it. You might be mad at me now, but tomorrow, you'll be glad. Because I'll be gone, and you won't have to feel guilty, or make any decisions about me." While I reassure him, I loop the rope around a rung in the ladder and pull it tight.

"Don't leave," he says, his eyes bleary as be peers up at me in the darkness. "I need you."

"I'm sorry." And I really am. Something squeezes in my chest, behind my sternum, and I think I might cry if I stay longer. I lean down and kiss his bristly cheek.

"Stay," he whispers. "Stay with me again, like last time."

"I can't," I say, taking a deep breath before rising to my feet. "But I forgive you. I might not be part of your pack, but I think I understand enough to know why you did what you did. I'm not going to carry around hatred for you when I'm gone. I'm going to forgive you. So you don't have to feel guilty. And neither do I, for leaving you here like this. Goodbye, Harmon."

"Stella," he groans. His voice is a horrible, twisted thing like his body. I turn away. "Stelllllaaaaaa…" The word is slurred, and it sends a shot of fear through me. If he transforms into a wolf right now, he'll be out of his ropes and at my throat in a second. He won't kill me. But he won't let me go.

I back away and hurry to the bedroom. This time, I don't bother with extra clothes. I take only my fork, my butter knife, and a crudely sharpened broom handle. The door next to the bathroom is unlocked, like he promised it would be, so I can go outside. He has no idea how far I'll go.

Before stepping through the doorway, I pause. Because as awful as it would be to stay in the basement with Harmon forever, it's something I know. I know his moods, when to leave him alone and when to invite him to play cards. Food will be delivered every day. I'll have clothes to wear, and someone to read plays with me and make silly voices for different parts until I laugh and, for a moment, forget how small my life is.

Out there, life is big.

It's also unknown. It could be even worse than a basement prison. I'll be free, but what then? Freedom isn't predictable or guaranteed. Freedom isn't safe. As if to remind me of that truth, a distant howl finds its way to me down in the basement.

There's a full moon. Somewhere out there, they will be doing their bonfire dance and transitioning. If I don't get out of here before they all make the change, I'll never get out at all.

"Stella," Harmon calls. "Wait. Before you go…"

I wait, listening for sounds of struggle, but I only hear his harsh breathing. After a minute, he speaks again. "Are you still here, Stella? Check the bathroom. Check the mirror."

A chill works its way over my skin when I think of the

wolf definition of *mirror*—a body snatcher. Or does he mean that my sister is here, my identical twin? The thought of her makes my stomach lurch. I don't know if she's a friend or an enemy, but my blood calls me to her, a silent voice vibrating along our twin bond. Part of me is sure this is a trap, that I'll open the bathroom to find something too grotesque to imagine—a portal to my mother's attic prison, a wolf waiting to rip out my entrails, my father's dead body.

Finding my father's body once was more than enough.

And yet, I can't seem to stop myself from stepping towards the bathroom, away from freedom. Maybe I'm stalling for a moment, being a coward, unable to face the solitude of freedom. Warily, I push the bathroom door open with one foot, standing aside as I do so, in case the trap is cruder, like a foot clamp. When nothing happens, I reach in slowly, my fingers trembling as I extend them towards the light switch. I squeeze my eyes closed, sure something will rip them off at any moment.

Instead, the cool plastic plate around the switch meets my fingertips. I hit the switch and yank my hand back. The bathroom is empty. But my gaze immediately fixes on the one thing that's changed. In the spot above the sink, where the mirror hung before Harmon shattered it, hangs another mirror. It's a familiar one, and my stomach knots at the realization of how far Harmon went to get it for me. He had to leave his house, show his hideous face to the others in the community. He had to convince my sister, somehow, to relinquish her hold on it. She loved the mirror, and I can't imagine what Harmon could have traded her for it.

But it's not enough. Sure, he's making the prison homey for me. That doesn't change the fact that it's still a prison.

I start to turn away, but just as I am about to step out of the bathroom, a movement in the mirror catches my eye. Heart hammering, I twist around, sure that someone is behind me. But the bedroom is empty. When I step closer to the mirror, my image blurs with another face, one I know well. Harmon promised we'd see my father, and here he is. In the mirror, my father's face appears haggard, his long hair disheveled.

"Dad," I gasp. "Are you okay? Where are you? What happened?"

But apparently magic mirrors don't work like Skype. He doesn't answer, and after a second, my view recedes and flickers.

"No," I cry, grabbing the edges of the mirror. The image crystalizes again, coming into sharp focus. Dad is sitting on a bed. A bed that I made.

Fury explodes behind my eyelids. I'd recognize that loathsome attic anywhere. I barely left it for three years.

If I was angry before, if I hated my mother before, there is no word to describe the feeling that slams into my chest when I see my father's chained wrists. For years, my mother acted as my jailer and tormentor, and she must have gotten a taste for it, because now she's acting as his. She probably told him I was dead. After all, she went along with the others, telling me my father was dead all those years. She even watched me grieve, used it as an excuse to keep me locked away, all the while knowing he was alive.

Everything she has done up until this point might have been forgiven. But there is no forgiving this.

"I'll get the key," I say, remembering the necklace of keys hanging from her neck. I don't care what I have to do to get it. I've been a prisoner in that attic for too long to sit back and let someone else suffer that way. And my father, of all people. My sweet father, the gentle giant who stayed up late talking to old ladies and pasted *Dora the Explorer* Band-Aids on my scraped knees when I was a kid, is now stuck in a barbaric prison.

A tear spills down my cheek. Though I know he can't hear me, I speak to the mirror anyway, my fingertips skimming its cold surface. "I'm going to get you out, Dad. I promise."

I reach for my weapon, the broom handle tucked into my waistband, and steel myself. It's probably the stupidest move I've ever made, but some unknown bravery takes hold of me. My father needs me, and I can't let him down.

Sneaking close enough to the bonfire to steal a key from my mother's discarded skirt with only a rough-hewn stake for protection against a pack of wolves is about as stupid as a turtle crossing the path of stampeding elephants, counting on its shell to save it. But it's what I have.

A thread of doubt follows me away from the mirror. What if I get there and he's gone? What if the mirror was some kind of trick, a trap to lure me back into my mother's clutches? But I have to believe he's there. I have to believe I can save him, even though I've learned how dangerous hope can be, how it can keep a person going but no more than that. It's like the crumbs that keep a starving man from dying—never enough to feed him, but never letting him succumb to the peace of death.

Fighting back the dark thoughts, I step into the light that falls across the bottom of the stairs and freeze. A vicious snarl comes from the bedroom. A chill races across my skin, up my back. Harmon doesn't sound pitiful anymore. He sounds as angry as I am. "Stella," he bellows from the basement. When I hear something wooden crash and splinter, the chill turns to a hot, liquid fear in my gut. I race up the steps to the door, fling it open, and dash into the yard—straight into a pack of wolves.

24

I stop dead in my tracks, sucking in a long, loud gasp. A dozen heads turn my way. All eyes fix on me, catching the scant light from the house and reflecting it back like dozens of tiny moons.

Slowly, I take a step back. It's a trap. They're all waiting for me. But who set it up? My mother? Harmon? It must have been him, sending some telepathic signal. There's no bonfire, no celebration. Just wolves pacing the yard, waiting.

My skin crawls with fear as I slowly creep backwards, not daring to take my eyes off them. The second I do, one will launch itself at me. Suddenly it strikes me that I know these people. There is the glossy golden wolf that tried to rip my throat out—my mother. There is the soft white wolf, my twin sister. There is the three-legged brown wolf that is my sister's half-brother. Two young grey wolves who are my sisters' friends.

"Don't hurt me," I say, holding out a hand, as if that would ward them off. I stare at the blunt stake protruding from my fist as if I've never seen it before.

My mother growls and lowers her head, advancing a step.

"I'm not going to hurt anyone," I say. "And I didn't

hurt Harmon. I've kept him company the last two months. I helped him through the last full moon."

Where were you? I want to add, but I don't. My mother snarls, the skin on her nose wrinkling as it draws back, baring her gleaming teeth.

"All I want is to leave in peace. I'll never tell anyone about you, never breathe a word. I'll sign a contract if you want. Swear an oath. Whatever will make you trust me. I just want to leave. I don't want to be a burden to your community, don't want you to feel responsible. You let my father leave once. So let us leave again. I'll take him with me, and you'll never hear from us again."

My mother lunges at me. I scream and bring the stake down on top of her head, but it's the wrong end. She draws back, circles around the pack. Did that just happen? I warded off my mother with nothing but the dull end of a broom handle. But just as my confidence grows, two wolves begin to twitch and shudder and spasm. After a few seconds, they stand upright. I recognize the two men who threw me down the ladder when I tried to escape before.

One is Fernando's father. My mother has also transitioned back into human form, her pale skin glowing eerily in the moonlight. "Put her back where she belongs," she says, her voice cold and commanding. She points to me like I'm a pesky dog that keeps getting out of its crate.

"Mother, please," I say. "All I want is to leave. Just let me leave. I know you don't want me."

And then she says the thing she's been saying to me every day since I arrived. "It's for your own good."

"It's not for my own good," I explode, jerking away

when the men try to grab me. "It's for your good. It's for your sick sense of revenge. You've always hated me. I've never done anything to you except come to live here against my will. If you really wanted to do what was good for me, you'd let me leave with my father like you did when I was a baby. That's the only thing you've ever done for my own good."

She flicks her wrist like I'm not worth the effort, and the two men seize me. I'm suddenly very aware of their nakedness, their animal heat, the scent of their sweat on the warm night breeze.

"Let me go," I scream, digging my heels in, arching my back. But they grip my arms and drag me backwards, towards the door. I turn my eyes to the fuzzy white wolf standing at the edge of the pack. "Elidi, help me. Get me out. I just want to go home."

She lowers her head.

Before I can get another word out, the men hurl me through the door and down the back stairs. This time, Harmon is not there to break my fall. My shoulder smashes into the dirt wall, my body tumbles down and down and down. My head slams against a wooden step, and darkness swallows me.

25.

The first thing I hear when I wake is Harmon raging. It takes a moment to find my bearings, to remember where I am. Slowly, I drag myself down the last few stairs. My ankle is on fire, flames shooting up my leg. My head weighs a thousand pounds. I curl up on the cool dirt floor for a few minutes, drifting along the current of consciousness.

"Stel-la," Harmon roars from the other room. I push myself up to sitting, and my head swims. Afraid I'll pass out if I stand, I crawl into the bedroom and kick the door to the stairs shut behind me. For another minute, I lie on the floor.

Then Harmon starts up again. "I know that's you, Stella. I know your smell."

Through the haze of pain and dizziness and thick-headedness, fury blazes up bright and clear. "It's your fault," I snarl back at him. "You called them here."

"What are you talking about?"

Something jabs into my side when I move, sending pain streaking up my torso like an infection. I reach for it without looking. My stake is gone, but my fork remains, protruding from my pocket with one of its tines driven deep through my skin. With gritted teeth, I ease my jeans down a few inches, lowering the fork with them. It comes out smeared with blood.

I grip it in one hand and crawl on my elbows towards the basement room, like that starving man who's lived on crumbs for too long. My body is ready to give up. But my fork is ready for more than crumbs.

Pain flares in my leg every time I move, but I continue forward, determination driving me on even as warning bells begin to go off in my mind. Something is happening to me, a pain that has nothing to do with my injury. Holding back the pulsating panic in my mind, I drag myself forward.

But I know this pain. Aching joints, undulating light at the edges of my eyes, distorted vision, as if seeing through a wavy glass. I stop and lower my head between my hands for a minute. Ironically, I've had these fits since I was a kid, when I—no joke—fell down a flight of stairs. My dad always told me we moved to Oklahoma to be near Dr. Golden, who specialized in traumatic brain injuries. Now, I don't know if any of that was true. All I know is that I had these strange fits when I was a child, but they stopped until last year, when I had one in my mother's attic.

That time, she was there to help me. This time, I'll have my father. I have to get to him. He always knew how to talk me through the fits, to get me to sleep. When I'd wake in the morning, I'd have only nightmare images I couldn't tell from reality, and sore muscles and joints.

"Stella," Harmon rasps from the basement.

I pause at the entrance to the tunnel. I can still go back. I could drag myself to my feet and stumble back through the sitting room, back through the bedroom and the door, up the stairs and out into the yard. My mother was sympathetic when I had my last fit. She'd take me to my father this time.

Maybe.

But I need to take care of Harmon first.

I heave myself forward, ignoring the pulse in my temples. When I emerge from the tunnel, I can see Harmon more clearly than before, and I wonder distractedly what time it is. The wolves will transition back at dawn. Is it close already?

"Traitor," Harmon snarls. He's sitting up halfway, bound from full range of motion by the the rope tangled around the ladder, which is lying on the floor beside him. His hands remain behind his back.

I guess I'm not so bad at tying knots after all.

"I'm the traitor?" I ask. "You had my father in an attic the whole time?"

"Your mother caught him less than a week ago," he says.

"And you let her put him up there?"

"What am I supposed to do about it?" he explodes.

"Stop being a coward just because you're hideous," I shoot back. "And if you want to talk about being a traitor, you're the one who called your wolf pack to stop me. I guess it takes a whole pack of wolves to stop one tiny human girl? You're all cowards."

"I didn't call them," he says, his voice grating and harsh. "They're waiting to see if I can transition."

That gives me pause. I hadn't expected that answer, hadn't considered they were there for anything other than stopping me. But why wouldn't he just call a guy or two if that was the case? They don't mind throwing girls down flights of stairs on a regular basis. Why call in the whole pack for backup? This time, he must be telling the truth. Which really, really sucks. Not only is he suffering and weak and in pain, but he's got the weight of the entire, expectant community resting on his shoulders. Tonight, he's supposed show them he's strong enough to be their Alpha. Instead, he's going to prove he's not. Again.

"Are you sure they're not there to be spectators when your thugs knock me out?"

"What are you doing with that fork?"

"I'm going to stab your eyes out with it."

He snorts and twists around a little, his heel digging into the dirt for leverage. That's when I see that he has two human feet. I sit up, then grab my head. The fork tumbles to the floor.

"What's wrong?" he asks, his voice suddenly urgent with concern.

"Your foot," I say through clenched teeth.

"My foot is bothering you?"

"You have two feet, Harmon. And your face."

"What about my face? It's still hideous? Because it hurt like hell, so I know something rearranged itself."

I drop my forehead to the floor, relishing the coolness, but the gritty dirt sears my skin. It feels more like I'm getting a gravel facial than resting gently on the ground. I shouldn't have come in here. I knew better. Right now, before it's too late, I need to go to my father.

"I think you're better," I mumble against the floor. "You're a human again."

"In case you missed it, I have a cursed paw where my left hand should be," he says. "I have a tail, Stella. Do you have a tail? Do most humans have tails? So I don't think they're going to accept me as Alpha anytime soon."

"Your face…"

I want to tell him it's better, almost normal. Sure, it's a little furrier than the average human face, but still. It could pass as a beard. Maybe. If I'm really trying to convince myself. But I can't say any of that, because a ripple of pain shudders through me. When I lift my head, my neck feels wobbly and unsteady.

Harmon is staring at me. "What was that?" he asks, his voice low and deadly.

"I need my father." I can feel it building again, like a wave beneath the surface of the ocean, powerful and unstoppable.

"Untie me."

"Get my dad," I say, my voice sounding far off and dreamy.

"I can't get your father," Harmon says, nodding towards his bound hands.

"My mother, then," I mutter. "Summon her, or whatever you do with your wolfie voodoo mind tricks."

Harmon is quiet for so long that I lift my boulder-sized head again. He's watching me, his eyes narrow and calculating.

"My mother," I whisper. I can't believe I'm asking for the woman who ordered me thrown down a flight of stairs. But the one time this happened, she took care of me. I can feel her arms around me, cradling me, can hear the panic in her voice. Maybe she did tie me to a bedframe when I started convulsing, but she also brought me the tea that helped me relax and fall asleep. And she told me why it happens, something my father never did.

"No," Harmon says. "I don't think I will call her."

"I—I need her," I say, flattened by the pressure ripping through my back. "You don't understand. Please, Harmon."

"I understand more than you know," he says. "You tied me up here and left me to go through this alone. At least you'll have me with you."

"A fat lot of good that'll do." A cramp jerks me forward, and I roll onto my side, curling in the fetal position, defeated. "Please…help me."

"Hmmm…." He considers me, as if I'm no more than an extra scrap of wood he's trying to decide what to do with. Throw away, or build something?

"Harmon…I need help. Get my father, my mother, anyone. Dr. Golden. I—I might die."

He smirks. "You won't die. Just relax. Go with it. Isn't that what you said to me?"

"Please."

His eyes are remote, detached. His voice is firm when he speaks. "No."

26

I swim in and out of consciousness. My body shivers, shudders. My muscles spasm and convulse.

"Just go with it," Harmon commands. "Embrace it. Move towards it, not away."

I scream. I vomit. I black out.

"Stella."

I open my eyes. Through a distorted funhouse mirror of pain, I see Harmon's face, as it was before, beautiful and perfect, his glossy black hair shot through with a streak of white. But his neck is black, too, his shoulders thick with a black pelt. He's no longer tied, but lying in front of me, his face inches from mine. He's stroking my cheek with the pad of his paw, his claws just scraping my skin, alerting me to danger.

"Stop fighting it," he says. "It'll be easier next time. Just relax, and think about something you love. Think about a tiger. How brave it is. How majestic. How power-ful." His voice is soothing, lulling my eyes closed. I picture the tiger at the zoo when I was a kid, with its huge head and its golden eyes staring out at me, just inches away from mine, on the other side of the glass. I remember the measuring post next to the enclosure where Dad took my picture next to the wooden tiger cutout that was ten feet tall.

I remember him telling me it was time to go. And when we got home, I was obsessed. Tiger sheets. Tiger t-shirts. Calendars. Posters. Stuffed animals. Dad promising to take me back to the zoo. And until we could go, I could wear a tiger eye necklace and think of him. Remember his promise to take me back. Somewhere along the way, it became a reminder of Dad, not the zoo.

"Holy mother of Diana."

I open my eyes. Harmon sits up and scoots away quickly. He hasn't changed, but he's somehow smaller. A lot smaller. So small that when I sit up, he's shorter than me. And sitting up is strange, dizzying, even. Suddenly, I know how Alice must have felt when she grew ten sizes bigger. I look down at myself, and I'm not there. My hands are gone, and in their place are two huge white paws.

I look up at Harmon again. He's scooting away, shaking his head slowly. "Stella," he says, a warning note in his voice. "You're still you. You know that, right?"

I open my mouth to say of course I'm still me. But am I?

The sound that comes out of my mouth says I am most definitely not me. It's not a growl or a roar or a bark, but more like a *chuff.*

"It's okay," Harmon says. "You'll shift back. I'm sorry it was so hard for you. They say it's like that, if you resist it your whole life. Your parents really should have told you that. Had you practice…"

My head is spinning. I lift my hand, and the paw lifts. It's freaking enormous. As I lift the other one and set it down, it sinks in. I'm not a werewolf. I'm a shifter. A freaking tiger!

Harmon has reached the wall, and he can't back up any more. He's so small. Even if he changed into a ferocious wolf right now, he'd be small compared to me. And he's not a ferocious wolf. He's a twisted hybrid freak, and he's stuck that way. He can't shift.

I stand. My body feels huge and unwieldy. I must look drunk as I take a few steps towards him, figuring out the whole four-legged thing. Suddenly, I remember his taunts when I was shifting. I stop, open my mouth, and roar at him. The sound is a blast of pure sound, the energy of it rocking through the basement in waves. It's huge and glorious. I do it again.

Harmon seems to shrink as I stand there roaring at him. If he hadn't knocked down the ladder, he could have climbed it. But guess what? Tigers can climb. Tigers can knock down flimsy little ladders. I could probably knock down this whole building. I roar at him again, glorying in the immensity of my voice. No wonder my mother "helped" me when I started shifting. No wonder she never told me. She wasn't protecting me. She was protecting herself.

At the thought of my mother, a flood of anger pours like blood from my heart, enough to drown my veins. I leap forward. Harmon strikes at me, his fist smashing squarely into my nose. Pain shoots up my nostrils. I growl in frustration, and it reverberates through my body, through the basement, like a living thing.

"Stop," Harmon barks, his voice sharp and commanding. But I'm not a wolf. I don't have to obey his commands. This time, I strike him. He tumbles sideways, and before he can recover, my jaws close around his neck. My jaws are enormous! I could rip his head off in one swift pull. And doesn't he deserve as much? Why should I have mercy on him, when he's never shown me any?

"Stella, you don't want to do this," he says quickly, his palm bracing against my throat. "You're high on the power of it, but this is still you. It's not separate from your human self. When you go back to your human form, you're still responsible for what you did. Do you really want to kill me? Is that how much you hate me?"

He must know my teeth could sink into his flesh in a heartbeat, and he'd be gone. I can feel his blood pulsing in the veins in his neck. It's disturbingly alluring. I don't hate him. But he betrayed me.

I remember him asking if I would kill anyone, if I'd seek revenge, when I got out. The realization of what that conversation really meant rocks through me. He wasn't my partner in this, asking what I would be willing to do for my freedom. He was securing a promise, knowing this moment would come.

And it has. I'm not a helpless, ordinary—and therefore useless—girl. All this time, I believed I wasn't special enough to be part of my own family. That I was ungifted, and that's why my mother didn't want me.

I'm a freak and an outsider, all right. But not for the reasons I thought.

I'm dangerous not because I know what they are, but because I'm stronger than they are. Because I can turn into something bigger and fiercer and stronger than they are. Something that can snap the neck of their Alpha in a second. Something that could kill each and every one of them, if I chose to do it. No wonder they didn't want me to know.

Now I know.

I tighten my teeth on Harmon's neck. His pulse throbs against my canines, his thick wolf fur warm against my tongue. He buries his hands in my fur, but instead of struggling, he goes still. No begging and rationalizing, no bargaining and explaining and warning. No one will stop me if I choose to do this. I could be this person.

If I choose to be this person, this is who I will be for the rest of my life. Powerful. Ruthless. Treacherous.

No one can stop me.

That thought brings a strange, stark clarity to my mind. If I want to do this, I can. It's my choice. But the choice is mine to make, and only mine. In this moment, I understand my mother. The knowledge of my complete power is intoxicating. One pulse of my teeth and a whole, promising, glorious life snaps to an end.

I drop Harmon.

He rolls away, flattening his back against the wall. I want to ask him everything at once, but I can't ask anything. My voice is huge, but it's also without language. After a minute of staring at each other, he laughs nervously. "Are you...yourself?"

I don't know if I'm myself. I don't even know who that is anymore. Suddenly I'm not just me. I'm much more. And I want him to know that even though I chose not to crush his skull in my jaws, I could have. I still could. Placing a paw on his chest, I press him down into the dirt until his cheek twitches. I ease back on the pressure, baring my teeth.

Instead of cowering, he slowly reaches up with both hands. His paw touches my face, and even though there's a layer of fur between his hand and my skin, I can feel it every bit as well as if I had bare skin. He buries the fingers of his human hand in my fur, a look of pure wonder spreading over his strange face.

"I knew what you were," he says, stroking my fur with his paw. "But I didn't *know*. This is incredible. *You're* incredible."

I dig my claws into his furry chest, just enough to let him feel them. He's still at my mercy. He grimaces in pain, but he doesn't look afraid. He's too busy marveling at me, stroking my ears, my neck. He touches my whiskers, and my lips instinctively pull back from my teeth. He smiles and runs his hand along my powerful jaw.

And after all this time, after sixteen years of my father, my mother, my sisters, and everyone else knowing but me, he's the one person who was brave enough to tell me. To force me into this, however painful it was. He didn't have to do that. He probably shouldn't have done that. But he did.

I lean forwards over him, bringing my face close to his, and growl. I don't want to sit down here in the basement. I want to run through the woods, over the hills, back home. He wouldn't stop me. Couldn't. I have strength I never knew.

But for the first time since entering the Three Valleys, I'm not sure I want to leave.

27.

For a long time, I lie on the floor next to Harmon, ready to pounce if he moves. But eventually, I fall asleep. When I wake, he's curled up against me, his body resting against mine. I stand and stretch, relishing the powerful length of my limbs.

Harmon sits up and rolls his head on his neck, rubbing his shoulder with his good hand. "You might want to transition back to human," he says. "Or not. You know, if you wanted to talk about this. Maybe I can answer some of your questions?"

My first question is, how do I transition back? When I remember the pain of those fits, the nightmare shifting vision, the headache, I don't know if I do want to. But he's right. I have questions. I have a lot of questions.

"If you do, you know where to find me," he says, rising to his feet. His human feet. But he's not all better, just because his feet look normal. His legs are still uneven, his stance crooked. His knee bends at a strange angle as he limps to the tunnel and ducks through. I pace the basement, which now seems impossibly small. It occurs to me after a few minutes that they can't hold me here anymore. I'm bigger and stronger than all of them. Which means I'm free.

The thought scares me and thrills me in equal

measure. I pad into the tunnel, which must have been made for animals and not humans. As a tiger, I don't have to duck when I walk through.

I find Harmon at the table, playing solitaire. I place my front paws on the edge of the table and rise up over it, peering down at Harmon. He smells even better when I'm a tiger. I snuffle at him, at the cards on the table, which shift slightly when I blow out a breath.

"Okay, you don't get to act like a cat," Harmon says, pushing at my neck. "You're not a tiger, Stella. You're a shifter. You don't get to lose your human side completely, even when you're in your animal form."

I drop down from the edge of the table and turn away. My tail moves with me, like an extra arm, always extended for balance. It swishes back and forth now.

"Go on, transform back," Harmon says, setting down the deck of cards in his hand. "The same way you did last night. Only think human, not tiger. It'll get easier every time, and pretty soon, you'll be so used to it you almost look forward to the pain. It feels good, like popping your back."

I snort, and Harmon laughs.

"When you're ready, I'll help you," he says. "The most important thing is that now you know, so when it happens, you can go into it instead of resisting."

I step back and lower my head. Closing my eyes, I think of my human form. Harmon's voice coaxes me on, telling me to reach for it, to pull it into me. Picture it, seek it, call to it and embrace it when it comes. Don't hold back or hesitate or be scared. I've done it before, I can do it again.

Soon, the pain starts, and I pull back from it. But it only intensifies when I tense up, scared to let it consume me again. Harmon moves to my side and massages the spot between my shoulder blades. He talks me through it, one wave at a time, until I finally let go and let myself fall, spinning into the pain as if I love it.

This time, the blackness seems to last only a second or two. And then I'm blinking, pushing myself up off the dirt floor.

"I did it," I say, momentarily elated. It takes me a second to notice that I'm stark naked. With a shriek of surprise, I turn and run back through the tunnel. I'm naked. I look around the basement and find my clothes in a rumpled pile. My face hot, I hurriedly pull on my underwear and jeans, then my shirt. It's silly. I know it's silly. Harmon has seen everyone in the community naked hundreds of times. He's even seen my identical twin naked, which means he's basically seen me. It's nothing to him.

I smooth my hands over my clothes, take a deep breath, and return to the sitting room. "Did you undress me?" I ask when I'm seated opposite him. "When I was blacked out, you took my clothes off?"

"I didn't look at you," he says, sounding slightly offended. "It's like if you needed medical attention. There's nothing sexy in that context, trust me. I would have been happy to let you do it yourself. But those jeans were not going to do anything but cause a lot of pain when you were transitioning."

"I guess," I say, still feeling weird that he's seen me

naked. Of course, I've seen him naked, too, when I spied on him. So I guess we're even.

"I promise," he says, holding up his hands. "Not that you put much on a promise from me. But really. I wouldn't look at you like that when you were going through what you did."

"Okay. I believe you."

"You're not the one who has anything to be ashamed of," he says, turning his attention back to his cards, his face darkening.

"You don't, either," I say. "You're not a wolf or a human, but you're still you. Like you said to me."

He snorts and lays down a card. "You're a beautiful human and a beautiful animal. What do you know about being ashamed?"

"I'm a girl," I say. "I think it's in our DNA."

"Why don't you ask me what you want to know before you go," he says, frowning at the card he flips up.

"Am I going?"

Bitterness creeps into his voice. "Why would you stay? I knew the danger when I made you shift. Not just for me, but for the pack. But you said you didn't want to kill anyone, and I trusted you. There's no reason for you to stay now. You wouldn't tell anyone about us, because you're the same. And you hate it here. You hate us. There's nothing keeping you."

"You're just going to let me go, just like that, after all this time."

"Yes," he says, flipping over three more cards. "That's why I didn't go get your mother when you asked for her. I knew she'd stop you again."

"Why let me go now, after holding me hostage all these years?"

"It wasn't my decision until these last few months," he says. "I should have made it sooner. But I didn't know how to tell you. I didn't know when it would happen. You're not a wolf, where it happens at the same time every month."

I run my thumbnail along the edge of the wooden table, leaving a faint line. "How did you know I'd ever shift?"

"You're a shifter," he says with a shrug, moving a pile of cards to another. "You'd do it eventually. When it started last night, I knew it was time to let you do it. Time for you to know who you really are."

"Why now?"

"Why not? I was selfish to keep you here as long as I did. And a coward."

I smile a little. "I don't know. You risked me eating your face off."

"I didn't want to be alone," he says, ignoring my attempt at humor, his tone scathing. "So I made you stay with me in this misery. You shouldn't have been stuck with me for the past two months. But you were. The best I can do now is to make sure it's only two months, and not two more years."

"More like sixteen more years."

Finally, he looks away from his game. He sets his cards down again and pushes up on the edge of the table, bracing his palms on the surface while he navigates his body out of the chair. It's easier for him now, more normal.

"I think you should talk to your father about that. It probably would have been better if you'd seen him before you shifted. But I told you I'd take you to see him, so let's do that now."

"I already found him."

Harmon pulls up short and studies my face. "Right," he says. "I forgot. I summoned him in the mirror."

"You did that? How? And how do I know it's real?"

"I thought I was the one who had a problem with mirrors."

"I don't have a problem with mirrors. I have a problem trusting you. So if you summoned that image, how can I trust that it's real?"

"Why would I lie about it?"

"Because you knew I could shift into a tiger and eat you. I can't believe you kept me down here with you for this long."

"At first, I thought you knew. I figured once you saw your father as a mountain lion, he'd explain it to you."

"We didn't have much time for pleasantries," I say. "First, we were escaping from you, and then we were rescuing Mrs. Nguyen, and then we were being attacked by shifters. The question-and-answer portion of the evening was brief."

Harmon scowls. "You were escaping from me? In case you forgot, your father is the one who did this to me."

"Because you were trying to kill me."

He pulls back, looking genuinely surprised. "Why would I kill you?"

"Oh, I don't know. Maybe because I almost killed your Alpha, who's basically like your god and master, not to mention that he's your literal father. And then there was the little matter of me pretending to be Elidi and tricking you into Choosing me at the coronation."

"I wasn't trying to kill you," he says, his voice tinged with hurt. "I followed you to protect you. And I knew who you were when I Chose you."

"What are you talking about?" I feel my face warming at the thought of that night, of the way Harmon held me, and kissed me until I couldn't think of anything else.

"I knew it was you." His eyes search mine, and in them, I see all the hope and fear and vulnerability of that confession written all over his face. "I Chose you for my mate, Stella."

I don't have time to ponder the meaning behind some boy's words, even a boy who kissed me like it was the last the world would ever know. So I just ask. But…why?"

"Because you're my mate," he says. "Now that I know you, I know why. And I…I love you, Stella."

I swallow hard, an ache swelling in my throat. But I have other things on my mind. I still want what I've always wanted. And that's not Harmon.

"I'm sorry," I whisper, and I mean it. "I…I liked being your friend. But I can never trust you again, and I can't love someone I don't trust."

"I know," he says, his eyes moving away from my face, to his mismatched hands.

"I need to see my father," I say after a pause. I square my shoulders and force myself to look at him as if he didn't just tell me he loved me. A year ago, I would have died to hear those words. But things are different now. I'm different. "Not in the mirror," I add. "Tell my mother to let him go."

"I don't know if I can make your mother do anything," he says slowly.

"Don't you have power over them? They have to obey you, right?"

"I told you, I'm not the Alpha," he says, as if pushing the words out is physically painful. His fist clenches. "But I will be. I'll unite our people with the other valleys. That's the prophecy, so it will come to pass."

He sounds more angry than sure.

"Fine, then I'm going out as a tiger," I say. "It's on you if I eat someone."

"Don't," he growls.

"You know, you're pretty loyal considering your pack hid you away in the basement for the past two months."

"They're still my pack," he says. "If I wanted to force them to acknowledge me as Alpha, even though my father didn't confirm me, I could try. But who would follow me? I don't even have the pack bond yet. *That voodoo*, as you call it. And I can't transition. I'm not an Alpha. I'm an abomination."

"No, you're not," I say. "You're just…you."

"And I'm doing what's best for the pack. Waiting to see if I can transition at the next full moon. If I can't, I won't be Alpha, and I'll do what's best for the pack then."

I swallow hard, my heart suddenly pounding. "What's that?"

"I don't know," he says, staring down at his cards. "I could leave and become a lone wolf. Maybe I'll join the goblins. I already live underground. I'll fit right in." He smiles, and I can tell he's attempting a joke. But it makes me ache.

"The pack wouldn't take care of you?"

"They would," he says. "But I don't want to be a burden on them. They're my pack, whether I'm Alpha or not. They always will be. I'd live and die for them, Stella. This is where I'll always belong, but if I'm not a wolf anymore, I'm nothing but an inconvenience. I want them to be healthy and happy and complete. A wolf who can't shift is not helping to make that happen."

"That's sick," I say fiercely. "There should be room for people who aren't all the same."

He smiles. "There is. They wouldn't kick me out. And I'm not angry about leaving. I'd do it because I want to. I will always want what's good for the whole. What's best for the pack is best for me."

"I guess I can't understand because I'm not a wolf," I say with a shrug. "I don't belong to your pack, and I'll never think that way. And I'm kind of glad. I want to be happy, too, not just make a bunch of other people happy."

"And you will be," he says. "You can be. Go and see your father now, Stella. You've been in here too long. It's time for you to go."

28

Though Harmon is right, and it's time for me to leave this godforsaken place forever and never look back, I falter. Even as I climb the stairs, my chest tightens. As crazy as it sounds, I don't want to leave him. He betrayed me, but I still... I want him to come with me.

But he belongs here. And I haven't yet found where I belong. I emerge from the basement into the light, blinking in the bright sunshine. No one attacks. No one throws me down the stairs. No one is there at all.

Every step I take, I am waiting. Waiting for them to attack. But this time, the fear is mixed with something else. I almost hope they will attack me. They'll see what happens when they try to throw a tiger down the stairs. All that time, they thought I'd never figure out who I really am. But now I know.

I march straight up to my mother's front door without seeing anyone but a couple kids playing in the woods beside one of the cabins. At Mother's, I hesitate. I've never come to her door before. I was always dragged through it, or hidden behind it. Now I don't know if I should knock or smash down the door. Even though I'm in human form, the power of my knowledge gives me courage and strength I didn't know I possessed. I am a tiger. Not a helpless girl among vicious wolves.

After a second of indecision, I turn the knob and walk in. No one in the community knocks. They walk into each other's houses like they own them. I know much more than the fact that they are werewolves. I know all their customs and habits. For three years, I was an observer, a spy gathering bits of information as if they were the crumbs keeping me alive.

When the door swings open, my sisters both turn from the sink, where they are washing a tub of beets.

"Stella," Elidi gasps.

Zora snorts as if holding back laughter. "Oh moons, what happened to your hair? It looks like you haven't combed it since I last saw you.'"

Once, I was obsessed with my appearance, and that comment would have sent me scurrying for cover. Now, I barely register her scorn. I haven't seen a mirror or a hairbrush in months, thanks to her pack's decision to throw me in a basement with their disgraced Alpha. My hair is the least of my worries.

"Is Dad here?" I ask. When I saw him in the mirror, I didn't know if it was an illusion. But I guess I do trust Harmon, because I'm sure he's here. Still, I want them to say it.

Elidi's gaze moves from the dripping beet in one hand to the scrub brush in the other.

"You can't come back and live here," Zora says.

"Why, because Mother has a new prisoner to torture? Surely she has enough cruelty for two."

"Then why are you here? She said you'd found somewhere else to live."

"Mother's out back in the garden," Elidi whispers.

I turn away from them in disgust. I used to idolize Elidi, to fantasize about trading places with her and living her blessed life. She had a family while I was alone. She was powerful, while I was vulnerable. But Mother was right when she said I'm not like Elidi. I may have been as timid as her before, when I had no choice. When one wrong move meant punishment at the hands of an entire community whose weakest member could kill me without struggle. But if I'd been raised knowing I was strong and deadly, I wouldn't be so spineless.

For a moment, I can't help but despise both my sisters, but especially Elidi. At least Zora has some fight in her. Elidi could be fierce and fearsome, but she cowers under my mother like a beaten dog.

Without another word to them, I turn and stride to the back door and throw it open. Mother looks up from her small backyard garden, where she's weeding a row of collards. "Where's my father?" I demand.

Mother stands, her shoulders square, her eyes blazing. "Who let you out?" she demands.

"I let myself out," I snap. "I'm not a dog to be kept in a cage and let out for walks."

"Does Harmon know you're here?" she asks. "He's supposed to be watching you."

"Oh, Mother," I say. "Despite your every attempt to convince me I'm worthless and unlovable, it turns out I have a certain charm after all. Did you really think Harmon would be as cruel to me as you were?"

Her eyes narrow. "He let you out?"

"Or maybe you were hoping I'd kill him, get rid of your competition," I muse. "Is that it? You're leading the pack now, after all. If the Alpha recovers, you'll be relegated to second-in-command status again. You always did love lording your power over me. Now you get to lord it over the whole pack."

Even as I speak, the bitter words rolling off my tongue, my insides tremble. The fear of her is ingrained into every muscle fiber in my body. My hands are sweating and my heart palpitates. Entering this house again is like being swallowed by a nightmare. But I won't back down.

"What do you mean, kill him?" Mother asks slowly. "You wouldn't kill Harmon."

"No," I say. "But I could. I could kill every single one of you. And you know it." I relish the words as I speak them, relish their truth. I can feel my tigress stirring, as if she's scratching at my insides, reminding me to let her run. A surge of power floods through me. Defiant, I meet my mother's eyes.

Understanding flashes across her face. She may be cruel, but she's not stupid. She hardens her expression, her eyes locking on mine, letting me know she's not afraid of me, either. For a long moment, we stare each other down, silence stretching between us.

"Now give me the key," I say.

She lifts the chain from around her neck and tosses it onto the porch at my feet. "Take him away," she says with a sneer. "I'm sick of his whining anyway."

I turn and race back into the house and up the stairs. Fingers trembling, I shove the key into the lock and turn. The door swings open, and there is Dad, lying on the bed with his back to me.

"Dad?" I whisper, my throat tight. He rolls over

slowly, throwing off the dark wool blanket as he does. He sits up and blinks at me from a face thick with matted facial hair. For a second, he doesn't speak.

"Stella," he says after a pause. "I thought it was a dream. How'd you get the key?"

"Why didn't you tell me I was a shifter?"

Once, I would have run to him and fallen into his arms, sure he was the saint I built him up to be. But he lied to me longer than my mother. His betrayal is deeper.

He rubs his eyes. "Who told you that?"

"No one. Someone *showed* me that."

"How about that," Dad says. "So you finally did it, after all that time."

"Why didn't you tell me?" I ask again, gripping the loose door knob.

He sighs and shakes back his stringy, greasy hair. It breaks my heart to see him like this. But not enough to blind me to everything else. I'm tired of having my questions put off for later. "It's complicated," he says at last.

"Then uncomplicate it," I say. "I've got all day."

For a long moment, he studies me. "You've changed."

"It's been three years, Dad. I'm not thirteen anymore."

"I guess you're not." With another sigh, he shuffles towards me, and I see then that his hands are cuffed together and secured to a chain around his waist. He's wearing a pair of dirty, navy blue shorts and a dingy t-shirt. He's changed, too. His hair is thinner, now straggly and almost to his shoulders. I don't remember if it's changed since spring, when I saw him last, or if I was too busy being attacked by shifters to notice then.

"I'll get you out," I say. "But I want answers. Now."

"Okay, okay," he says, holding up a hand, which lifts the other one with it. "Let me get my thoughts straight. What do you want to know?"

"Everything."

"Everything," he says with a chuckle. "Let's start at the beginning. Your mother and I, when we found out, thought it would be difficult to raise you here, among wolves. You were bigger, harder to control. And so headstrong…" He breaks off and smiles into the distance. After a moment, his eyes narrow with calculation, as if he's trying to decide how to best tell me something unpleasant. At last, he goes on. "As it became apparent that you wouldn't take orders like a wolf, your mother and I decided to divorce. It was better for everyone if we moved somewhere else, gave you a normal life. But it wasn't fair to your mother or sister to make them leave, too. They belonged here. We didn't."

"Because we're shifters."

"Yes," he says. "The wolves don't trust us because we broke a few treaties with them over the years. But they're the selfish ones. If they shared what they had, we wouldn't have to make these bargains with them, giving them whatever they want just so we can hunt on their land."

I open my mouth to tell him that the wolves use that land, but then I remember that my loyalties aren't supposed to lie with them. I'm not one of them, no matter how much I've come to think of myself as part of my mother's family. The mad daughter in the attic.

My hands slowly ball into fists as my throat tightens.

"And you didn't think you should tell me all this at some point?"

"I was going to tell you," he says. "I was, Stella. Don't go getting mad. I was waiting until you were a little older. I moved us near Dr. Golden so she could keep an eye on you. And I had Yvonne help with your memories."

"So I never fell down the stairs? Or did you toss me down the stairs on purpose, so I'd have something to blame for my suffering, when it was your fault all along?"

"Hey, now," he says, holding up a hand again. "No one hurt you. We suppressed a few of your memories, that's all. And you really did fall down the stairs—no magic involved. We focused on that enough times, and your mind filled in the gaps all by itself. The human mind is a remarkable thing."

"It was all a lie," I whisper. "All that to keep me from knowing my true self?"

"You were your true self," he insists. "When we found the tiger eye, I had Yvonne do an enchantment to keep its wearer from shifting. See, I ended your suffering. You didn't have the fits after that, did you?"

"The necklace," I say, my hand going to my throat. He made me promise never to take it off. That's why. When I lost it in the woods last year, I had one of the fits for the first time in years, because the enchantment is on the necklace.

"Yes," he says. "When you were so obsessed with tigers, I knew you'd dream of being one again and maybe remember. We had to stop you. For your own safety and everyone else's. A tiger roaming around downtown Oklahoma City? You would have been shot. I didn't know it would end up around my neck, keeping me from escaping this prison here."

"Wait, that's why don't you shift and get out of here?" I ask, looking around. If I'd known I was a tiger all that time, I would have busted down the door and gotten the hell out of here years ago.

"It's on me now." A rough cord peeks out from the neck of his shirt. My necklace. The tiger eye that kept me from shifting all my life is now keeping him from shifting.

"You still have it," I say, reaching for it automatically.

"I was bringing it back to you, but they caught me before I could." His face darkens with anger. "Seems I've been captured by every kind of being in the Three Valleys since I got here."

My own anger bubbles under the surface. He wasn't coming to rescue me. He was coming to bring me a necklace he used to trick me into being ordinary, human, and obedient. No matter what he says, he was never going to tell me. He was still trying to keep me from shifting a week ago, when he was captured.

Eyes narrowing, I glare at him. "You could have told me what you were. What I am."

"I know," he says, shifting his feet on the wooden floorboards. "But I didn't want you to have to live with the secret I did, to have to hide it from your friends and everyone else. I wanted you to have a good life. A normal life, where you didn't feel different. And you did, didn't you?" He smiles hopefully, his eyes pleading.

My father used to be such a big, imposing man. Now he's just pathetic.

"I did," I admit. "But I wish you had let me decide

what to do with that information. It's my body. My animal. My life."

"Maybe I should have."

"And how could you just leave me, let me think you were dead?"

"There's something else you should know," he says. "Something we can do, besides shifting."

"Projecting. I know."

His eyebrows shoot up. "You do?"

"Mrs. Nguyen told me."

"Ah, of course," he says, nodding to himself.

"You projected out of your body and came here to check on my sisters."

"Once or twice a year," he says. "I never disturbed anyone or made my presence known. I just checked on them and your mother. Made sure they were doing okay."

I smile a little. This is the dad I know, always looking out for me. My sister, too, it seems.

"But it seems projecting is not such a desirable skill," he says with a wry smile. "In fact, your mother's people are violently opposed to it."

"I've gathered as much."

"The only people who really want to do it are witches," he says. "I only meant to check on your sister, same as usual, that night. But Yvonne caught me, and she kept me here."

"Mrs. Nguyen?"

"That's right," he says. "She wanted me to teach her daughter how to project. She kept me here, and then arranged things at home."

He doesn't sound at all upset by this. In fact, he's smiling. But my blood is boiling. He and Yvonne have been orchestrating my whole life. "How did your body get here?" I ask, already knowing the answer.

"Again, Yvonne," he says, confirming my suspicions. "She set it all up, brought me my body. She said they even had a funeral. It took a little help from Goldie to pull it all off, but Yvonne...she's always been clever." A smile plays over his lips, amused and admiring. Dad's always been a jokester, but I can't believe he thinks any of this is funny.

"Do you even hear what you're saying? I found your body. I thought you were dead. They had a funeral for you, Dad. You couldn't have, I don't know, sent a note? Had one of them tell me?" My hands begin to shake as I squeeze them tighter and tighter. How could he do this? How can he act so casual about it, as if it didn't affect me at all?

"You were with your mother," he says. "I thought you'd get a chance to know her. A girl, she needs her mother, especially at your age. You were getting a little headstrong for a single dad to handle, anyway."

Rage boils inside me, and something loosens within. All this time, I've held onto this. While I was in a dirt hole, I repeated these thoughts like a mantra. I will get my father out and leave this place forever. I will save him and myself. We'll go back to Oklahoma City and live there like this never happened. Life will go back to good again.

But he doesn't want to go back. He doesn't even want me back.

"Whoa, Stella," he says, retreating a step. That's when I

realize I'm starting to shift, that while I've been seething, my limbs have begun to pull and strain.

I snap back to myself. "You knew I'd get sent to live with my mother, and you thought that was okay?"

"I thought it was time you got to know her. I know she's a little stricter than I was, but that seemed like what you needed then. I projected here and visited every year. Your sisters always seemed happy."

"Dad," I say, my voice measured. "I'm not my sister. Mother was horrible to me."

"I'm sorry, sweetheart. But it was for the best, don't you think? Now we're all together again. We can be a family again."

My temple throbs, and I don't think I can hold back this time. That's what I've always wanted, even when I was a prisoner here. Just to be part of the family, equal to everyone else. But it's too late now.

"I don't want to be a family," I yell. "I hate her. I hate it here. All I've wanted every day since I got here was to go back home, to go back to when you were alive. Now I finally find out you're alive, and you don't want to go back?"

"Go back to what?" he asks. "We've been gone three years, Stella. Our house was sold a long time ago. Your mother says you already got your GED, so you wouldn't go back to school. What would we go back for?"

I can't answer. My head is pounding with blood, black spots flowering on a canvas of red behind my eyelids. Not my father, too. Everyone my whole life has let me down, betrayed me. He was the one person I could always count on to be strong, and solid, and good. But he's not. He's just another flawed, selfish human being like the rest of us.

I turn and run down the stairs, my feet pounding the wooden steps, my joints loosening, transforming as I go. I scramble to the door on hands and feet, burst out onto the porch, then pitch forward into the grass. Instead of falling on my face, I land on my hands. My fingers snap like twigs, and I scream in pain. But instead of stopping, the pain stabs deeper. I watch as my fingers expand, lengthen. Hair begins to sprout from my hands, and a band of iron seems to be caught around my stomach.

I jump to my feet and unbutton my jeans, rip them down before I lose the ability to use my hands. Now I know what Harmon meant about this not being sexy. I have no time to think of modesty as I rip at my clothes, tearing them off on the lawn in broad daylight. All I can think about is getting out of them before they strangle me. When I'm mostly rid of my clothes, and my hands are no longer able to remove the rest, I collapse onto the ground. My skin feels raw where the fur came through, and my head is so heavy I don't think I can lift it. For a minute, I can only lie on the grass and pant.

After it passes, I stand. It takes a few strides before I'm comfortable on four feet, my legs moving in sync. But it happens faster than I expected. And let me just say, my tail is amazing. I've never really thought about an animal's tail before. I know the regular things—dogs wag when they're happy, cats wave theirs when they're mad. But this isn't just something hanging off my butt. It's a limb. I don't even have to think about it, but it's there, helping me balance, gain my stride. It's almost like a wing, helping me be lightweight, floating along. It streaks behind me, catching the wind, dancing with it, curling around it.

I bound up the driveway in seconds. I'm fast, and each stride covers more ground than I expect. The rush that came over me last night comes again as I race down the path. I race away, over the hills, heading away from the Second Valley and its wolves.

29

I don't have a plan. I don't know where I'm going. After prowling up hills and down valleys, along ridges and bluffs, I end up at a sparkling green river. Standing on the rocky bank, I lean my head down and drink. It's a little odd at first, but soon my tongue scoops up the water, delivering it to my parched throat. It's summer now, and in my thick fur coat, I'm roasting.

When I've had my fill of water, I flop down in the shade of an oak tree and fall asleep. Some time later, I wake to the sound of voices. I raise my head, on alert for the wolves to be here, ready to capture me. Instead, I spot a procession of canoes floating down the river. The smell of them assaults my nostrils—sunscreen, beer, bug spray, and the blood and sweat of human bodies.

My father's words echo in my head. *You'd be shot.* Harmon's words come back, too. *What are you going to do, live in a zoo?*

And a small part of me understands why my father kept this secret from me. It is dangerous to be seen by humans. There's a reason the wolves live in the valley, in solitude, protective of their privacy. They are both right. I can't go back now. And even though a part of me has known it for a while, the stark realization only now sinks in. My dreams disappear, floating down the slow-moving

Buffalo River and disappearing around the bend. It's taken me too long to realize it. But I'm a part of this place. A part of their supernatural world. I belong here as surely as Harmon does.

I stand and step back towards the woods just as a shout of surprise echoes down the river. I've been spotted. A girl shrieks. A few others yell and laugh, pointing and talking excitedly over each other. Someone has a phone out, trying to snap a picture. If I thought I was done being a freak, I couldn't have been more wrong. Everyone wants to take a picture of the white tiger in the Ozark Mountains. And if they get it…they'll call the police, or animal control, and they'll comb the forest for me.

I dart away into the woods, my heart hammering in my chest. I have to get back. It's not safe here. Even in my tiger form, I recognize the irony. I'm going back to a place that kept me in captivity for years. Out of all the places in the world, I never thought I'd voluntarily return to the valley or think of it as safe. But my legs take me, bounding over rocks and between trees, grateful for the cover of the full foliage of summer.

Maybe I'm not a werewolf, but I'm also not a human. Not entirely. I'm a tiger now. If I belong anywhere, it's in the Three Valleys with the rest of my people. Not in Oklahoma City, and not among ordinary humans. I am not ordinary.

The thought fills me with more rage than I know what to do with. I may not be an ordinary human girl, but I'm not a freak. I'm not a monster. I'm not a worthless, weak, useless burden, the way my mother made me feel for years. She could have told me the truth, let me go live with the shifters, or explained to me how it all works. I may not be like them, but I'm more like them than like those humans who want to take pictures of me. She could have helped me. Instead, she chose to shun me, to imprison me, to make me believe I was nothing.

But she was wrong. I am something. I'm a strong, fearsome, capable tiger. And she's about to see what I'm capable of.

30

Within minutes, I'm back at the sharp turn into the rutted, sloping drive with rocks showing through the soil. The same driveway I watched from my window for the past three years. My stride slows just a bit, and I have a brief thought that I shouldn't be here, but I ignore it.

And then I see her. My mother is standing at the clothesline along the south side of the house, a single line strung between two wooden posts. A row of clothespins juts from between her lips, the old-fashioned wooden kind with the rounded heads that we once made into tiny dolls in craft class at school. She pinches the corner of a t-shirt around the line and pushes a pin over it before reaching for the other corner. Out hanging laundry on this warm summer evening, she looks like a woman who could be a good mother. Anyone looking at her might make the same mistake my father did.

Anyone but me.

As I watch her, the weight of the last three years crushes down on me. The hope and despair of the first few weeks, when I'd lost my father and everything I'd ever known, and I needed a mother more than anything. When instead of being a mother to me, she threw me in the attic and slapped my face when I dared to question it. Then there were all the times she told me to go to my room because someone came over, and she didn't want me to be seen. And the times when I tried to speak to my own sisters, and she punished me for it.

Any hesitation I had is swept away by the anger burning through my veins. She could have been the person my father thought she would. She could have treated me like her own daughter. I am. I'm just as much her daughter as Elidi, every bit as much her flesh and blood and DNA. But she treated me like an imposition, an imposter, and a parasite.

I bound forward, covering the driveway in seconds. I misjudge the corner of the house, or my body, and scrape the edge of a board. The wood bites into my skin, tears out a chunk of fur, and sends me stumbling. My mother looks up.

A scream cuts through the air as I leap at her. But it's not her scream. It's my sister, who was hidden from view by the house. She screams again, a mindless, terrified shriek, as I bowl my mother over. My mother flies backwards, hitting the ground with so much force she bounces a few inches off the grass. Elidi screams again, but to my ears, it is nothing more than the annoying whine of a mosquito.

And that's as much as she should mean to me. In the years I've been here, she's done nothing to defy my mother, nothing to protect me. The most she's dared is a covert smile, a longing glance, a few stolen sentences, and once, a lie that was quickly discovered. That was the very first time I ran away, when I saw them turn to wolves. Since then, she hasn't stood up for me once. All she's done is ask me to help her escape.

It's my mother who rules this house like a tyrant. My mother who terrorizes us all, who not only let me believe my father was dead but exploited my loss, using my grief to control me. She didn't just ruin my life for the past three years. She ruined me.

Now it's my turn.

I strike at her with my huge paw, relish her cry of pain. Placing both front paws on her chest, I stand over her, open my mouth, and blast a deafening roar into her face. Another scream joins my sister's, this one on the road. I don't care. I want my mother to suffer, to experience a quarter of the terror and humiliation I experienced at her hands. Still holding her down, I roar into her face again as she squirms and flails under me.

I roar again, as loud as I can. For all these years, she hasn't listened to my pleas to go home, to get out of the attic and be part of her community, to be seen as a human being. She ignored my questions and withheld answers. She turned her back and pretended not to hear me when I cried for help, for mercy. No more.

Spittle flecks her cheeks, and her hair blows back from her face with the force of my breath. My teeth are inches from her skin. I could rip out her cold, frozen heart right now. But that would be too kind. First, I will revel in my power, in her fear and helplessness.

Somewhere far away, people are screaming. Running footsteps pound the trail. I drown them all out with the volume of my new voice. Can she hear me now?

I want everyone to hear, not just my mother. I want them all to come running, to see what the commotion is about. I want them to see my haughty, arrogant mother on her back, cowering and begging for her life. I want them to see the terror in her eyes, to see how small she really is, how pathetic and mean. And I want them to recognize the strength in my massive body.

"Stella." Harmon's voice is not loud, not panicked. It cuts through the chaos of voices, screams, and shouts. It's calm and strong.

"You need to stop now," he says, stepping towards me.

As if coming to, I raise my head. They've all come to see me, just like I wanted. The whole pack has seen me triumph over my mother. They know I've won, that I'm stronger than she is. Standing around the yard, the wolves clump together, every one of them staring at me in shock. White faces gape as Harmon limps forward until he reaches us.

"That's enough for today," he says quietly, his human hand reaching for me. He buries his fingers in the fur on the back of my neck, digging in until he's gripping me firmly. I could swat him away, rip his hand off. I could send him sailing into the valley below.

"Stella," Harmon says, an edge of warning in his voice. He gives a firm tug at my hair. "You're strong, but you're not stronger than a whole pack of wolves. We will defend one of our own."

Those words slice something inside me, cut me away from what I'm doing. I will never have their sympathy, will never be better than my mother in their eyes, no matter what she's done or how intimidating I am in my animal form. They are wolves, and they are loyal to each other first, no matter what. Even Harmon.

I step back, letting him pull me away.

He holds out a hand to my mother. It's a wolf paw, half covered in black hairs and half bare, a deformed thing. I can see the others grimace, swallow, and avert their eyes. My mother reaches for his hand, but when she sees it, she hesitates, her hand hovering halfway to his. "Are you injured, Talia?" Harmon asks, his voice as brittle as the ice skimming a puddle in winter.

Before she can answer, Fernando's father pushes through the crowd and rushes to her side, taking her outstretched hand and helping her sit. Behind her, near the house, my sisters stand clutching each other, their faces ashen and stunned. I did that. I caused that. But the power to put that expression on their faces brings me no satisfaction.

"Let's go," Harmon mutters. He snatches up my clothes from the lawn as we go. When we pass the first group of people, he holds his head high, his jaw tense. They step back, the children hiding behind their parents, staring out from behind their legs while the parents shift and look away. Harmon won't hide his gruesome face. But I will. I lower my head in shame, walking beside him like a scolded dog. He came out here, paraded his humiliation, to stop me. Now I can't tell if they're staring at me or at him. But I know what this is costing Harmon.

When we reach the road, he releases his grip on my fur and stalks ahead. His loping, crooked gait is painful to watch, and shame washes through me. I don't know where else to go, though, so I follow Harmon. At his house, he drops my clothes on the porch before disappearing around the side of the house. I hear the door to the side stairs open and close, but I don't follow. For a few minutes, I stand on the porch, then shift back. It takes longer than it took to become a tiger, but the transition is less painful. Like Harmon said, it's getting easier already.

When I'm human, I grab my clothes and pull them on as quickly as I can, glancing around as I dress. Now that I'm just me, a small human girl in cropped jeans and a cap-sleeve tee, I feel stupid and…strange. Like that was a dream that happened to someone else. How can someone as meek as me be a Siberian tiger? How can I have almost killed my own mother?

Still reeling, I stand on the top step, more hesitant than ever. But finally, I go downstairs, because I have nowhere else to go. Harmon is in the sitting room, staring at a haphazard pile of cards strewn across the table.

I sit opposite him and sweep them into a neat stack. "I'm sorry."

"I think you should go home," he says.

I drop the cards, and they scatter across the worn wooden surface again. "You're kicking me out? After you kept me here against my will for months?"

"I'm not kicking you out," he says. "If you want to stay, you're welcome as long as you want. As long as you're not hurting anyone."

"I didn't hurt her."

"I know." He begins to gather the cards slowly, with his human hand. "That's why you can stay. This is my pack, Stella. I have to take care of it. This is what I was born to do. They are my responsibility. There's not another life out there, waiting for me somewhere else. This is it."

"What if you can't transition?"

"Then leading the pack won't be my responsibility any

longer." His voice is so flat, I know it must be killing him just to say those words.

"And?"

"And I'm not going to make them look at me the way they did today. That's not good for morale. Your mother, she's not an Alpha, but she's good at organizing them, and she's smart. She grew up in an Alpha's house, so she knows our ways better than anyone else."

"Except you."

"I don't have a choice the way you do," he says. "This is pack life. Talia will keep things running smoothly until they find someone else to lead. It's better than not having anyone in charge. That's happened before, for a few years. It's not good for the pack. They need someone to take charge."

"Harmon."

He continues, slowly stacking the cards, speaking as if to himself. "Right now, if they need me for something, or to advise, she comes and asks. It can work this way for a while. She's been doing it for the past year, with my father injured, anyway. It's not so different."

"But what about what you want?"

"I'll stay and help train a new Alpha. Maybe it will only be four or five years. Fernando's father grew up with mine. He's older, but he can still lead. Together, we could train Fernando to take over."

"What then? What happens to you when they find a new Alpha?"

He frowns at the cards, his fingers pausing on one. "Whatever he wants me to do, that's what I'll do."

"And what do I do?"

"You don't belong down here, hidden away with me," he says, tearing his eyes from the cards. "You're not meant for this, Stella. You should be out there, taking over the world, like you wanted to today. Didn't you? That's how it feels sometimes, when you transition. I know that. I used to, anyway…"

"You'll do it at the next full moon," I assure him.

"This is no place for you," he says. "I've told you what I know. If you have more questions, your parents can answer them. You should be with them. And you…you don't have anything to be afraid of, Stella. Look at you. Look what you did today."

"Yeah," I say with a snort. "Look what I did. I'm afraid of…of what I might do."

"Just remember yourself," he says, finishing the stack of cards. "Remember that you are who you are, no matter what form you take. You're still you."

"And you're still you."

His eyes are pools of sadness when he raises them to me. "Yes. I am."

"So that's it? I just walk out of here. I'm free to go."

"You're free to go," he says with a sad smile on his perfect human lips, set above a nonexistent, furry chin. "Find your father. He can answer your questions better than I ever could. Go home and be with him. Be happy."

"I don't think I have a home."

"You can hold your own against anyone. Go talk to your mother. It might be easier than you think. She and your father, your sisters, can help you make this decision. Figure out what you to do and where you want to go. It's not my place to tell you, and it wouldn't be, even if I was

Alpha. You're not a wolf. It was never my call, Stella. I just helped you see that."

"And if it was?"

He smiles again and pushes the deck of cards aside. "I'd let you go conquer the world."

"Or get shot, like my father said."

"Then I'd let you go home, to where you used to live. To be happy. When you talk about that, there's a look that comes over your face… You never look like that when you talk about this place. It's the only time you're happy, when you remember that. That's where I'd want you to go."

That's not there for me anymore, but something holds me back from telling Harmon that. If he wants to think of me that way, happy and headed home, then I'm not going to take away his false idea of me. Some part of me is still as proud and vain as he is, even after all this time. I like seeing myself that way, through his eyes.

"Thank you," I say at last.

"Don't thank me," he says, shaking his head. "You know I'm not the one letting you go. I couldn't stop you if I tried."

"I know."

"One last hand?" he asks, cutting his eyes towards the deck of cards.

I stand, not sure what to say to him now. I've been his prisoner so long, it doesn't seem real, that I can just walk out, be set loose in this big world with no one chasing me or hunting me down. "I should go."

"Yeah, you should." He smiles up at me, his brow still sloping and prickled with black hairs, his eyes too round, too full of that glacial white-blue color. The shape of his head is still wrong, oblong though no longer pointed. But not human, either. It's strange how normal his strangeness has become. Even with new changes, I can hardly remember what he used to look like. He's still Harmon, no matter what he looks like.

For a minute, I stand watching him, unsure of what to say or how to leave. And then it occurs to me that I can simply go. And so, I do. I turn and walk out, all the time expecting him to call me back, or leap to block my way. When I reach the top of the stairs, I pause. Some part of me wants him to stop me. But I'm leaving that part behind. I open the door, and step outside into the sun.

31.

As I walk along the path to my mother's, this time on human feet, I have time to marvel at everything. The trees are jungle-like in their lush greenery, draping over the dirt path. Bird and insects sing all around me, not just in the trees but everywhere. The scent of leaves, dirt, plants, and the forest is strong and warm. And I'm free to walk through it, to examine it, to make decisions about it. I'm not watching it from high above or down below. For the first time since I arrived, I'm part of the world around me.

My muscles quiver with anticipation, and I know what's about to happen. But I don't want to lose control again, so I quiet the energy brewing inside me. My tiger growls in protest, but I hold firm, and she stills at last. I can't spontaneously burst into tiger form every time I get excited. Wolves don't do that. I don't know about shifters. I don't really know anything about them, except what the wolves have told me, and I know better than to trust them.

What I need now is a home. So I walk on, even though it feels strange, like the world is suddenly too big, too bright, with too many possibilities. I'm a mole, thrown into the body of a bird, soaring high above the world and seeing all it has to offer. How do I choose what to do next, what to see, what I want? Those choices have belonged to someone else for so long I'm not sure I know anymore.

Just as I do every time, I pause at the end of my mother's sloping driveway. But not for long. Ahead, I hear voices and catch a glimpse of people walking towards me along the wide dirt track that leads through the community. I duck my head and hurry down the driveway, my heart pounding. I have no idea what they think of me now, after what I did. All I know is that Harmon's invitation to join them is never going to happen. There is no way they'll accept me as one of them after I terrorized my mother, their interim leader, in front of the entire pack.

When I reach her front porch, I hesitate again. But they must hear me, because after a second, someone inside calls for me to come in. Zora. I take a deep breath, reminding myself that I'm no longer their prisoner, no longer their doormat. I don't have to accept their derision and scorn any longer. And they sure as hell know it now.

I turn the knob and push the door open.

Everything stops.

Zora, who is standing at the table, drops the envelope she's holding. Little black seeds spill out and roll across the table. My mother, who is halfway reclined on the sofa, stops talking to Dr. Golden, who crouches beside her. Dr. Golden turns and freezes like the rest of them. Elidi, who is standing at the head of the couch, drops her gaze when I try to communicate something to her through our eyes, like I used to when I was trying to get out of here, begging for her help.

She said she wanted to leave, but she'll never leave. Like everyone else, she belongs here. Where do I belong—

with the wild, violent shifters? The way everyone is looking at me gives me a pretty good idea what their answer to that question would be.

"Hi," I say.

"You're back," Zora says, giving me a derisive once-over. I don't think I imagine the touch of wariness in her voice, though, as if she's waiting, testing to see if she can still get away with looking at me like a squashed bug on the bottom of her shoe. This time, I give her the look right back. If shifters are their enemy, then wolves are mine.

"I came to get the key," I say to my mother. "To get Dad out."

"I'll be going, if there's nothing else," Dr. Golden says, standing. "I think you'll be fine. No permanent damage."

I swallow hard. Permanent damage? I didn't think I'd even hurt her. I didn't mean to. Not really.

"That would be fine," Mother says to her, in the same voice she'd use to dismiss a servant. Maybe she speaks to everyone that way, not just me.

"Stella," she says, turning to me. "I gave you the key, didn't I?"

I have to swallow again. Seeing her, being back in this house with her and my sisters, feels as if I'm being sucked down into a whirlpool that I just managed to swim clear of. But I steady my nerves and plunge ahead. "That's right," I say. "And now I'm taking him. He told me what happened. That you were supposed to be my mother all these years, not my jailer. He told me everything."

She looks at me skeptically. "Everything."

"Yes, everything. There's no reason for you to keep him in the attic. He hasn't done anything except be who he is.

Obviously being a shifter is a criminal offense to your people, as I know firsthand. It might have been nice to know my crime before you locked me up."

She keeps looking at me that way, a way that says I'm beyond stupid and irritating, and she has no time for such outbursts.

I glance at Elidi one more time, hoping for…something. But she's still a stranger, even if she is my twin. A stranger, and more than that. A chasm exists between us, one she always knew existed, even when I didn't. I tried to bridge that, tried to be her sister, but she always knew we couldn't be normal twins. We may look the same, but we're not even the same species.

I turn back to my mother, who has risen from the couch. "Very well," she says, heading for the stairs without waiting for a reply.

She's doing what I asked. I can hardly believe it. Is she scared of me? Or just sick of me?

This is what it feels like to win. It's eerie.

"Thank you," I say. "I hope I didn't hurt you earlier."

"You didn't."

"Dr. Golden was here…"

"I had some pains in my chest." She clomps up the stairs in her work boots, never glancing my way. "But it's just some deep bruising."

"I'm sorry."

"No need."

"And you're really letting Dad go? Just like that?"

"On the condition that you go, too." She swings the door open and beckons me inside. Every instinct tells me not to go through, that she'll slam the door and lock it.

But I could break out.

I drop my voice to a whisper when I see Dad lying on the bed, snoring. "Do I need to sign something, or...I don't know, shake on it?"

"I've made the decision. You are shifters, and now that you know, you can go back to where you belong."

"Perfect. A guy who can't shift and someone who didn't even know she was a shifter two days ago, in a community of violent outlaws. Any advice?"

To my surprise, she smiles. "I guess your father didn't tell you everything."

"What?" I ask, the beginning of hope edging into my words. "They aren't violent criminals and you lied about that, too?"

"No, they are," she says. "Let's just say your father is quite familiar with them."

My father finally stirs, then sits up and swings his feet off the bed. "Talia."

"Owen," she says coolly. Seeing them together for the first time in my life, I try to picture them as a couple. As Mom and Dad, sitting around drinking coffee in their pajamas on Sunday morning, hugging at the window and watching snow fall outside, rushing us all to gymnastics practice. Somehow, the picture doesn't quite materialize. I can't imagine why they ever married at all, let alone why my father would love this ice queen.

But maybe he had no choice. Harmon could have been wrong about that. A shifter and an important were-wolf marrying to unite the tribes makes sense. And it explains the chilly silence between them as my mother hands me the keys, which I must have dropped in my haste to shift.

"You are to leave immediately," she says. "And this time, don't come back. If you trespass again, expect to end up right back here." As she speaks I unlock the chain around his waist, then his handcuffs.

"Ah, that's better," Dad says, flexing his wrists. He gives my mother a wink. "I'll be just over the mountain if you need me."

My mother pulls herself up to her full height, which isn't enough to account for her imposing presence. "Take your daughter and leave," she says coldly. "And don't try to pawn her off on me again, Owen. We had an agreement. I didn't saddle you with Elidi. I did my duty to our daughters. Now do yours. Don't let me see either of you again. Shifters are not welcome in our valley."

"Come on, Stella," he says, putting an arm around my shoulders. "I guess we're not welcome here. Better get going."

Again, I can hardly believe it's happening. I'm free of the wolves at long, long last. We step past my mother. Her lips tighten as we pass, as if she smells something unpleasant, which isn't totally unjustified. After a week in a hot attic, my father doesn't exactly smell super fresh.

Dad shoots me a grin and ambles towards the stairs, as giddy as a boy going to see a surprise out in the garage on his birthday. I can't help but smile back at him. I shoot a look over my shoulder, but my mother's face is set in its usual pinched scowl.

Turning back, I take in my father's light steps as he

descends the stairs towards freedom. At least my mother didn't torture or starve him—or lock him in a shed. He looks fine. No limping, no weakness, no injuries. I'm so busy checking him for signs of mistreatment that I run straight into him when he stops in the doorway. As I step around him, *deja vous* swims before my eyes for one awful moment. I'm sure the yard will be filled with wolves when we step outside.

But this time, the yard is empty.

32

As my father and I walk through the community, people stop to stare. My mother walks some distance behind us, assuring everyone that we're leaving with her blessing, and we won't be back. Strangely, after all this time, I can't seem to find words to say to my father. I've asked him the questions, gotten answers. Not all of them were reassuring, but they were answers nonetheless. Now I don't know what to say. He's not the person I thought he was.

"Dad?" I ask as we approach the clearing. "Where are we going?"

"We're going home," he says. "I have that house here, where I grew up."

We walk in silence a minute before the nagging thought that I haven't wanted to surface finds its way to my mouth. "You have a house here. While I was stuck in Mother's attic, you were buying a house and settling down like I never existed."

"Stella," he says. "Don't be dramatic. I didn't buy a house. It belonged to me before I moved to the Second Valley to marry your mother."

I hold my breath as we step into the clearing. *Deja vous* sweeps over me again, sending a chill racing over my skin. A handful of kids my age are playing Frisbee on the lawn. The old toothless woman is lying on a picnic blanket in the sun, her veined legs exposed. Kids are digging in the dirt with sticks. It's all so much like the day three years ago when I arrived that I can almost believe it's the same day. That I got here and found my father and immediately left. None of this crazy, impossible world exists.

"Always nice to be admired," Dad mutters as people stop what they're doing to watch us pass. And then, because it's not awkward enough, he starts to smile and wave, as if we're in some sort of demented parade.

When at last we step out of the clearing, I breathe a sigh of relief.

"Almost out of wolf territory," Dad says. "Then we can shift. Faster that way, you know." He grins and reaches behind his neck to untie the necklace.

"You haven't shifted since the eclipse?" I ask carefully, testing him out to see if he'll tell me the truth.

"Shifters don't have time limits like werewolves. We can do it any time we want. And any animal you want, although it does take practice to shift into other things besides your natural form." He holds it out and smiles. "I believe I have something that belongs to you, daughter dear."

I close my hand around the stone, then open my fingers to study the swirling brown and gold patterns. I wore this for so long, never knowing its power. "What happened that night, Dad? The last time I saw this, Mrs. Nguyen had it, and she disappeared when trouble showed up. You were passed out on the porch, and I got thrown against a tree and knocked out."

"That about sums it up," he says cheerfully.

"So then what?"

"The wolves had me for a minute, but my brother and his son got me back. They said you'd asked the wolves to take you instead of me, and the wolves seemed agreeable. Everyone was happy."

"Um, except I was a prisoner in a basement?"

"I didn't know that," he said, pulling back to look me over. "Yvonne said you chose to stay when she came to get you out. And you don't look much worse for the wear. Nothing a hairbrush couldn't fix."

"I guess it's good that I stayed with Harmon, or I'd never have known how to shift, would I?"

"Exactly," he says. "Don't wear that necklace if you want to shift. You could even throw it away if you don't want it anymore. Now that you know how to shift, you don't really need it."

"No," I say, slipping it into my pocket. "I think I'll keep it." I try to quell the resentment building inside me. Dad will never understand what it was like for me. He's always known who he is. In a way, he's always belonged here. He can't know what it was like for me to live here as a disgraced daughter. Even if he could understand, he wouldn't want to. I see that now.

He leads me into the woods, then stops. "This is probably far enough. Time to let your wild animal run."

"Is there a protocol?" I ask, remembering that I'll have to take off my clothes. "Who goes first?"

"I'll lead you to the house," he says. "I'll keep a lookout while you go in and find something to wear."

"Keep a lookout."

"I should probably tell you, I'm still not on the best

terms with the shifters," he says with a goofy grin. "They let me go after that night, but I've laid low."

"Wow, Dad. You got along so well with people back in the real world. Are you sure you don't want to go back there?"

"They'll come around," he says. "But see, I kind of abandoned them when I married your mother."

"Oh, right. Because it was an arranged marriage."

He gives me an odd look. "No, it wasn't. Where did you get that idea?"

"Harmon," I say with a sigh.

"It wasn't arranged," Dad says. "We were very much in love. But I left the shifters without a king to marry your mother, give up my natural form, and become a wolf."

"Wait...what?"

"I agreed to join the pack," he says. "As part of the truce, I promised not to shift into anything but a wolf. I was going to be one of them."

"Yeah, but what's this about a king?"

"I'm the last shifter king," he says, his chest puffing out with pride. "The last leader they had. When I left, they didn't have a leader. People moved away, like Dr. Golden. And those still living here...well, they haven't quite forgiven me."

"You're the one who left them with no leader? That's why they're lawless?"

"Shifters don't have the same reverence for law and order that wolves do," he says, peeling off his shirt. "But yes, I did leave them without a king. Now that I'm back, though, I'm going to make it right. I'm going to take the reins and bring us back to our former glory. And you can help."

"Okay," I say weakly.

"Great," he says. "I just have to figure out how to do it. Guess I can't marry your mother again. That was my crowning success. Making peace with the other tribes of the valleys, so we could all live in harmony. That's always been my goal."

"You sound just like Harmon," I mutter.

We turn our backs to each other and undress. I don't want to leave the necklace, but I can't shift with it on me, so I stash it in the hollow of a small tree so I can come back for it. As I take my tiger form, my father's words begin to sink in. When I'm an unstoppable beast, they become more believable. My father was once a king. He says he will be crowned again. Which means that in some strange twist of fate, I've gone from werewolf prisoner to tiger princess.

33.

When we're back to the little house where Dad grew up, he changes into clean clothes while I put on a pair of his sweatpants and a t-shirt. They swim on me, but I don't have any of my own clothes. The second bedroom smells like stale old wallpaper and musty carpet, and the bed looks like it could be harboring more than a few spiders. I stand there, feeling so lost I don't know what to do. All these years, I've wanted to go home to Dad. But this isn't home.

And Dad…I can hear him whistling in the kitchen, so I make my way there. Stains mar the linoleum flooring, which is peeling in places and makes a crackling noise when I walk across it.

"It's good to be home," Dad says, casting me a glance. I can't read his expression, and it strikes me that I've never really known my father at all. Maybe I never bothered to try. I loved him, but it was the blind love of a child for her only parent. I never thought he had his own life with secrets too big for me to fathom. When I try to imagine what life would have been like if he'd told me the truth, I can't. There is only a big red blank.

"So we're shifters, and you're a king. What else did you lie about?" My voice comes out harsher, more accusatory than I meant. I wince at how much I sound like my mother.

"I didn't lie," Dad says, opening the refrigerator and retrieving a beer.

"Really? What is it with people around here thinking that there's nothing wrong with deception as long as it's not an out-right lie? You kept me prisoner inside my own body for fourteen years. Didn't you think I could handle the truth about my own self?"

He sighs and sits down at the ugly brown Formica table. "Come on, Stella. We just got home. Give me a chance to relax. I've been chained up for the past week."

"I've been locked in a basement for two months," I say, my eyes narrowing. "Where were you all that time?"

"I was…here," he says, popping open the can of beer.

"Here." I shove my hands onto my hips and press them into my flesh until it hurts. I concentrate on the ache so I won't feel the ache in the back of my throat. "You let them haul me off and throw me in a basement with an angry, injured wolf. And then you didn't think you should, I don't know, check in on me, until last week?"

He throws up his hands. "What do you want from me, Stella? You told them to take you instead of me. You've lived there for years, anyway. So yes, I let them take you back home."

I bite my own tongue so I won't scream at him. "You didn't even come after me? You stayed here, living your sad little life, and didn't even try to get me back."

"Yvonne checked in on you a couple times at the beginning," he says. "She said you were doing fine. And when you refused to leave, I assumed you'd chosen to stay with your mother permanently. I can't blame you. I don't have much to offer you here."

"I should have left you to rot in her attic," I mutter.

"I'm not perfect," he says. "In fact, I guess I was always a bad father. That's what you think, right? Because I didn't teach you to shift and take you hunting? Because I sent Yvonne to check on you, because she could slip in undetected by the wolves, instead of risking my life to do it myself?"

"You're not a bad father," I say grudgingly. But I'm not sure I believe it. I used to think he was the best Dad in the world, but now, I imagine what Elidi felt like growing up. Mother is harsh, but she's strong. She shifted with her daughters, ran beside them through these perilous woods, taught them how to hunt and kill and survive. Dad made a deal with a witch and hid behind her magic so he wouldn't have to do the hard things.

"What did you give Yvonne for the necklace?" I ask.

"What?"

"Yvonne enchanted that necklace for you, right? To keep me from shifting. What did you give her?"

"It doesn't matter," he says, taking a large swallow of beer. "It was a long time ago, and it was between me and her."

"I have a right to know," I say. "You paid that price for me, right? It was for my benefit. For my own good. That's what Mother always said. It wasn't that you were too weak or scared or lazy to raise your own daughter as herself, right? You hid who I was, what I was, for my own good, I'm sure. You didn't want me to know what I was capable of, or let me make the decision whether to live as a regular girl in the real world or come here and get to know my other side. My animal side. After all, that was too wild, right? I wouldn't be able to control myself."

"Stella, be reasonable."

"I'm done being reasonable," I say, slamming my palms down on the table. "For all those years, I thought I lived a great life, but it was all a lie. You're as bad as my mother. At least she didn't pretend I was free. But I was never free with you, either. I wasn't free to be myself, my whole self. I was forced to be the person you wanted me to be. I didn't get a choice. I had to be what was easiest for you."

"I was a single dad," he says. "And I never said I was a great one. It's not my fault that you had some skewed idea about me. I mean, sure, I liked you being my little girl. What father doesn't? But I'm only human, Stella. I have flaws like the next guy."

"Except the next guy isn't also a lion," I say. "The next guy probably couldn't raise a tiger. But you're not just a human. You could have taught me how to control myself, how to enjoy both sides, just like you did. Didn't you? All those late nights when you were working late? That's what you were really doing, isn't it? Shifting into your animal form and enjoying that. You didn't give it up. You just made me give it up."

"You didn't miss it," he says. "I had her wipe your memories of here so you wouldn't have to live with the knowledge of this place and everything that happened here."

I suck in a breath. The blackouts were caused by trying

to shift when I was under a spell. The nightmare images were flashbacks. "No," I say, suddenly fighting back tears. "You gave me a necklace that was supposedly a gift to bring us closer, and had my memory wiped by a witch so I wouldn't ask questions. All you really did was look out for yourself. You didn't care if it was best for me. If you had, you wouldn't have blocked everything special about me."

"Everything dangerous," he corrects. "You're special all on your own, Stella."

"You could have let me decide that," I say, my voice flat. "Now I know the truth. Never trust you, or anyone else. You're all shifty shifters. And I'm done with all the lies."

"Fine," he says, holding up his hands. "No more lies. Happy now?"

I'm not happy, but I have nowhere else to go. The wolves don't want me in the Second Valley, and I don't want to go back. I'm free, but I don't feel free. I keep waiting for a knock at the door, for someone to leap out behind me and throw me to the ground and try to murder me.

Dad may not be the person I thought he was, but he's giving me a place to stay. And so, I stay.

34

Over the next month, we clean up the house, which is a disaster. Thanks to my mother, I now know how to really make a place shine, and I have a great work ethic, according to Dad. "You never used to work this hard," he says admiringly as I scrub the cracking linoleum floor in the kitchen. "And I've never heard you go more than five minutes without complaining."

I sit back on my heels and flick my frizzy white hair out of my eyes. "I probably complained because I had you standing over my shoulder saying stupid stuff like that."

"Guess your mother didn't kick all your bad habits," he says. "You still got the attitude."

Instead of answering, I go back to scrubbing. The house is old and small, with two bedrooms, a bathroom, and a living room with a new patch of drywall Dad installed but hasn't painted yet. While he works on putting putty around the drywall sheets, I clean the kitchen, which is full of things a house accumulates over the years when no one lives there. Apparently, during the past few years, he didn't live here much. And when he did, he only cleaned enough to make it livable—sweeping the floors, washing the countertops. The drawers are full of mouse droppings and dust. The corners are full of cobwebs and grime.

"I think it's best if we establish ourselves here, let them know we're not leaving," he says. "Let's slowly work our way into the community before we start making claims about being their ruler. That was my mistake last time. I thought they'd be happy to see the prodigal king return. Turns out they're still bitter about my leaving."

I try to imagine my big happy Dad ruling anyone, or having enemies, but it's impossible. He's like a big silly oaf, more the court jester than the king. Although, after he explains that the king is basically just an old title referring to family lineage and means next to nothing, it makes more sense.

One day, he goes into town to get loads of paint, and we start painting the house, inside and out. I have plenty to do, fixing up the house and helping Dad put in a late garden. And though my hands are always busy, my mind wanders too often back to the wolf community. I think about Harmon every single day, wonder what he's doing and if he's still in his basement, if he's alone now. When it rains, I wonder if the scent finds its way in the windows to him, and if the roses are still blooming. I wonder if he wonders about me.

I'm free now, not my mother's servant. I'm Dad's daughter again, as I've wanted to be for the past three years. Everything is as it should be. But something in me is still restless. For years I dreamed of going home, having my life back. And now that I know who we are, I recognize the truth, that we can never go back to that life. But the dream of *something more* lingers.

As I climb into bed late one evening, exhausted from working in the garden all day, I think of my sisters. Of my mother, her secrets and mysteries buried somewhere no one can find. Of Harmon, prowling his basement, waiting for the full moon to deliver his sentence. I turn to the window, where the big, round moon hangs in the clear sky, the light washing the night in its eerie, pale glow. No storms or clouds hide its ominous face tonight.

For a few minutes, I lie there, unable to sleep. I think of Harmon, his bones and ligaments snapping. I remember his head in my lap, his delirious voice asking me to stay with him. His burning frost eyes as he told me he loved me, and the resignation on his face when he told me it was time for me to go. He's alone there now. Alone in that dungeon, without even the comfort of an angry girl with a fork on the other side of the wall. With only his aunt to lower down his basket of food each day.

I sit up in bed. This is ridiculous. He's probably not even down there now that I'm gone and he doesn't have to keep up the pretense.

But what if he is? What if my mother decided she wanted to keep the leadership role a little longer? What if the pack decides that, since he's unfit to lead, he should eat poisonous mushrooms and rid them of the burden of his care?

I swing my legs off the bed and stand. My father is already in bed, too, though it's only just past nine. After working all day, going to bed early feels natural. But now, I'm wide awake. Bright moonlight spills across my rumpled sheets. I slip my feet into a pair of tennis shoes and ease the screen out of the open window, a smile forming on my lips. For the first time since we've lived here, I'm doing something normal. Something I'd be doing back in Oklahoma. Sneaking out after bedtime to see a boy.

As soon as I'm outside, I realize this is not going to work. It would take hours to hike over the mountain and down into the valley of the wolves. Checking to make sure I'm alone and no cars are approaching on the road that goes by Dad's house, I kick off my shoes, drop my pajama shorts, and peel off my long-sleeved top. I push everything into the body of my shirt, tie the bottom, and tie the arms loosely around my neck. Perfect.

I crouch against the wall as a car approaches and then passes. We don't get visitors, but Dad's not exactly hiding that we're here. If the shifters decide to get together and haul him off to jail again, they know where to find us. So far, they've left us alone, which Dad says is normal for around here, where everyone minds their own business. Once a week, Dad goes out to play poker with a couple friends from childhood, but otherwise, we keep to ourselves.

When the car is gone, I think, feel, and reach for the tiger inside me. My body shivers in anticipation, and I know I've snagged her. I've been practicing this every day, with a few pointers from Dad, and I'm already faster at it than a wolf. As I embrace the pull of her, my chest swells with warmth and power. Adrenaline floods my blood-stream, and my muscles ripple and bunch, pain rushing over me in a dizzying, blinding wave. And then I'm shaking off the initial disorientation, padding out from the shadow of the house, my white coat glowing in the silvery moonlight.

35

It takes a few minutes to find the place where we left our clothes the last time. But after a bit of roaming the woods around the area, I catch a whiff of stale sweat. I weave through the trees and find Dad's clothes, filthy and discarded, hanging from the branch where he left them. My jeans have fallen from where I hung them and are lying on the ground, half covered in leaves and bits of bark and dirt. My shirt remains where I hung it, tied to a branch.

I sniff at the tree where I left the necklace, excitement growing inside me. This could work. It worked for me. It worked for Dad. If I can get it to Harmon in time…

I glance up at the big white moon rising higher by the second. Where is the necklace? Suddenly, the fur along my back bristles. I am not alone.

My muscles bunch, and I turn slowly, lowering my belly towards the ground, getting ready to pounce. But only trees surround me. I search the woods with my tiger eyes, prick up my tiger ears, inhale the night air, searching for a scent, but there's nothing there. Still, I can feel a presence.

I turn back to the small hollow tree and scrape at it with my claws. I'm scared to shift now, to be a vulnerable human when I'm still unsure. My tiger senses might not be as accurate as a wolf's. In the month since I've had them, I haven't practiced using them. I press my nose to the small opening, searching for the necklace.

A tremor works its way across my skin, and my fur bristles again. I reach into the little hole with a claw and snag the string of the necklace, tugging at it as something shifts under my other paw. I step back quickly, and the necklace string slips from my claw. Something is holding it in place. I step forward, peering into the little hollow. Tiny twigs and vines have twined around the necklace, plastering it to the wall of the hollow, with only the stone showing.

Another shiver goes through me. I can't fit a paw into the hole, but I reach in with two claws, ripping and slicing at the little vines to break their hold on the necklace. Under my feet, the dirt shifts, stones grinding together. Something is moving. I strike at it with my paw. Leaves and dirt go flying, revealing a root slithering across the ground like a snake.

I swipe at the necklace again and miss. The root begins to wind itself around the small tree with the hollow carved out. As it climbs closer, then reaches out a tendril for the entrance to the hole, I swipe at it again. It falls away, then rears back like an angry snake, and dives forward, into the hole. Just as it wraps itself in the string, I reach in and snag it with my claw. With a quick yank, I jerk it free from its moorings. But the root winds around the other end of the string. The loose end swings free of the hollow, and the charm races down the string and drops through the air.

I lunge for it, catching it in my mouth just as the root whips across my eyes. Blinking in shock, I hold in the roar of pain, cradling the enchanted stone on my tongue. I turn to flee, but a vine swings down from a tree, curling around my hind leg. I swipe at it with my powerful claws, just managing to yank my foot free before a branch comes hurtling towards my shoulder. Ducking aside, I bound forwards. A branch whips across my chest, but I continue, dodging branches and tree trunks, vines and roots. A rock hurtles through the air and bounces off my hip.

In my human form, I'd already be dead. But now I race through the trees, weaving my way back to the road that leads into the wolf community. Just as I think I'm safe, a vine comes swooping across the path. I leap over it, only to land with my foot in a trap of roots. They tighten around my front paw even as I swipe at them with the other. I tear at the fibrous root with my claws, laying bare the moist inner layer. The living part of it, of some person. I rip through it with my teeth, and surge forwards.

The haunted trees come less often now, but every minute or so, a branch draping into my path snatches at my legs or tail. One of them snags on my bundle of clothes, and I leap forwards, barely noticing the tearing sound as the shirt rips. It bounces awkwardly on my back, barely hanging on. I dodge another rock, another vine. At long last, I come within sight of the clearing, and the attack ceases. But ahead, a fire glows through the trees, and my chest tightens. Am I too late?

On alert, I creep forwards, remembering what Harmon said. I'm a tiger, but I'm no match for a whole pack of wolves. And I've been warned not to come back. But when I come within sight of the fire, it lies abandoned. Only embers glow in the pit, and for a moment, I think I missed the transition.

But surely it didn't take me half the night to run a few miles as a tiger.

And then I remember. Like last time, they'll all be gathered outside Harmon's house, waiting to see if they have a leader. Tonight, especially, it will be crucially important. It's his last chance before he loses the ability to transition forever.

Picking up my pace, I streak along the path, through the clearing, through the short stretch of trees, and onto the path that leads past all the little log houses. At the end of the dirt track, the big community center which doubles as the Alpha's house stands watch over the others. I slow and raise my head, trying to determine which unfamiliar scent might signify wolves rather than humans. But I don't have to wonder for long. A lonesome howl from ahead gives me all the clues I need.

They've already transitioned. I don't know what that means, if it's too late to help Harmon or not. I don't know all the powers of the stone. But if it can make a person turn human and stay that way, maybe there's still a chance. If only I can get past the pack of angry, mourning wolves in one piece.

They've congregated on the grass behind the house again, between it and the rose jungle. Unfortunately, that is also the side of the house with the flight of stairs leading down to the basement. Harmon demolished the ladder, so I can't use that. Still, there is a door inside the house that leads to the basement, so I creep that way.

As I approach, I'm hit with a round of spasms that I

know all too well. My body jerks painfully one way and the other. My joints pull and ache, threatening to tear my shoulders and hips from their sockets.

The tiger eye.

I can't drop it, though. I take another step, and a twig snaps under my foot. Before I can catch myself, I stumble forward and fall to my knees. If I'm not making enough noise to alert the wolves now, I will be by the time I reach Harmon's house. But if I give up my one advantage, my strength and power, there's no way I can fight off even one wolf. My best bet is to head for the front door, and by the time the wolves realize I'm here, I might be close enough to fend off the first few. I'll barrel through the front door and leap down into the basement.

Obviously, that plan is not going to work if I'm human. The tiger eye falls from my mouth as another convulsive burst of energy shoots through my muscles. I have to fight not to cry out in pain, which would surely alert the wolves. They may be used to the night sounds of the forest like snapping twigs, wind, and insect noises. But they will notice the foreign sound of a tiger crying in pain.

Before a rogue spirit can snap up the stone, I place my paw on it. I'm just going to have to go in as myself. Within seconds, I'm back in my human body, shivering with relief. Now that I know shifting ends the pain, it's much harder to hold back when one of the fits begins. I pick up the stone, only then realizing that somewhere during my escape, the bundle of clothes gave up its hold on me.

Oh, well. No one here pays nudity any mind, and it

will be easier to shift. If I have to throw the stone away and shift to save my life, I will.

Now in my human form, I duck low and run hunched over towards the house. The smell of a human can't be as suspicious to them as that of a tiger, anyway. And they might be too preoccupied to notice one more human.

I stop when I reach the end of the road that circles through the community. The houses are all off this main road, with Harmon's house at the end of the circle. At the other end of the house, I catch a glimpse of a white wolf walking back and forth, patrolling.

Elidi.

I freeze, pressing my back to the tree closest to the house. Between the big oak tree and the wooden porch, the narrow, rocky road now seems impossibly wide.

I hold my breath, praying for a miracle. Maybe she didn't see me. But then she stops, lifts her nose, and scents the air.

Please don't smell me, please don't smell me...

Her head swings my way, and adrenaline pumps through me. For a long moment, her black eyes fix on mine. And then, she lifts her head and howls. The mournful wail is deafening. It echoes through my blood, tugging at something deep within my chest, my bones, my DNA.

Maybe there is a bit of wolf in me after all.

When my sister turns back to pace the other way, I dart across the drive and up the steps. At any moment, they'll be on me. She alerted them. I yank open the screen door and reach for the doorknob, sure that it will be locked. But no one around here locks their doors. I twist the knob and slip inside, my hands shaking as I ease the screen door closed. I wince at the squeak of the hinge and the soft click as it latches. Then I close the inside door and lock it. If they want to get in, they'll have to transition to human first.

I turn and grope my way through the unfamiliar house towards the door that for months, was my only hope for escape. The door through which my food was delivered, and through which I was thrown when I tried to escape. That day, Harmon came up the ladder after me. If he hadn't broken his arm, would he have been strong enough to heal in time? Is my one ill-planned dash for freedom going to cost him a lifetime of leadership, the fulfillment his dream and his fate?

"Psst."

The voice comes out of the dark, and I freeze, my arms outstretched, searching for the door to the basement. Around me, the blackness deepens, suddenly full of terrible possibilities.

A tiny flare of green light bursts into life, no bigger than the flame of a single matchstick. In its light, I can just make out a beautiful woman with long dark hair, somewhere in her twenties, sitting halfway across the room on a barstool at a small, round table. Though she looks vaguely familiar, my eyes are drawn to the ball of green fire in her hand, and I know she's no wolf. For a second, I try to place her, thinking she must be another person from my old life who was hiding some magical ability.

"What are you doing here?" she hisses.

"I'm here to see Harmon," I hiss back. "Who are you?"

"I'm just waiting for him to come around," she says.

"Once he realizes what he'll have to give up if he won't marry my daughter, he'll agree to it."

"Mrs. Nguyen?" I ask, taking an involuntary step back.

"Don't look so shocked," she says. "I told you that old bag wasn't my real body. I'm just Yvonne when I'm not borrowing Mrs. Nguyen's body."

That's not why I shrank back, but I'm not about to tell her that I know she's the one who trapped my father here. If she wanted me to know that, she would have told me herself. Dad may not hold that against her, but I do.

"Why do you want Harmon to marry your daughter so bad?" I ask. "Don't you want your daughter to marry someone who loves her and actually wants to be with her?"

"Oh, darling, that was cute when you were thirteen," she says with a smug smile. "Surely you're not that naïve anymore."

"But why? What do you stand to gain from it?"

"Ah, that's better," she says, shaking one finger at me and smirking. "That's the question you must always ask. Who benefits? And how?"

"If not for love, why would you want Harmon for your daughter? You've seen him. You called him a monster, and he hasn't shifted back since then. He's not going to be Alpha if he can't transition. He won't live in this big fancy house. He's not even handsome anymore."

"And yet, you're here," she says, tilting her head and giving me a calculating look. "Why?"

"I asked you first." I raise my chin, trying to ignore the fact that I'm naked and, for the moment, defenseless. It's hard not to feel vulnerable when I'm so completely exposed.

"Fair enough," she says. "I cast a little spell on your friend, kept him ugly all this time. So I'm here bargaining with him. When he agrees to marry my daughter, I'll remove the spell, and he can transition back. If he doesn't do it by morning…" She grins triumphantly. "Tick tock, deal's off."

I swallow hard, squeezing my fist closed around the stone. It suddenly feels hot in my hand. She'll notice it at any moment. "So if he marries your daughter, you'll let him transition back. But if he refuses, he'll be stuck like that forever, so you have no use for him?"

She shakes a finger at me again. "Now you're catching on."

"He'll never agree."

"Oh, I wouldn't be so sure," she says. "That's a lot to lose. Beauty, status, a wife. You know how wolves feel about their mates. If he accepts her, he'll have everything. If he refuses, he has nothing."

"He has me," I say quietly. "That's why I'm here."

She laughs, sounding delighted. "You are naïve," she says. "It won't last. You'll see. You're enamored with the image of his tragic fall, and you think you'll rush in to rescue him. But you can't save him. He'll grow tired of hiding in your basement, but you can't take a monster out in public. You'll despise him for holding you back, and he'll despise you for your embarrassment at being seen with him. Do the kind thing, Stella, and tell him to marry my daughter."

"You're wrong," I say, stepping towards the basement door. "I love him. I don't care what he looks like."

"Love never saved anyone," she sneers.

"Tell me that tomorrow." I reach the door, slide my fingers down until I find the knob, and twist. This one is locked. That's when I realize the wolves haven't gone crazy outside, fighting to be the first to get in and tear me to shreds. Maybe that howl didn't mean what I thought it meant. Just as I'm about to give up, my palm presses against the lock. Of course it locks from this side. I twist the tiny mechanism in the center of the knob and turn.

"Need a light?" Yvonne asks from her spot halfway across the room.

"I got it."

"Hm, I don't see one," she says. "Unless you've invented invisible light. Or wait, if you're a cat, you can see in the dark, right? But that only works when you're in animal form." As she speaks, she comes closer. Suddenly, her little light blinks on like a tiny firefly. She peers past me, down into the blackness of the basement. Faint moonlight glimmers from the far window.

"Why are you helping me?" I ask. "I thought you wanted your daughter to marry Harmon."

"She will," Yvonne says. "Harmon may be ugly, but he's a smart boy. He knows it's not really a choice."

I'm tired of stalling, so I pop the enchanted stone in my mouth, preparing to shift.

"What was that?" Yvonne asks, her eyes narrowing.

Before I can answer, she shoves me hard, and I plummet into the basement below.

36.

I land in a heap, my head spinning. For a second, I don't know what happened. The door slams above, and Yvonne's gloating laughter echoes from above. I try to stand, but it takes me several tries to push onto my hands and knees. Except, I don't have hands or knees. I have paws.

My tiger took over by instinct, saved me from the fall. When I stand, I feel suddenly indestructible. I just fell ten feet onto a packed dirt floor, and I'm fine. More than that, I shifted in two seconds flat. Excitement roars through me, and I open my mouth to roar. But then I think of Yvonne up there cackling, thinking she got me. I'll just let her keep right on thinking that.

On silent paws, I slink forward through the dark. I know this place well enough that I don't even need my tiger vision. The remnants of the ladder are gone, but I make my way to the spot under it, where Harmon always slept.

The spot is empty. The dirt is cool to the touch, and no sign of his presence remains. No blanket, no books, no Harmon.

My tiger heart quavers.

I shift back to my human form and whisper his name, feeling along the wall in search of him. But he's not here.

"Harmon?" I say, my voice just above a whisper. Maybe he's gone. Maybe he did it. He's transitioned and gone upstairs to join his pack. I know it's what he wants, what he's always wanted. He's in his rightful place. But the cavity inside my chest squeezes at the thought of never seeing him again. I'm not ready for him to be gone.

All month long, while I thought of him, I knew he'd be here when I got back. Some part of me always knew I'd come back. But he's nowhere to be found.

"Harmon?" I say again, rising to my feet and speaking into the tunnel.

I'm the one who was betrayed. I'm the one who left. What am I doing here, risking imprisonment again, when I just escaped a month ago? I shouldn't be here. I shouldn't care what happens to him. I shouldn't even wonder.

"Harmon?" I duck into the tunnel and hurry through it, bent double to clear the ceiling. When I step into the sitting room, the moonlight streaming in the window grows brighter. It falls on the tiny glass vase in the center of the table, a bunch of withered white roses spilling from it. A soft white circle of petals surrounds the vase like a halo.

"Stella?" At the sound of his muffled voice, I begin to laugh. Hope, in all its terrible wonder, bursts open inside me like a blossom.

"You're here," I cry, rushing into the bedroom. He's lying in the bed, with the blanket pulled up to his chin. His arctic eyes are glassy in the moonlight, but his chin is still missing, his cheeks still dotted with fur.

"I thought I was dreaming," he says. "I heard you

calling my name. I thought I was going crazy from the solitude. What are you doing here?"

"I brought you something," I say, opening my hand. "It's a charm, from my necklace."

"I know what it is," he says quietly.

"So maybe it can help you."

"You hate me, Stella. I'm a liar and a hypocrite, remember?"

"I don't hate you," I say, suddenly very aware of my cold, exposed skin.

For a long, painful moment neither of us speaks. Then Harmon scoots to the far edge of the bed and opens the blanket. "Come here," he says. "I want to talk to you."

"Just talk?" I ask, cutting my eyes toward the open blanket.

"Your call," he says, a smile twisting his beautiful boy lips.

"Just talk," I agree, slipping under, relieved for the coverage. The bed is warm, heavy with the smell of him, his spicy apple scent layered with boy scent. "There's a witch upstairs."

"I know."

"When they interrupted the coronation, she said she was a shifter, though," I say slowly. "Didn't she? So she was trying to trick you to marry a witch instead?"

"I don't know what she was doing," Harmon says. "But it didn't work then, and it won't work now. We don't change our minds and get divorced when we get bored like shifters. We don't have harems like witches. We Choose one mate."

I pull the blanket tight around me. "What are you going to do about her? What if she comes down here?"

"She can't," he says. "As soon as she left the onion bin, we paid a witch to lay a protection spell on the basement. That's why I wanted you down here with me."

"But you let me leave."

"I knew I couldn't protect you once you left. But I couldn't make you stay any longer. It was killing me to see you miserable."

"I wasn't miserable," I say. And maybe it's true. Now that I've left, this place doesn't seem so bad.

"You could have fooled me," Harmon says, a shudder wracking his body.

"She gave my father this tiger-eye charm," I say, reminded of why I'm here. "It did its job. It kept me human for years. And it forced my father to stay human. If I put it on you tonight, it could force you into your human form. Which means, you will have transitioned. You won't lose that. It can't hurt."

"A witch's charm can always hurt." He turns onto his side to face me, laying his cheek on his paw.

"You have to have it on you," I say, holding it out. "Sorry, it might have a little saliva on it." I stop talking, feeling silly, and watch another spasm work its way through him. Now that I've experienced those, I know exactly what it is.

"Sorry, what?" he asks when it's passed.

"Do you think it will work?" I whisper. "Do you even need it? I mean, you're a little more normal every time. Maybe you'll change back anyway."

"Maybe," he says without conviction. "She put a spell on me. That's why I can't transition. I've recovered enough to do it, but I insulted her and her daughter, so she's keeping me this monster until I agree to her demands."

"But she put a spell on this stone first," I tell him. "My father says an earlier spell always takes precedence over one cast later. It can work. Let me get something to hold it on you. I'll make a necklace. And tomorrow, you'll be human again." I sit up and drop my legs off the bed, ready to go and find a rope.

"Wait." Harmon's warm fingertips brush my bare skin, and goosebumps sweep across my body. "Wait," he whispers again, his fingers sliding slowly down my back.

When I swallow, it echoes through the tiny room. I turn and quickly pull the blanket back over myself. Harmon sits up and fishes a t-shirt off the floor beside the bed. He clamps his teeth on the edge and tears it with both hands, pulling off a thin, curling strip of fabric. I hold out the charm again, but he holds out the makeshift string at the same time, and our hands bump and fumble awkwardly.

"Can you?" he says, dropping the strip and sliding back under the blanket. He stares out the window, the muscle in his jaw working.

"Don't be mad," I say, feeding the fabric through the loop of wire holding the stone with some difficulty. It's too big for the tiny loop, and there's no way Harmon could have done this with a wolf paw. "You'll be back to normal in no time."

"If this works…"

"Then you'll be able to lead your pack."

"I'll make it right for you," he says, turning fierce eyes my way. "If this works, if you fix this and give them back their Alpha, we will owe you forever. The pack won't like it, but wolf people don't take these things lightly. They'll repay you. Your…people."

I hold out the necklace, then hesitate. "Let me do it."

When he sits, I reach for his neck. I'm about to ask him to turn his back, but I don't want to embarrass him in case the scars and thick fur there remind him of his monstrosities. Strangely, after not seeing him for a while, his odd face and body don't bother me at all. His familiar distortions are comforting rather than shocking after a month's absence.

I slide my arms around his neck and tie the cloth ribbon, unsure where to look, since I can't look at my hands as I do it. His face is so close, his breath on my cheeks. I fix my eyes on his neck. His Adam's apple bobs and then sinks again. The necklace rests in the hollow of his throat.

"Thank you," he murmurs. His big hands come to rest on my shoulder blades, their warmth prickling my skin at the slight touch. I trace the line of the necklace around his neck to his throat, my fingertips exploring his collarbones, my palms brushing across his chest. His skin is warm, his heart beating hard under my palm.

"Are you wearing anything?" I whisper through my tight throat.

He slides back down under the blanket with a soft chuckle. "I was hoping to transition. And I was alone. So no. I'm not wearing anything."

I swallow so hard my ears click. Following his lead, I lie back down on the far side of the bed, which seems so close now. It's only a full-sized bed, not a king, and I can feel the heat of his body just an arm's reach away. Another shudder goes through him. When it ends, he takes a deep breath and reaches out, taking one of my hands and squeezing. "This is it for me, Stella. If this doesn't work, I'm finished."

"You make it sound like you'll be dead."

"I might as well be. What is life worth if it's spent alone in a basement?"

I try to imagine it, to find some way to convince him, but I know I'm the hypocrite for even trying. I wouldn't want to live that life, either. But it's way too soon to be making those decisions. "I was alone in an attic," I point out, my voice more bitter than the brightness I had intended.

"You had hope," he says quietly. "If this doesn't work, what do I have to hope for?"

"So maybe the pack wouldn't let you lead. That sucks. But you could still get married and have kids someday."

"Be realistic, Stella. You can't even look at me. Who's going to love a monster?"

"I am." The words slip out before I can think them through, before I can stop them. I wait for Harmon's scornful scoff, but he's silent, which is a thousand times worse. I open my mouth to make excuses, to tell him I meant it hypothetically, that I meant that I could love someone who wasn't perfect, who couldn't shift, who doesn't look the way he used to look. And if I could, someone else could. But I'm afraid to make it worse, to take away something that might give him enough hope to get him through this night, if not the rest of them. Because this is only the beginning, the first night he'll despair over what he lost.

"You can't," he says at last. "You don't mean that."

Somehow, despite everything and against every logic, I do. I close my other hand over his, sandwiching his human hand between mine. I don't care if he has a paw or a tail or crooked legs. I'm part animal, too. And there's a strange beauty in his half-animal features, something that catches the eyes off guard and makes them look again, until they see past the surface abnormalities.

"I think I do."

He scoots across the moonlit space between us, pulling me to him. In the dark, his frost eyes glow with the burning depth of buried coals, warming my cheeks as he searches my face. Suddenly, I'm no longer shy of that look. I want him to keep looking at me like that forever, to burn off the artifice until there's nothing there but the real us. I lift my face to his, but I don't close my eyes. I want to devour him with every part of my being, my mouth, my eyes, my body.

"I know I do," he says. His lips caress mine, but unlike hope, desire is not a flower blossoming inside me. It's a raging firestorm. I bury my fingers deep, deep in the thick fur on his back, twine my limbs around his, open my mouth and pull him in. His body is hot as fever against mine, his core pulsing out a deep, animal heat that mingles with mine.

After a minute, he pulls back, but I can feel his heart

hammering against mine. "I love you, Stella," he says. "I Chose you. You know that, right?"

I struggle to swallow, my throat suddenly deeper than before. Remembering. The line between truth and deception, mine and his, blurs and shimmers like a mirage. "But you thought I was my sister."

"No." He smiles and slips his hand around my back, securing my body to his. "I definitely didn't."

"But…I mean, it got interrupted. Does that count?"

His eyes search mine again, searing into me. "It counts. It's not something I'm trying to get out of on a technicality. I meant it, and I still mean it."

"I thought…she said if you Chose someone, they had to marry you."

"No," he says. "You don't have to do anything. You don't even have to answer. But you should know that I did. That I do. That I always will."

"If you don't have to marry someone, then I don't understand what it means. Choosing someone."

"It means I Chose you to love and only you. You're the only person I ever will love. The only person I can. You're the only one. Before. Now. Always."

Suddenly, it's hard to breathe. I don't know what it means to love someone like that. I only know what it means to love someone the way I do, in my shifty shifter way. But I also know that although I might not be capable of wolf love, I'm capable of something more than I was as a human. My human mind is still trying to wrap itself around how this is possible, but my heart knows.

My body knows. I stroke his hair, his naked ears, and pull him in until our lips meet and our heartbeats meld. I revel in it all, the movement of muscle under skin, the smell of our sweat, the heat of his breath on my face, the way our flesh and blood bodies are so solid and raw, so visceral and present, breathing and bleeding and unyieldingly, unapologetically fused.

37.

When my breath and heartbeat return to their normal rate, I wriggle around in the cocoon of Harmon's arms until I'm facing him. "If you knew it was me at the eclipse," I say slowly, tracing the outline of the tiger eye against his tan skin, "Then why did you pick me? You didn't even know me. How did you know you'd like me?"

"I know you now," he says. "And I was right, wasn't I?"

I give his shoulder a little push. "I'm serious. Tell me."

"You know how people call it love at first sight? Well, it's not really like that. It's like knowing at first sight."

"So you knew you were going to Choose me before that?"

"Sometimes it happens at third or fourth, or ten thousandth, sight. It's not about knowing all the little things about you or even liking you. That's what I'm trying to say. It's about just knowing that you're my mate."

I try not to laugh at the word. He's being serious, but ever since my sister said it, it's always made me feel strange. "What if I don't know?" I ask.

"That's okay," he says. "You will."

"Does that ever happen? That someone Chooses a mate who doesn't Choose them back?"

He hesitates, then shakes his head. "No."

"What if I don't? I'm not a wolf."

"I don't know," he says, pulling me closer. "I guess I'll be happy alone. Like your mother. She Chose a shifter."

The thought makes me sick. Is that how it will end? Is that why wolves are supposed to stay within their tribe, their species? And what if they know their mate is outside the wolf world? Will I leave Harmon bitter and cold like my mother?

"If you don't change back," I say. "If it doesn't work. Will you come with me? We can be together outside this community. We'll keep to ourselves. But at least we'll be together. And if you can't be Alpha, you said leaving might be best for the pack."

He grimaces, his jaw clenched, but then he nods. "And if I change back?" he asks. "Will you come here and be with me? The wolves will be grateful for what you did for me tonight, and they'll welcome you. And you're the heir to the shifter legacy. I'm the pack leader. We can do what your parents failed to do. Make peace with both our peoples."

I want to remind him that I'm only sixteen. I can't lead anyone, let alone a bunch of violent outlaws. The shifters don't know me. Most of them probably don't even know I exist. They don't trust or respect my father. I'm the last person who could make them want to make peace with the werewolves.

"What if the pack doesn't accept me?" I whisper, searching his eyes.

"They will," he says, his voice fierce. "And if they don't, I'll leave with you. I'll be a lone wolf. We can start a new pack. Make our own pack laws."

If he would leave his people for me, why wouldn't I

leave these same people I don't know for him? I nod mutely, and he smooths my cheek with his paw. "Don't look so scared," he says, a smile playing on his dark lips. "It makes me think you regret bringing this necklace."

My cheek presses into his caress like a cat. "I don't," I promise him. "I want you to be happy." I stop myself before I finish that sentence. Because despite what I just agreed to, I know that it's not going to make me happy to stay here. No matter what he says, the wolves don't trust me. And I sure as hell don't trust them.

"Thank you, Stella." He smooths back my hair and kisses my forehead. "That's what I want for you, too. And for us. Together." His lips find mine this time, tender and fierce at once. When he finally pulls away, he smiles his strange smile. "Let me hold you while we wait?"

I nestle into the warmth of his body and try to relax, as if the rest of my life does not depend on the next few hours.

38.

Harmon's shudders subside as I lie there. At last, the darkness begins to lift, and light creeps in through the small window. I haven't slept all night. I lie in his arms, feeling like an imposter, like I've stolen something precious and sacred. Like I've stolen some kind of innocence from him—his innocent promise to love me forever.

But I'm not a wolf. I don't make vows that last a lifetime. I'm a shifty shifter.

Sadness seeps into my bones like poison as I lay in his arms. I don't deserve this. He doesn't deserve to be stuck with me, someone who has no interest in being a wolf. And he deserves a wolf, a mate who will choose him for life. A mate who will shift into a wolf and hunt beside him, who knows and obeys the customs of his people. I don't even like his people.

But he can come with me. We'll find some place in the mountains, like Dad has. An unassuming little house in the woods. It could work. It really could. We won't have to worry about the wolves—they think what's best for the pack is for him to leave. But he won't be alone. He'll have me. And I'll have him. We'll be together like this every night. During the day, I'll hunt as a tiger and bring home food. He won't have to leave the house at all, won't have to endure the stares and shock of outsiders. We'll have each other.

As I turn and look at Harmon, my breath catches in my throat. His face is still in the scant light of dawn, but I know. His skin is smooth and brown, his lashes resting gently against his cheek. His lips are slightly parted, his strong jaw and chin sharply defined by shadows in the basement.

He's healed.

I swallow hard, reaching out to shake him awake. But then I stop. Only then do I realize that I loved that strange, furry face. That I loved it as much as this one, maybe more. I loved who he was down here, with just me. I loved getting to have all of him. I don't want to share him. In that moment, I realize the depth of my selfishness. Some part of me, maybe the larger part, hoped it wouldn't work. Some part of me liked the life I was picturing, with just us. No part of me likes the thought of staying here.

For three years, I was trapped in this community. And though I no longer want to go home, I don't want to stay here, either. I want to be a tiger, to explore that part of myself. I don't want to hide it away and shift into a wolf to fit in with these wolves, though it's not my natural form. That's what my father did.

And I don't want to go back to my father, to hide away in a musty old house and pretend I'm nothing, shirk my responsibilities to my own people. I don't know if I want to be a shifter, either. I just want to be a tiger. And I want Harmon. And I want to be free.

But I can't have all three of those things.

I can't tear my eyes from Harmon's sleeping profile.

He's so beautiful it almost hurts to look at him. But it hurts because I know it's not fair to him to stay. And I can't ask him to leave. He belongs here, leading his pack. He's born to be an Alpha—proud and regal, protective and strong. This past year, he's suffered enough. His father's injury, at my hand. His own injury, at my father's hand. The death of his father, at my people's hands. His inability to shift. Having to sit down here in the dark, watching my mother take his spot in the pack.

No, I can't ask him to leave with me. And I can't honor my promise. I told him I'd stay, but I've been doing what other people ask for too long. If I stay here, I'm staying for Harmon, not for me. I'll still have to deal with my mother, my sisters, the whole community. I can't stay here and let my life slowly bleed away in this place where I don't belong. I'm not sure where I do belong yet, but I know I won't find it here.

I need to let my tiger show me how to be a shifter before I can decide to give that up and be a wolf. I've barely scratched the surface of my shifter nature, and if I stay, I'll never get to do more than that. Even if it is my birthright, I have no loyalty to the shifters, though. They are strangers to me. My own shifter side is barely more than a stranger to me. I need to let her out.

And so, I slip from under the sheets. Looking down at Harmon, I almost climb back into the bed. I could curl up in his arms and stay, accept the love of this incredible man. But if I do, he'll never have a chance to love anyone else. If I leave, he can still back out. He said he wasn't looking to get out of his Choosing on a technicality. He didn't say he couldn't. Choosing me is not doing what's best for the pack. And he needs to put them first. It's in his nature.

Before my resolve crumbles, I slip into the sitting room. By the scant light slanting in the window, I find a pen and tear out the end page from one of the books on the shelf. I scribble a note to Harmon, tears blurring my eyes as I rush through the words, trying to say everything I want to say, trying to make him see that it's for the best. I can't stay here, can't make his people doubt his wisdom. They won't respect his Choice if it's me. My sister is a better choice. She's a shifter princess, too, but she's also a wolf.

I tell him all this. And because I know he'll know exactly what I'm doing if I am too gentle, I tell him that now he knows what it feels like to be betrayed. That I don't Choose him. I tell him to find someone else. To love someone else. That I want him to. That I want him to be happy, to lead his people, to fulfill the prophecy. His destiny is here, with the wolves.

Mine is not.

39

Just as I finish the note, before I've even signed my name, I hear the door in the bedroom swing open. I freeze, my heart skipping a beat. Harmon said witches could not enter here. But someone is here.

The sound of footfalls on the stairs sends ice through my veins. "Has he transitioned?" my mother asks.

The wolves have come for their leader.

I stand, my legs shaking. Inside me, my tiger strains to break free. Thanks to Harmon, I know what the pains are. I slide into her form and slip through the short tunnel into the basement. That's when I see the doorway to the basement is open, too. Above, I can make out a figure, but I don't stop to wonder if it's a smart idea. I'll take my childhood babysitter over a pack of angry wolves any day, especially when I hear my mother say my name. Gathering my strength, I make a run for it and leap. My huge front paws land on the floor, my claws digging into the wood, leaving huge tracks as the weight of the back half of my body drags me backwards, into the basement. Yvonne stands over me, her arms crossed, not moving.

I turn pleading eyes to her, but she only glares. "What have you done?" she snarls. "You ruined everything!"

I scramble my back feet against the wall, the ceiling of the basement. Below, the first wolves exit the tunnel, snarling and yipping. They haven't forgiven me, as Harmon naïvely assumed they would. They hate me, as always, and their instinct when an outsider sneaks into their midst is to kill, kill, kill. I'm not one of them. My mother drilled it into my head a thousand times, though I never knew the whole truth. Now I know. I am a shifter. They are wolves. And they will never see past that.

I bunch myself up, and with a last burst of energy, grip the door frame with one hind leg. My tail braces against the frame, pushing my weight forwards. At last, my balance tips and I hurl myself forward, into the big lodge that the wolves use for a community center. The front door is closed, but I don't have time to shift into a human and use the knob. I charge the door, and it flies open.

I barely hear the sound of splintering wood. I'm already halfway across the road, and then passing the big oak tree, before I realize Yvonne is clinging to my back, holding around my neck the way I did when my father carried me out of this valley. But I am not deterred. Someone calls my name, but I don't stop. A rock slams into my hindquarters, and I wince in pain, but it doesn't slow me down. Nothing can slow me.

My mother's voice trails after me. "Don't come back here again. Ever!"

I don't turn around to tell her that for once, I have no urge to disobey her. The last thing in the world I want is to come back here now. Harmon is better. He got what he wanted—to be healed, to lead his pack. And I got what I always wanted—freedom, and my father back. We can both be happy, I tell myself.

As I reach the top of the mountain and leap onto a

boulder, Yvonne's arms slip. She drops from my back, rolling in the leaves a few times before jumping to her feet. Shaking her fist, she screams after me. "You better run. And if you're smart, you'll never come back. If I catch you before Harmon, I won't be so kind."

I don't stop to talk. I have nothing to say to her, to my mother, to anyone. I never want to go back there, to go back to my human form. I am invincible now. I am happy now. If it's a little hard to feel it, I'll just have to wait until my heart catches up with my mind. I'm good at waiting.

Though I may not be a werewolf, I chose Harmon, too. And now I'm choosing to leave him. I can't make him give up his destiny to be with me. Loving him when he was less than perfect was nothing compared to this. Letting him go so that he can have the life he deserves, even if it kills me, is the hardest thing I've ever done.

But I'll do it for him. For the first time, I understand what he feels for his pack. Not just willingness to put them first, but a selfless desire to do what's right for them, even if it hurts them. I loved him enough to set him free from that curse, enough to save him, though deep down, I knew it meant we could never be together.

So I run faster, putting as much distance between myself and the wolves as I can. That life is over for me. That world is behind me. My cruel mother, my strange sisters, my flawed father. And Harmon. But I won't look back. I won't miss them, or think about them, or mourn them. I'm a tiger now, and tigers don't cry.

Also by Lena Mae Hill

Young Witch Series

(companion series to *Girl Among Wolves*)

Twisted

Caged (2019)

Winslow Witch Chronicles

(prequel series to *Young Witch Series)*

Magic of the Void

Sister of the Sea

Hosting Gods Series

Emerge

Ignite

Ascend

The Superiors Series

Blood Moon

Blood Thirst

Blood Oath

Blood Sport

Blood Lust (2018)

Blood Night (short story)

Lena Mae Hill

Hey, y'all!

I'm a southern author of fiction of many flavors. I was born and raised in Arkansas and make my home there today, along with my family, a cat, two dogs, and eleven chickens.

I've been writing in one form or another all my life. I adore fairytales, especially the way they portray the dark and twisted parts of human nature. Those original tales inspired this series. To read about the witches who appear throughout Stella's story, check out the *Young Witch* series.

My related prequel stories, the *Winslow Witch Chronicles* may also appeal to you. Check out these and more by searching for my name on Amazon. And don't forget to leave a review!